T0195989

Praise for *Retribution* by Anderson Harp

"Tense and authentic—reading this book is like living a real-life mission."
—Lee Child

"Want to see what the military's really like? Harp knows his stuff. *Retribution* proves that the scariest story is the true story. Here's the real intelligence operation."
—Brad Meltzer, bestselling author of *The Fifth Assassin*

"I seldom come across a thriller as authentic and well-written as *Retribution*. Harp brings his considerable military expertise to a global plot that's exciting, timely, and believable. His characters are exceptionally well-drawn and convincing. If you like Tom Clancy's work, you'll love *Retribution*. Harp is very much his own man, however, and to say that I'm impressed is an understatement."
—David Morrell, *New York Times* bestselling author of *The Protector*

"Anderson Harp's *Retribution* is a stunner: a blow to the gut and shot of adrenaline. Here is a novel written with authentic authority and bears shocking relevance to the dangers of today. It reminds me of Tom Clancy at his finest. Put this novel on your must-read list—anything by Harp is now on mine."
—James Rollins, *New York Times* bestselling author of *Bloodline*

"*Retribution* by Harp is an outstanding thriller with vivid characters, breakneck pacing, and suspense enough for even the most demanding reader. On top of that, Harp writes with complete authenticity and a tremendous depth of military knowledge and expertise. A fantastic read—don't miss it!"
—Douglas Preston, #1 bestselling author of *Impact*

"*Retribution* by Anderson Harp is a fast-paced, suspenseful thriller loaded with vivid characters and backed by a depth of military knowledge. Top gun!"
—Kathy Reichs, #1 bestselling author of the Temperance Brennan and Tory Brennan series

The Will Parker Thrillers by Anderson Harp

NORTHERN THUNDER
BORN OF WAR
RETRIBUTION

Misled

Anderson Harp

LYRICAL UNDERGROUND
Kensington Publishing Corp.
www.kensingtonbooks.com

LYRICAL UNDERGROUND BOOKS are published by

Kensington Publishing Corp.
119 West 40th Street
New York, NY 10018

All Kensington titles, imprints, and distributed lines are available at special quantity discounts for bulk purchases for sales promotion, premiums, fund-raising, educational, or institutional use.

Special book excerpts or customized printings can also be created to fit specific needs. For details, write or phone the office of the Kensington Sales Manager: Kensington Publishing Corp., 119 West 40th Street, New York, NY 10018. Attn. Sales Department. Phone: 1-800-221-2647.

Lyrical Underground and Lyrical Underground logo Reg. US Pat. & TM Off.

First Electronic Edition: May 2020
ISBN-13: 978-1-5161-0976-0 (ebook)
ISBN-10: 1-5161-0976-7 (ebook)

First Print Edition: May 2020
ISBN-13: 978-1-5161-0980-7
ISBN-10: 1-5161-0980-5

Printed in the United States of America

To Gaines Parker

мосцош
МОСКВА
(Moscow)

"To hear a coyote is dangerous. To see one is death."
—Apache saying

Chapter 1

Deep in the Yukon

The arctic fox did not move when the aircraft narrowly cleared the tree line and crossed the open field. The animal was caught in the open, far from the protection of the tall pines and spruce, paralyzed by fear and sickness. His nearly pure-white fur blended perfectly into the blinding sunlit snow of the Yukon. The air had a sting in it from the subzero cold. His breath caused the faintest vapor cloud to form as he panted, his white-frothed tongue hanging from his mouth. The exhaustion had overtaken him. He was dying.

In a daze, the animal tracked the airborne object above, head canting left and right as if he were drunk. As the engine's throaty sound grew louder, he jumped and fell back into the snow. He tried again to run, but at a tilt, stumbling as if his internal gyroscope were off. He recovered his balance and made a desperate break for the protection of the trees.

The DHC-3 Otter's pilot circled the field, lining up what had once been an Army runway, putting his flaps down, and landing softly on the single strip buried under the snow. The sleds of the aircraft barreled through the drifts as the aircraft's propeller churned the dry, powder-like snow into a cloud of white that followed the bright yellow Otter to the end of the runway.

A lone person waited next to the runway with a backpack and a rectangular object next to her feet. The shape of her parka gave a clear impression that this was a woman, petite, not nearly tall enough to reach up and touch the aircraft's wing. She held up an arm to shield her face from the blast of icy air from the propeller. A black, canvas-covered rectangular object near her feet shook as the aircraft approached, seeming to wobble on its own. Something alive inside moved the covered cage.

The aircraft stopped at the end of the runway near the passenger and her cargo. The old Otter had black oil streaks across its yellow engine cowling. The tall propeller blades came to a stop and the engine silenced. With the motor halted, the sudden silence of the outback weighed heavily until movement in the airplane broke the quiet. The sound of metal echoed as the door handle was turned. The pilot's door swung open and a man climbed down. Tall and built firmly, he jumped down from the cockpit with a subtle air of confidence. It didn't seem to be his first trip to the backcountry.

"Did you see that fox?" Will Parker glanced toward the other end of the runway.

"Did it have two tipped black ears?" the woman asked, carrying her backpack to the airplane.

"Yeah." He leaned against the cargo door. "Didn't think he was going to move."

"Surprised he moved at all. That's George." She took off her mitten and pulled the strings on her backpack at her feet to ensure it was closed.

"Another infected one?" He had already seen a few types of animal in the area infected with the rapidly spreading rabies virus. Mostly, the small varmints were the targets of the dreaded disease.

She nodded.

What a way to go, he thought. As a Marine who had served in special operations in some of the most dangerous places in the world, William Parker knew all about "ways to go." Having spent much of his time in the arctic prior to leaving the Marines, he also knew that rabies was rare in such cold climates. Will had been a member of a small band of experts that instructed Marines in how to survive above the Arctic Circle. He knew what eighty-below could do to the human body. But brutal cold was an old and well-known threat up in the north. The rabies epidemic, on the other hand, was new. And growing.

To pick up his cargo, Will had flown to this remote, abandoned airfield in Snag, Canada, deep in the Yukon and well east of the Alaskan border. Snag was an abandoned outpost of the Royal Canadian Air Force from World War II and it no longer hosted regular visitors, instead becoming a backcountry ghost town.

Perfect for my Otter, Will thought as he walked around his aircraft, performing a post flight check. The Otter aircraft was designed to get down fast and land hard in a very short space. But flying in the arctic required much of a bush pilot. Something as simple as a slightly damaged strut could, in extreme, subzero temperatures, easily snap off as the airplane landed.

Yet the unusual demands of flying in the bush were what had brought Will here. He'd long ago passed the ultimate challenge for a bush pilot: landing a Super Cub on a riverbank no wider than the wheels of the aircraft. But winter was something else again. Regardless of season, though, Will had found no place on earth that had flying like the Yukon.

He had also come for the cargo.

Dr. Karen Stewart visited Snag on a regular basis. Lying to the east of the Saint Elias Mountains, the flatlands ranging north and south drew a variety of wildlife to the local habitat. Karen had left Médecins Sans Frontières to take a position with the CDC's unit in Alaska, monitoring zoonotic infections. Zoonotic diseases followed the movement of animals, and the most dangerous of the zoonotic illnesses was rabies. Alaska and the northwest had gradually become warmer each year and, as they did, the rate of rabies had increased. The rabies virus burned through the brain and progressed relatively quickly. But as winters became milder, the sick animals were able to move farther north before dying, thus interacting with more animals and continuing the rapid spread of the fatal disease. In joining the CDC, Karen Stewart had followed in her father's footsteps, but by studying the spread of viruses among the animals of the extreme north, she'd blazed her own trail in this relatively new field.

She and Will Parker had some history—he had saved her from a kidnapping by Al-Shabaab in the western frontier of Somalia. The purpose behind the raid on the Doctors Without Borders camp had been simple: Capture those whose families could pay the ransom. Like her father before her, Karen had worked with Doctors Without Borders in the meningitis-stricken Horn of Africa until it and terrorism caught up to her. After her close call in Africa, she'd taken the CDC job and been posted to Alaska. That's when her father had called in a favor from Will Parker.

"Just keep an eye on her," was all Dr. Paul Stewart had asked after hearing that Will was flying as a bush pilot out of Anchorage.

Will had agreed gladly. He owed the man who had saved his life.

"Did you get one?" He hefted Karen's backpack and fitted it into the Otter's cargo space.

"Yeah."

He walked to the canvas-covered cage, slipping on his leather gloves. "This one have a name?"

"Juliet."

"She going to make it?" He managed to fit the cage in the rear seat of the cabin.

"No."

Karen had been in the backcountry for several days already. Parker had wanted to join her, but she'd refused. She was fiercely independent and he respected that about her. Having been a prisoner of a terrorist group in Somalia and living face-to-face with death every day, Karen had plenty of reasons to take a nine-to-five in Atlanta. But, like Will, she'd had enough of being walled in by an office.

"We need to get out of here." Will glanced west at the Saint Elias Mountains and the darkening skies above. "A bad one's coming."

She nodded, hauled herself up into the copilot's seat, and pulled back her parka hood. Her short, shaggy haircut and well-tanned face made for an attractive, athletic woman who could live in the outback with no makeup and look no worse for the wear.

He climbed into the pilot's seat, buckled in, and started running through his preflight checklist. "You know, that's a good name," he said as he worked.

"What?"

"Juliet."

She gave him a false frown.

"Dr. Juliet." Will smiled, knowing it was her middle name.

The Otter's engine roared with a throaty growl. Will spun up the turboprop to a deafening roar, turned the aircraft into the wind, and sped along the runway until the sleds started to leave the surface. As the plane lifted, he banked to the southeast, heading away from Anchorage.

"Why this way?" she asked through her mike.

She had donned earphones to hear Will above the guttural sound of the engine. The radial Pratt & Whitney engine on the Otter was as old as the 1967 aircraft, but more than once it had been taken apart piece-by-piece and rebuilt. An engine like this was meant to be overhauled. Its parts were made of heavy castings for repeated use until it ended up in a graveyard or short of a runway in a bad crash. No matter how it died, the Otter's body would be cannibalized for its knobs, handles, and gauges like a transplant donor. In that way, it would keep on living for decades. But for now, it had thousands of landings to go and many years of flying to come.

"We need to skirt the storm." He pointed to a dark line that crowded the tops of the peaks that stood between them and Anchorage. "There's a valley to the south that we can pass through." Some of the mountains in the Saint Elias Range topped out at 19,000 feet. Will's Otter was not made for such high altitudes.

Suddenly, the cockpit's electronics panel shuddered. At the same time, the aircraft's engine sputtered.

"What?" Karen's voice betrayed her fear.

"We're okay."

Will knew immediately what had occurred: A solar flare. The weather report that morning on takeoff had mentioned a risk of the flare's arrival. The sun had unleashed a magnetic shockwave that had traveled millions of miles through space until it collided with the earth and overloaded the electronics of the airplane. Like being knocked down by a wave, the avionics on the cockpit's panel sputtered, then went black.

It shouldn't have affected the engine, Will thought as he loosened his grip. A nervous pilot only made matters worse. He kept the yoke steady and the wings level, going through the mental checklist that an experienced pilot would use to check each system quickly. He looked at the fuel gauge, then tried to turn the engine over, but the big radial simply coughed and went silent again.

Probably some bad fuel. Will scanned the panel again. He had landed at a small airport to refuel after crossing the mountain range. It didn't take much water in the fuel to cause havoc, especially when combined with an electrical failure.

Will Parker knew one thing about the Otter: It was made to land in any condition and on any surface.

Give me the space between home plate and first base...that's all I need. Ninety feet and he could put the airplane safely on the ground.

He scanned the terrain ahead for that much room, keeping the nose of the aircraft tilted down to maintain his airspeed. Without power, some airplanes can glide for miles as long as a calm hand can keep the nose down.

"Hand me that radio." Will pointed to a small handheld in a storage pocket next to her seat. The battery-powered radio was a must for flying in the bush. It could serve as a most important backup.

He radioed air traffic control. "Anchorage Control, this is November one-one-two." He hesitated to use the word *mayday*. A quick landing, with an equally quick passing of the solar interference, did not qualify for a mayday.

The SP-400 radio only crackled.

"We can land this...no problem." His voice was intended to calm his passenger—and himself. He looked straight ahead for a likely landing spot, as a turn would only cause the plane to lose critical airspeed. Air slowing down as it passed over the wing meant the loss of lift.

Easy, Will thought as he relaxed his hands again. It never helped to fight an airplane, even in a situation like this. He scanned his panel to make sure that something obvious was not missing. Engine failure in the arctic didn't happen every day, but this was not Will Parker's first.

Nothing.

He looked across the horizon. A ridge stood in front of the nose. There was no telling what was on the other side. It didn't matter. Their situation required commitment without hesitation. He steered the plane steadily, holding on to as much altitude as possible and for as long as possible.

"Altitude is our friend." He spoke the words unconsciously, forgetting for a moment that he had a passenger. It was an old pilot's saying that went back to the most basic instructions and first flight lessons.

"What?" Karen was turning pale.

The Otter's sleds brushed the top of the trees at the crown of the ridge.

"There you go." He pointed to a small, ice-covered pothole lake just to the left of the nose. The pothole lakes of the Yukon were Mother Nature's version of the same small, deep holes found in the Yukon's road surfaces. These were filled with ice and water. If he could hold on to a gentle turn, they had a chance. The Otter slowly slid down the hill as it lost altitude. The crown of a pine tree brushed the strut. Lower, lower, finally reaching the lake.

The aircraft slammed down on the ice and snow, the banking turn having caused the airplane to lose all of its remaining lift. The speed rapidly bled off as the skids scraped across the frozen lake until Will saw a log sticking up out of the ice.

"Hold on!"

The crunch of metal echoed through the woods and all movement stopped. The right skid had been sheared off, and the remaining sharp point of the landing gear had gotten stuck in the ice. At least the airplane had come to a stop.

"Let's get out of here." Will pointed to the door on his side. The aircraft was tilted with her starboard side angled down, causing the cargo to slide to the right. He pulled Karen across his seat and helped her down onto the ice, which seemed more than adequate to hold their weight.

"You okay?" Will was still holding her on the ice. She'd felt so small and light in her parka as he'd helped her out. He'd forgotten what the woman he'd saved in Africa felt like.

"Yeah." Her face remained ash-gray, but she seemed steady enough on her feet. Suddenly, she jumped at a noise from behind.

The cargo door on the other side had popped open; they heard another sound.

"Watch out." Karen shielded him with an arm and backed away from the wrecked aircraft.

Will saw motion on the other side as a white form crawled out of the wreckage and scurried away across the ice and into the woods on the far side of the lake.

Juliet had escaped.

"This storm isn't going to be pretty." He looked back to the Saint Elias Mountains. "We need shelter."

He knew that the clouds would bring a blizzard; after that, the temperature would drop precipitously. The clear Siberian air that followed a major front could be deadly. He pointed to a space in the timberline on the other side of the aircraft across the lake. The gap in the trees made an oddly straight line from the edge of the lake deep into the woods. In the center of the timber cut was what appeared to be a rock formation covered in deep snow.

Will pointed at the outcropping. "Let's go there. We need to get out of this wind."

A cold breeze swept across the lake. The tail of the Otter squeaked as the rudder was pushed from side to side by the wind. It was the only sound.

"Whitehorse is south." He pointed in the same direction as the swath of broken trees. "But no one will come." He calculated the process. The airplane would not be missing for some time, and air traffic control was likely overwhelmed with others affected by the solar flare.

"Even though we crashed?" She looked up at him with eyes that seemed larger than normal.

"Not a crash." He smiled. "A landing." He looked back at the storm coming in. "Anything you walk away from is a landing."

"Great." Karen gave him a sarcastic smile like the teenager told about a curfew. But at least he got a smile.

They were several miles from Snag and a massive, thickly forested hill deep in snow stood between them and the airfield. Although the pilot-training strip had closed decades ago, pilots still recognized the name Snag. It had a distinction in Canada that Will didn't choose to share with Karen. Gasoline froze at forty below, but Snag was known for temperatures that turned oil into fudge. Metal would break off in your hand when the mercury hit seventy or eighty below zero, like stale icing falling off of a leftover cake.

"Follow me," he said, taking her arm. "We need some shelter, Dr. Juliet."

Chapter 2

Area 41, Camp Pendleton, California

"Sixteen-hundred!"

Lance Corporal Gordon Todd Newton hit the button to close down both of his computers. One was his work PC, provided by his employer, the United States Marine Corps, and the other a supercharged Alienware laptop loaded with everything he could afford on junior enlisted pay. But it was also his special baby, used for the recreational hacking he did on breaks and weekends, as well as the competitive online gaming he still enjoyed in his remaining free time.

"It's Friday," Todd said, stretching his arms and rubbing his eyes. "And I'm outta here."

No one heard him, as he was the sole occupant of the small, dark computer room. He packed up his Alienware in his backpack and slung the strap over his shoulder. His orders mandated that he not bring his personal computer into a room full of computers containing access to classified networks, but Todd took a flexible approach to the rule. Inside, he still had a little of the errant student who had once accessed his high school's computer network to tweak his friends' grades. He liked to push authority.

He also loved his job as a temp. On special TAD (temporary additional duty) to the 1st Raider Battalion, he felt slightly out of step with his command. He was as 180-degrees different from the super-Marines of the Marine Raider Battalion as a computer geek could be. The critical skill operators, or CSOs, would go out for twenty-mile runs while Newton spent eighteen-hour days in front of a little green screen. When the Raiders were out drinking, Todd would play around with John the Ripper or THC Hydra, hacker programs, and try to break into nonmilitary computer systems — not to do harm, only to see if it could be done. Normally, Todd's duty station was MarForCyBer, Marine Corps Forces Cyberspace Command at Fort Meade, Maryland, the home of the 0651s: the military's cyber network operators. But the chance to be in California's Camp Pendleton for a few weeks had worked well for several reasons.

For one, Todd thought as he hurried to the barracks to change out of his Marine camouflaged utilities, Area 41 at Pendleton wasn't far from the beach. Stretching north and south for twenty-one miles, the landscape—aside from Interstate 5—was practically untouched. Todd also had a car, which meant he could spend weekends in San Diego, where the weather was always warm and he could be left alone. Not that the Raiders bothered him much. Most knew little or nothing about his 0651 specialty, but they knew that they needed him. Like cable television, when computers shut down due to a glitch, things got frustrating very quickly.

The assignment also meant something. The Marine Raider unit was working with the integration of tablets wirelessly connected through encrypted networks. Combat patrols and missions would have access to everything the networks could provide. Satellite feeds of enemy locations, for instance, came up instantaneously. A call for close air support or artillery fire could be made by tablet. The stealthy F-35B fighter jets overhead could be called in for air support like a pack of dogs hungry for a target. And a Marine on the battlefield with a tablet knew exactly where he was. GPS not only gave him a location, but also helped the troops avoid friendly-fire mistakes.

Finally, Todd's temporary duty at Pendleton was a trip to his own past. Newton had lived in San Clemente as a kid when his father was stationed for a couple of years at Marine Corps Air Station El Toro to the north. His dad had flown F/A 18s when they first came out. The Hornet topped out at 1100 miles an hour with its pilot strapped to two General Electric F404 turbofan jet engines. A Hornet pilot didn't make any mistakes. If he did, it was only one. At 1100 miles per hour, a sneeze could put a man into the side of a mountain. Of course, it took a special kind of person to fly a machine that didn't allow for the slightest error. Such people tended to be… unforgiving. Todd's dad's flying years came right before the divorce, which hadn't been a big surprise. His father and mother were total opposites. Dad ran over people. Mom tended to get lost in her books and vodka.

Normal would have been nice, Todd thought.

Back when his folks had still been together, the three of them had lived in an apartment on Avenida Montalvo looking out over the Pacific. That's also when Todd's high school had produced a small gang of hackers. The

San Clemente Tritons' computer science club started with just a few, but almost doubled before Todd had graduated.

The term *hacker*, while unavoidable, had never been his favorite word. Hacking sounded violent and malicious, but it had never been about committing crimes for Todd. Instead, it offered the irresistible challenge of solving puzzles.

In the end, Todd was his mother's child: Less of a straight arrow and more of a puzzler than his father. And as the years passed, the world changed on his father. Todd found himself part of the rising digital tide that affected everything—military, government, medicine, business, even reaction by society. The Marines still needed jet jockeys, but they also needed troops who could handle a hacked computer.

Todd looked at his cell phone to check on the time as he changed to jeans and grabbed his backpack, which he'd already prepacked for the weekend.

He dialed the number of another 0651 who had come with him from the East Coast.

"Hey, how are you looking?"

"Are we going to get in trouble?" Lance corporal Lucy O'Hara's voice usually was calm, but she sounded uncertain now.

"Hell, no." He slung the backpack over his shoulder as he went out the door, passing his barracks roommate who sat on the side of his bunk with his crutches, still recovering from a broken leg as a result of a bad parachute landing. They'd only been paired as roommates because they had both been assigned temporary billeting, and they'd been assigned a ground-level room to give Todd's roommate easy access with his crutches. As a Marine on temporary duty, Todd had to take what was given.

"Besides," Todd said into the phone as he left, "it's Hackfest."

He'd come up with the idea months ago when word first came down at Fort Meade. Their plan was to drive together up to San Francisco and attend the singular convention. DARPA's (the Defense Advanced Research Projects Agency) Hackfest took place at NASA's Ames Research Center on Moffett Field, in the heart of Silicon Valley. It was a cutting-edge conference on tech and tech innovation—perfect for Todd and his colleage-friend.

There was, however, one problem. Both 0651s had top-secret clearances, so headquarters would not be thrilled about them going to a computer conference full of speakers like technical activist Cory Doctorow. Doctorow was a popular speaker at hackers' conventions. His belief that technology was on a rapid pace to invade privacy put him at odds with the government. But DARPA was that rare government-military agency that understood that the nation's defenders could not bury their heads in the sand when it came to technology. DARPA sought to create unrestricted think tanks, and Hackfest served precisely that purpose. For their part, though, the Marine brass had made it clear that Hackfest was not a convention that two 0651s with top-secret clearances should attend.

"Your boyfriend gonna let you go?" Newton asked, pulling her chain.

"Oh, grow up." Lucy O'Hara's boyfriend was a ground-pounder, infantry, with the Third Battalion of the 1st Marine Regiment. He was like Todd's roommate. The two enjoyed sweat, pain, and generally being physical; they lived for the endorphin high. By contrast, Todd and his friend enjoyed cracking the virtual safe of a computer code. For fun, they would play with security systems, going just far enough to see if there were cracks in the walls of a General Motors or Johnson & Johnson R and D lab—but never far enough to fully open the safe. They weren't stupid.

"Hopefully he won't kick my ass for taking you," Todd joked.

"Nah. You're okay." She and Todd shared a platonic relationship that went back to their initial training school for their 0651 specialty. For the weekend, they had a motel reserved in Mountain View, where they would split a room with two beds for two hundred bucks. They'd scored tickets to Hackfest with help from a mutual friend they'd met during their days at the University of Maryland's Center for Advanced Study of Language—a training ground for the NSA and the same program that had produced one particularly notorious fellow graduate: Michael Ridges.

* * * *

"Have you emailed him lately?" Newton was walking out of Ames at the end of Hackfest. He hadn't asked his friend this question for over a year now, but she immediately knew exactly who he was talking about.

"Once."

"Me too."

Sending such emails amounted to living dangerously.

"Boy, he would have loved this." Newton put on his sunglasses. The West Coast sun was bright in a California-blue, cloudless sky.

"Better not even mention his name." Lucy whispered the words as if the small crowd heading to the parking lot with them was listening.

Michael Ridges was persona non grata with the federal government. He was considered a traitor to his country, but no one knew exactly why.

"Yeah, you're right." Todd was looking for his 1997 Toyota Camry. Two decades ago, the auto had been sold with what the car manual described as an "almond beige pearl" finish, but time and the sun had resulted in a worn-out, dirty brown. Now they'd have to drive through most of the night to get back to their duty stations by 0700 the next morning.

"This deep web is unlimited." Todd took his backpack off of his shoulder and tossed it into the backseat. "And the dark web is just crazy."

"I know." She changed the subject. "We need to stop for gas and roll." They would have to make a few stops to get back to report to duty on time.

"Yeah."

Neither of them noticed the black van parked on the other side of the parking lot.

Chapter 3

Near Dulles, Virginia

The silver BMW X3 pulled into the garage below the gleaming building that looked out toward Dulles in the distance. It was one of the new towers that dotted the four-lane to the DC-area airport. The top floors were reserved for a particular consulting firm that lived off of secret defense budgets. When the building was constructed, the tenant for the top three floors had a special contractor come in to finish out the space. The interior walls had not even been framed out. And this was just the way the tenant wanted it. The walls would be soundproof and secure from any kind of eavesdropping. Few knew just exactly what the tenant did, but they knew that there would be no access to the top floors.

Members of the Senate Committee on Intelligence knew the tenant well. When they met in the secret room of the Hart Senate Office Building, room 219, to discuss the world's secrets, the tenant was mentioned often. Room 219, like the top floors of the tenant's office building, was considered one of the most secure places in Washington. Both had soundproof doors and walls built to ensure no one would be listening in. When the CIA or DIA had a problem that they could not fix, room 219 heard of it, and then paid the bill that the tenant would charge. And no one ever saw the money.

The decade had been good to the military-industrial complex. Continuing wars fed the beast and security was king. Companies that promised security could name the price—their client CEOs knew they had no choice.

"Yeah, I know it's the finals. Got it. Four p.m. at Witter." He had learned how to quickly get down to the Witter soccer complex in Alexandria by often using the back streets.

The driver of the BMW ended his Bluetooth call as he pulled into his reserved parking spot. The SUV had less than a thousand miles on it. The dealer tag had not yet been removed. It had that fresh, new leathery smell that only a brand-new expensive auto could bring. It was the first new car that he had ever owned. In fact, it was the first car that he had ever owned. Everything before consisted of pickup trucks with six digits on the odometer.

Frank Caldwell liked his new job. The only problem with being the project manager for Alexander Paul's consulting firm was that it required unlimited dedication. He had missed his son's last three soccer games. But the work gave him something he badly needed.

The thrill of still being in the game.

After a tour as a lieutenant with the 75th Army Rangers, Caldwell had finally decided to pull the plug on a career of combat tours. He'd had seven deployments in just two years at Fort Benning. A Ranger's life was not meant to include a wife, a son, and soccer games.

After carding through the building's front door, Caldwell was met by an armed guard inside, the second of three primary layers of security he had to pass through. Security here was tighter than in any operations center he'd seen in the military.

Frank nodded at the guard. He didn't know the man's name. It was like another agency he knew well that rarely used names and, when they did, used false ones.

The guard nodded back. He looked the part. Few people at this company didn't have a military background. Even most of the executive assistants had previously served in the military or Department of Defense. This one had the look of someone chiseled out of rock with shoulders much wider than his waist. His hair was cut close on the side. The top was covered by a black baseball cap with no logos. In fact, the man's polo shirt, also black, was also missing any logos. His pants were the 5.11 Tactical-type cargo pants with plenty of side pockets. And he was armed.

Caldwell was working on a particular project that had been ongoing before he had joined Alexander Paul's company. The project had a secret price tag that was rumored to be well into eight digits, and the money was all offline. Nowhere did the project appear in any budget. And Caldwell reported directly to the man in charge. This was private money, so room 219 would never have heard of the company's project or the troubles that needed solving.

Alexander Paul had served in the Army for many years, rising in a career that took him to the rank of brigadier general. Until he chose to speak out against management, publicly criticizing the administration and calling its decisions in Syria foolish. It didn't take long for the door to be handed to him. But then the White House changed. His words sat well with the new administration, which made Paul head of the Defense Intelligence Agency.

Despite the new start, Paul's career at DIA didn't go much better. He earned a reputation for being inflexible and, more dangerously, apt to bend the facts to his agenda. Once more, he stood out as a maverick, and once again his career ended badly when he became a liability, this time when the administration was embarrassed by an incident at the agency he ran.

"Don't talk to him about DIA," Caldwell had been told by more than one person when he'd joined Paul's private firm.

Word was, Paul's early departure at DIA had fueled a passion for vengeance, though no one ever said against whom. If anything, he'd channeled his anger into his new consulting company, which thrived. Even though his tour at DIA had been cut short, Paul was still thought of as being on the cutting edge of military, security, and intelligence issues. Not everyone thought Paul was outspoken. Some thought he said what needed to be said. And some of those were in the upper echelons of corporate America. Those contacts ensured a comfortable transition for him, with money flowing into his new company.

When offered the job, Caldwell had been unable to pass up the challenge. In fact, he had taken the position without even talking to his wife. Although she didn't know everything he'd done in his career, which was mostly a good thing, she'd endorsed his choice.

She understood, Frank thought. It meant a home, soccer games at Witter, and a new car.

He'd met his future wife at a thirteen-mile trail run. He'd been sporting a short, carrot-red beard that he'd originally cultivated during his many secret missions in and around Pakistan. She ran slightly in front of him for most of the race and only started to tire at the end. As she flagged, Caldwell found himself doing something he'd never done before: He let her stay in front.

At that point, Caldwell had still been a Ranger, volunteering for missions that dropped him deep into the mountains of the Hindu Kush, where he worked with people he could never tell his fiancée about.

"I'll marry you if the beard goes."

She'd made the offer one night after they'd finished a particularly tough trail run. The beer was cold, tasted good, and they both looked as if they'd been dragged through a mud puddle.

He had laughed and immediately agreed, of course. It hadn't been unexpected; he'd given enough hints that the ultimate question would be inbound soon anyway. Shaving the beard also meant no more trips to the Hindu Kush. A clean-shaved man in the mountains was only a blinking sign that he was an American.

But even without trips to the Kush, the packing and unpacking of Army life quickly grew tiresome. She would plan for races and marathons that he'd have to drop out of at the last minute. It was time to leave the military.

But Caldwell quickly found that he was not meant for a day job. He missed the action, and this job with Alexander Paul's consulting firm had served as the perfect middle ground between repeated combat tours and something that was meaningful and at least slightly more predictable.

He took the private elevator to the twentieth floor, where his badge and a unique key unlocked access to his office.

Alexander Paul's secretary was waiting for Caldwell as he walked in. "Integral wants to meet."

"Again?" Caldwell didn't ask it sarcastically. He'd learned quickly at his new job that the customer ruled the day.

This would be the third meeting of the month with ITD—Integral Transaction Data— a global company that processed payments for nearly every form of credit cards or debit cards in the world, and which was being victimized by a very talented hacker. The phantom was endlessly chipping away at ITD's security, launching thousands of hacks on a daily basis. ITD was accustomed to millions of lesser hacking on a daily basis, but this hack was different. The trail was faint; it came from inside their firewall but originated in Russia, relayed through several servers around the world, but using hacking scripts that contained the fingerprint of Russia. At the very least, the hacker wanted ITD to think he was Russian.

"I know what we need to do," Caldwell's boss, Alexander Paul, had commented about ITD's hacking problem several times, as if there were some other agenda he couldn't share with Caldwell. The only other thing Paul had told him about the ITD job was that Caldwell should keep a firearm handy. So, apparently, the ITD job was dangerous, but Caldwell still had no idea why. He'd locked up all of his guns back when his son started to climb out of the crib. But since the ITD project had gotten underway, he'd been carrying a .38 Smith & Wesson revolver in the glove compartment of his car.

Caldwell had to admit that it felt good…facing unknown danger, carrying a weapon again.

Still, it would have been nice to have a little more background about the job. It had quickly become clear that Paul would only be granting Caldwell access to limited information. Thus far, each time he'd met with the ITD people he'd felt a little like a babysitter—on-site to calm the customer's fears. And perhaps a spy for his boss.

That's fine, he thought as looked at his calendar before calling to schedule another visit with ITD. *It's still a great gig. If Paul wants me to babysit the client, I'll babysit the client. But what kind of babysitter packs a gun?*

Chapter 4

A Remote Frozen Lake in the Yukon

Will Parker pulled his backpack from the aircraft with two sleeping bags and his .300 Winchester Short Magnum rifle. The Otter's cargo had shifted with the broken skid. It left the airplane in such a tilt that the lower wing nearly touched the surface of the ice.

At least it held, Will thought as he put the strap of the rifle over his shoulder.

The pothole lakes in the Yukon were famous for being very deep. An airplane that had sunk to the bottom would be hardly worth the expense of bringing it up to the surface. Once the electronics had been dunked, the Otter would never see a blue sky again.

More importantly, they were in one piece and dry. A dunking for either him or her could be as dangerous as being soaked in gasoline and lighting a match, with the bitter air and approaching storm. Even a fire might not be able to dry one off quick enough in temperatures well below zero.

"We'll get you out of here." Will stroked the Otter's airframe like a father rubbing a sick child's head. He had had too many close calls in his bird to let this be the final word.

He helped Karen onto the shoreline. It was not dark yet and there was still some daylight, although darkness fell early in the Yukon this time of year.

"I've got to get the word out."

He traversed the lake ice again, climbed into the aircraft, and retrieved the portable radio from the dash panel where he had left it after landing, then took it back to the shoreline.

"ATC, this is November one-one-two. Mayday, mayday, mayday." He'd escalated the call to a mayday now that the aircraft could not be flown out without major repairs.

He only heard static.

Will reached into his backpack and pulled out his cell phone. The signal was dead.

"What's going on?" Karen, as a scientist, liked the facts.

"My guess is the solar flare." He had seen one screw up the avionics only a few times of his flying in Alaska, but still wasn't sure why it had caused the Otter's engine to stutter.

"There must have been water in the gas." He said the words to himself, but she was close enough to overhear them. Two bad events that came together were not uncommon in this harsh environment.

"What?"

"Nothing." Will had checked the fuel port and knew an additive had been poured in with the gas. Bad fuel was just one guess.

He tried radioing the mayday message again on the SP-400 handheld radio, but again didn't get a response. All he heard was the garble of static.

The problem was that they had headed south from Snag. His flight path should have taken him to the northwest. Any concerned search party would be heading in the wrong direction. And with the storm coming in there wouldn't be a search party for days.

They were on their own.

"November one-one-two is down to the southwest of Snag. Crashed on a pothole lake approximately ten nautical miles southwest of Snag." There was hope that another aircraft might hear the call and relay it to Center. He repeated the message several times, then shrugged and turned to the more important matter. "We need to get ready for this storm."

The darkness would arrive soon and with it the drop of temperature. Well to the north in Barrow, residents wouldn't see the sun for more than sixty days. In Snag, they'd be lucky if they got more than five hours of light at this time of year.

"The snowstorm won't let the temp get too low." Will pulled his parka up over his head. He didn't mention that the drop that followed the storm would be deadly. "Let's get some protection." He pointed to the snow-covered outcrop up the rise from the lake. As they started up the bank from the edge of the lake, Will stopped. A movement caught his eye.

"She won't come back this way." Karen saw the rabid fox crossing the lake, heading back toward Snag. "She is in the early stages."

"What's that mean?"

"She is still a fox. She still thinks and acts like one."

Will pointed his rifle at what appeared to be a snow-covered rock that rose above them like the tail of an airplane. "We can make a lean-to at its base." He had taught young Marines how to make winter survival shelters in the wilderness back at Bridgeport, high in the Sierra Nevada mountains of California. The Mountain Warfare Training Center famously taught how to handle a dunking in a frozen lake with a full pack on. They'd also trained Marines to climb the face of a cliff, then rappel back to the bottom using an Australian descent, a method that involved traveling down the cliff face-first while standing upright. It was not for the faint of heart. And Will Parker had taught them how to do it all.

"I'll get the ax." He hiked back out to the Otter, worked his way to the back of the aircraft, and pulled out a short red-handled tool and a soft-sided duffel bag filled with much-needed survival gear.

Will put Karen to work at the outcrop. He built the frame of their shelter with a downed log that leaned from the top of the outcrop to the ground like the main pole in a tent. Next, he felled several small trees, cutting off the branches and tossing them to her so they could be stacked, one after the other from the tent pole to the ground. She pulled them tight together so as to make a nearly impenetrable wall and then laid pine boughs on the top, keeping her mind busy and her body warm as they worked together.

A long, dead log lay near the edge of the lake. Will trimmed all of the broken branches and pulled it up parallel to the wooden tent she had lashed together to form a long-log firepit. He used another log, which he stacked next to the first one, building a channel for the fire. He used a fire starter in his survival pack with some gathered twigs. Soon, the fire was burning from the center out toward both ends, in its channel between the two logs, causing the warmth of the fire to be like a space heater in a small room. He cut up two small pine trees and pulled them under the lean-to to form a bench under the covering and next to the firepit. Karen layered the pine boughs on the bench and put a sleeping bag on top.

Will leaned the .300 Winchester next to the outcrop, keeping it within easy reach. The fire would provide warmth, but the light risked attracting much more than a dip in the temperature. The glow of the eyes of the pack of wolves would soon be just beyond the light of the fire. He stuffed the survival pack in the corner of the shelter to act as a pillow and a brace from the bitter deep freeze that was coming.

The shelter could have easily protected them through an entire bad winter in the lower forty-eight states. But the Yukon could turn into a fatal deep freeze with the arrival of a single Siberian storm, and it would be nothing like any winter that Dr. Karen Stewart had experienced.

"Here, put this second bag inside the first."

They would need it for the storm that was coming.

* * * *

"November one-one-two is overdue." The air traffic control specialist at the Anchorage Air Traffic Control Center just outside of Anchorage was on the phone with the center in Juneau.

"Who's that?" The boss knew which pilots to worry about, even in the thousands that came through their sectors.

"Parker."

"Do we have an ELT signal?" The boss knew that it would take a significant crash for the emergency locator transmitter to send out an alarm.

"No."

"I know where he is."

"Snag?"

"Yeah, Dr. Stewart of the CDC has a station out there."

"Did you see this front coming in?" The specialist was looking at a radar screen showing approaching weather.

"From Siberia?" Hundreds of miles to the southeast, his Juneau colleague was looking at the same imagery on his screen.

"Yeah. Probably set a record."

"Not in Snag." The temperature would have to go to a record low to beat the history of the small airfield.

Chapter 5

A Remote Inlet on the Eastern Coast of the Baja

The cold floor and the headache from the blow to his head were the first things Todd Newton noticed when he finally stirred to life. He tried to focus with his eyes, but the room was pitch-black. He took in the smell of stale urine and something else, a putrid, decaying, rotting stench that almost made him gag. His vision was useless, but he sensed the presence of a wall opposite him, very close, making the room no larger than a jail cell. He moved his hand to his head to feel the dried blood, but as he did his hand was stopped by the chain that held his wrist.

"Uh… what?" His mouth was dry and he could barely speak.

It hurt too much.

He laid his head back down on the cold tile. There was a constant buzz in his ears. Soon he faded back into unconsciousness.

* * * *

A stream of daylight came through the crack of a window shutter and directly into his face. Todd tried to lean up and saw the shape of the other Marine, motionless in the far corner of the concrete room.

Todd's boots were missing and a chain was around his ankle.

Footsteps came down a stairway on the other side of a thick wooden door. He tried to hold his head up, but gravity seemed to grab it as if he were on another planet.

"Water," he croaked.

A brute of a man with broad shoulders and black hair cut in a short military style, came in, crossed over to him, and kicked him in the stomach.

"*Ooph.*" Todd Newton buckled and tried to hold out his arms to protect himself from another blow. The man crossed over to the other Marine, unlocked her chain, and pulled her up by her hair. He dragged her across the room to the door. Only a whimper of a sound came from her as he and another man pulled her through the door.

Moments later, Todd could hear Lucy's screams through the ceiling. There was a thud, then another, again and again, as if a large object were striking a watermelon.

He covered his face with his unbound hand, as a welcome wave of unconsciousness pulled him back down into the dark.

* * * *

"Todd?" Her voice was a whisper, slurred as if the blows to her head had broken her jaw or shattered teeth.

"Hey. What is this?" He tried to keep his head from spinning.

"They keep asking about Mike."

"Ridges?" Todd's body reacted with a shiver as he said the words. "We haven't talked to him in forever."

"They know we sent emails…."

"How?" In their few communications with their former classmate, they'd always used the deep web, making their emails untraceable.

"They want to know what we said."

"We need to get out of here." He felt as though he was catching his second wind. He understood that they were on their own. The Marines at Pendleton wouldn't miss them for a day or more, and when they did, he wasn't sure they'd even care to look. As far as the Corps was concerned, they were AWOL.

Newton looked around the room. The walls were thick adobe, causing an unpleasant chill in the space. The air held a pungent smell of a well-used fire pit.

"I think we're in Mexico." He tried to lean forward as he spoke the words quietly.

"How?" She was coughing up blood as she spoke. "Why?"

He reached down to the chain around his ankle. A padlock held the chain tightly, restricting the blood flow. The chain around his wrist was just as tight.

"We need a plan."

As he spoke the words, the door swung open again. This time, the man came to the room to Todd, unlocked the chains, and grabbed him by his arm. Todd tried to stand, but the man dragged him like a sack of potatoes. The other man grabbed his other side, and they pulled him through the door, up a short stairway, and into much larger room with windows covered by black plastic trash bags and a large chair in the center.

They carried him to the chair and threw him into it. The second man tied Todd's arms to the arms of the chair. The other, with the short haircut, oversized eyebrows, and a thin, pointed beard that followed his jawline, slapped Todd on the side of his forehead. The blow rattled him for a second. He looked at his captor in the light of a bulb swinging from above. The man had sleepy eyes with a squint that seemed to say that he knew much more than he was willing to say. His dark eyes were the eyes of a killer.

"What did Ridges tell you?" He said the words with a Spanish accent.

Todd tried not to look the man in his eyes.

"Man, I haven't heard from him in forever." Todd looked down as he spoke the words.

"How about emails?" his captor asked.

"I don't know anything." Todd couldn't hold it back. He started to sob.

"What about the dark web?" The man knew what to ask. It was a form of communication that left no trail.

"I don't know."

"Bullshit." He struck Todd again with a slap on the side of his head. "You use Tor."

The Tor browser was a pathway to both the deep and dark web forms of communication. It allowed the user to remain anonymous. The deep web was hidden from the many search engines that comb one's communications or downloads looking for cookies and identifiers. And hidden further in the deep web was the dark web. It was in the dark that the sinister world lived. Tor and a special software tool accessed the dark web. Both led to onion sites. It let the user create a private pathway that sent and received messages through a series of tunnels of interconnected servers. The dark web was like a Harry Potter stairway: The door you entered wasn't the same when you turned around and tried to go back through it. Tor and dark web browsers concealed who sent the email and who got it. They used the designator of .onion instead of .com or .net or .org, and it was impossible to trace or hack. Any 0651 Marine computer specialist with a top-secret clearance who used a .onion address without authority or on his own was looking for serious trouble. If one wanted to communicate with an outlaw in Russia, this was the way to do it.

Todd and Lucy along with Michael Ridges, had studied the dark web at the top-secret Center for Advanced Study of Language in College

Park, Maryland. At the time when Todd Newton had graduated from the program, the .onion network had still been impenetrable. No one could trace or intercept messages within it.

So how would they know he'd written to Michael Ridges? Todd tried to hold a thought while the bindings held his hands tightly to the arms of the chair. He'd heard that some agencies, like the CIA and DIA, were reputed to have a program that followed the use of email addresses into the deep web. If one got lazy and used the same email address on the open internet and in the deep web, those agencies could theoretically track you like a child with muddy shoes coming home and crossing the clean carpet. But even such a program would see the first track and possibly the last track leaving the carpet, but still could not be able to trace the footprints in between.

If, however, they were tracking everything Michael Ridges did, and if they could read his messages, incoming or outgoing, and find the corresponding prints on the other side of the carpet, then the CIA or DIA might be able to tell that Ridges and Todd had been talking.

Still, though, they weren't able to read the conversation.

At least, not until now.

Chapter 6

The Crash Site

The snow and wind ripped across the small lake almost horizontally to its frozen surface. Will covered his eyes and tried to look safely through a crack in his gloved fingers, but only saw a wall of whirling white. The icy particles stung even in the second he glanced through his glove.

"Is it stopping?" Karen was up against his body in the small shelter they had built at the base of the outcropping. She was shivering from the cold. The log fire could barely keep up with the wind and provided little relief.

While using the butt of his rifle to scrape the snow away at one end of the lean-to, Will had struck a piece of metal the size of a pie plate. The aluminum seemed to be some debris left from a hunting camp in years past; he'd gladly switched tools, using the pie plate to dig out the space for the log fire. Once the fire was going, they had both stripped down to their long johns and climbed into the nested sleeping bags, piling their parkas and clothes over the sleeping bags for extra insulation and tucking their boots underneath for pillows.

Now he used his arm to quickly pile more pine boughs on top of the parkas from ones set aside of the lean-to.

She looked up at him, a question in her eyes.

"We need to keep our circulation going." He didn't tell her that it wasn't the snowstorm he feared.

He felt her body heat as they huddled together again.

"What has you worried?" she asked, their faces close together. She was shivering.

"Snag."

"You said that."

"Snag got down to eighty-five-below in 1958."

"Oh."

Will knew what temperatures like that could do. On one mission with the Marines where they tested the worst of cold, he had been to Antarctic and the East Antarctic Plateau to visit the weather station, designated as AGO 3 at the South Pole, where they had recorded temperatures of more than130-below zero. As with men in space, death was a constant risk, but in Antarctica they'd had the equipment needed to survive. Snag could be just as dangerous at eighty-five-below, and they had nothing approaching a proper survival kit.

"Yeah, Snag has the record. The coldest spot in the Yukon. Ever."

The wolves had stopped howling. It was as if they too knew that the blizzard was only the beginning of the cold to come.

* * * *

The sunlight in the late morning seemed to bring no heat with it.

Will pulled the bag down, only to feel the pain of the brutal cold hit his face. As he breathed in, a sharp pain suffused in his nostrils as the icy air hit the warm mucus membrane. His skin soon became numb, his breath freezing as he exhaled. When he spoke, the words came out in a white mist and fell to the ground like a spray of talcum powder.

"Are we going to make it?" Karen looked scared in the sleeping bag below him.

"Yeah." He smiled. "You stay down deep in this while I get a fire going again."

He put on his clothes, parka, and boots and moved as fast as he could to keep his circulation moving. The cold struck so quickly that by the time he got to his gloves he barely could get them on. He held one under his shoulder and used his arm to push his paralyzed hand into it.

The log fire was now only cold embers. Will gathered some dead branches and stuffed them in between the logs. The starter kit seemed to be useless, as the twigs were frozen through. Will looked down to the lake and the airplane and began the hike. He made it to the Otter while rubbing his arms vigorously in an effort to keep his blood flowing.

The airplane had a bleed port on the underside of its wing that allowed the pilot to drain any of that unwanted water out of the fuel tank he had thought might have contributed to the engine stalling. Water and fuel do not mix, so the heavier water would drain from the port first. Will opened the bleed port, but nothing came out of it. If there was water in the tank, it had frozen solid, of course. He went to the underside of the engine, where a fuel line crossed over. With his gloved hands nearly frozen, he used his arms to pull on the line until it broke. He grabbed a cup from the cockpit and collected the slow-flowing, thick liquid into the cup. It moved like molasses.

He trekked up through the cut trees and snow, looking for something and found it: On one side of the clearing, a spruce stump that had been infested by beetles lay in pieces on the ground with one end sticking out through the snow. He knocked the snow off the wood. The tree's trunk lay in pieces on the ground, lightweight, air-pocketed wood rendered perfectly flammable by the pests that had killed it.

With the airplane fuel and the beetle-killed spruce wood, Will restarted the fire in the trench between the two logs. He pulled off the parka and his mucks and climbed back into the bag. Karen's body felt like a warm water bottle.

"We need to keep this going." Will knew the fire not only provided the heat that beat back the cold, but also served as a signal to any aircraft that might be on the lookout. The smoke curled up into the clear sky. The brutal cold brought one benefit: The blue was perfect, unlimited, and had not the slightest impurity like purified water.

"How long?" Karen was looking progressively weaker.

"They should get the word to Whitehorse." Will had used the airfield to the south of Snag as a refueling point when he traveled to this side of the mountains. It was now well into day two and the solar flare had long passed. Hopefully, all of the traveling aircraft had been accounted for except one and the search had already begun. The problem was that any search planes would be looking to the north of them.

"In the dark we may have a better chance."

"Why?"

"The fire should stick out on a satellite pass." If a weather bird was anywhere near an orbit that could cross near Snag, the fire would stand out in the dark. The one benefit of the Siberian front was that it had cleared away all of the cloud cover.

"Why did you come to Alaska?" Karen asked suddenly.

He'd never noticed how readily she could smile in the face of adversity.

"To fly." It was not necessarily the true answer, but it was the correct choice.

"Well, you did get that," she said, laughing.

"Yeah," he said, pulling her closer. "I got it good."

Chapter 7

The Hidden Casa on the Eastern Coast of the Baja

Todd Newton's wrists and ankles were both chained to the metal frame of a small bunk bed he had been moved to. He slid down to the base of the bed and was able to slide the chain down to the floor. His exhaustion smothered what little energy he had left. He was well into his second day with no food or water. It took all of the power he had to bump the bed up while he pulled on the chain. He repeated it several times and, on the third try, the chains finally came away from the bed. Just as they did, he heard the footsteps.

The door swung open and the blinding light from upstairs filled the room. The two men threw his companion onto the bunk bed on the other side of the room. Todd didn't dare move, hoping that they would not come his way. They left the room and slammed the door.

He dragged himself across the floor to Lucy's limp body. She had been beaten severely.

"We're gonna get out of here," he whispered into her ear.

"Okay." She slurred her words. He could tell that her life force was leaving quickly.

"Come on lance corporal!" He helped her stand with her arm slung over his shoulder and they made their way toward the door.

She could barely walk. He stopped and waited for her.

"I didn't know you had it in you." She looked into his eyes. Then, with great effort, began moving again toward the door.

"Thanks." Todd had always been the geek in the room. The son of a Marine colonel and the ninety-pound weakling when it came to sports, he'd long sought refuge in computers. He had never seen himself as the rescuing hero, except maybe in a computer game. Now, for once in his life, he felt like a Marine.

He checked the door. Unlocked.

If he or his companion had known that they were more than a hundred miles from the nearest Pemex gas station or police station, they would have understood that escape was impossible. The east coast of the Baja peninsula this far south was inhospitable; barren, rocky, and hot. Its only inhabitants were the cactus, scorpions, tarantulas, and the occasional lost donkey.

Todd had reached the top of the stairs when the blow to the back of his head knocked him to the ground. His face rebounded off of the wooden floor and he heard only the familiar ringing in his ears.

Once again, he felt only blinding pain. He had no way of knowing that his efforts had just guaranteed his friend's death.

Chapter 8

The Frozen Lake Southeast of Snag

The second night seemed more brutal than the first. Will kept the fire going despite no sleep. Strangely, the fire's glow seemed to attract the wolves. They had resurfaced as if hunger overtook the need for shelter from the cold. The howls seemed to get closer with every passing minute.

"How long can we last?" Karen had the sound of defeat in her voice.

Will knew that the cold could do that to a person. A laugh could change in minutes to a voice faint with desperation.

"We've got this." Will didn't plan on letting her give in. "The rescue planes will make a circle pattern around Snag. Tomorrow they should cover this lake."

He stoked the fire and then leaned back into the sleeping bag. Karen Stewart had started to shiver. He knew that it was the body's defense against the cold. Muscles would contract and expand in short blasts in an effort to create heat. The body was trained to protect the core. When the muscles in her jaws started to do the same, her teeth would begin to chatter.

He was so close that he could hear the chatter and feel the small body shake in almost convulsions.

"Hold on." Will pulled up his parka with one hand sticking out of the bag. He rifled through the pockets of his parka until he came across something. It was a Snickers candy bar, as solid as a piece of clay that had been forged in a kiln. He held it close to the fire as if roasting a marshmallow. It picked up some of the heat from the fire, but not enough to cause the wrapper to be singed. With time the block of chocolate soon became warm enough to chew.

"Eat this." The sugar would raise her core temperature. And the warmth of the bar would help stop the shivers.

"This can't be as bad as Somalia, right?" he asked as she ate the candy bar.

She nodded and shivered, but not from the cold. Being a captive of Al-Shabaab in Somalia had been a living nightmare that she hadn't expected to survive. It was there that they'd first met. And there that he knew her will to survive had kept her alive.

Will pulled her close, sharing in the warmth of the inside of the sleeping bag. "At least it wasn't cold in Africa."

She shook her head as she snuggled into him.

"So, what's next? Hot or cold?" he asked, referring to her history of working in both extremes.

"A beach would be nice."

"Something like Orange Beach?"

The sugar powder white sands of the Alabama coast were a reminder of a past trip the two had taken. On a bright, summer day the sun's heat was amplified by its reflection off of the white sand. The thought captured the best opposite of the extreme of this brutally cold Yukon.

"Yeah."

"Think of it. Put it in your head." He was suggesting she grab that visual memory.

"Okay."

"But you volunteered to come to the Yukon?" Will kept his arm around her, cuddling her head on his shoulder.

"It sounded good at the time."

There was movement in the dark just beyond the glow of the fire.

"What is it?" Her voice had the sound of a small child afraid of the dark.

"Most likely a curious wolf." His voice remained calm.

"If the pack's infected with rabies, they'll become unpredictable."

He nodded. Animals infected with rabies soon became confused and agitated, and ultimately violent, as the virus burned up their brain.

"Why's it here?" Will asked, using the question to keep her mind working and help it keep from wandering in the deadly freeze. "Why did it come this far north?"

"Climate change."

"What's that got to do with rabies?"

"Climate disruption means more warm spells during winter. Warm spells allow earlier and better paths of migration to the north. When an infected animal ranges north, it takes the disease with it. The dominoes connect."

He saw movement again in the shadows. The night had passed and it was morning, but in the Arctic, it was still dark.

"What about a wolf?" he asked the expert huddled in his arms.

"They can be the worst. A wolf is scared of a human, but a wolf with rabies goes into a severe aggressive state."

Will leaned up, pulled off his glove, reached for his rifle, and pulled it close, wincing at the painfully cold steel. It was a mistake to touch the metal with bare flesh. He handled it like someone taking it out of an oven, checking the bolt to see the gold brass end of the round in the chamber and then locking the bolt back down. He quickly put on his glove and moved his fingers to induce circulation. Will laid the rifle down in the little space between the sleeping bag and the log fire. He picked up the piece of aluminum scrap and used it to stoke the fire.

"Today they'll come," she said with certainty, as if the candy bar had given her a new perspective on life.

"You mean a rescue?" He didn't need any more wolves.

She smiled again.

Chapter 9

Cupertino, California

The corporate headquarters of Integral Transaction Data was a campus of green reflective glass and bright aluminum-clad buildings. The structures hadn't been in existence for more than eight years, and the company was only a little more than a decade old. The stock climbed through the roof after its initial public offering, its fate tied directly to the economy. The more people felt comfortable with their personal finances, the more they turned to their credit and debit cards. A large plastic credit card hung above the ITD campus's entryway.

It was a pitch-black night. Lampposts lit up the computer company's campus; instinctively, Frank Caldwell kept to the shadows as much as possible. Given his work history, he'd developed a paranoia about security cameras. He wore a black baseball cap and sunglasses, even in the low light, over an everyday black rain jacket and jeans. His clothes and hat bore no logos.

If he met a man on the street, it would have been difficult for the man to later recall a description. Caldwell knew enough tradecraft to blend in with the background and people around him.

There was a side entrance to the second building. A man waited there, also staying in the shadows.

"Thanks for coming." The man held the door open and handed Caldwell a clip-on pass marked with the word *Visitor*. Unlike a normal visitor's pass, though, this card would enable access to every corner of the facility.

Caldwell nodded back.

The contract that Paul had was with the firm Baker, Alexander and Hamilton, which had its own agreement with ITD. The bill-processing company used Baker for security, as did many others. In fact, Baker nearly dominated the field of cybersecurity contracting in government-related industries. In turn, Baker sometimes subcontracted Alexander Paul's firm to carry out its work. Hundred-million-dollar contracts were typical for both companies, as were "black agreements" that ensured complete secrecy regarding exactly who was doing work for whom. Similarly, the dollars for those black projects typically came from unmarked or mismarked funds buried deep in the budgets of corporations and governments.

Caldwell and his escort walked down a narrow hall to another set of locked and secured doors. After several passes and inspections, he walked into a small computer room insulated with brown, foam-like soundproof walls.

"You know the team." The ITD guide pointed to the two sitting at computers. They looked like they were on break from a twelfth-grade AP computer science class. A young woman with a shaggy bob haircut dyed with ombré green highlights and thick Tom Ford glasses glanced up from her computer. A guy in a bright yellow shirt with the word *Geek* stenciled across it and wearing black Converse high-tops also acknowledged Caldwell by lifting his Red Bull can in a salute.

"No names," Caldwell reminded his guide. The ITD manager didn't know Caldwell. Caldwell, however, did know the team and their backgrounds.

"This is the latest spear-phishing. Just came across today." The host stood behind the woman's chair.

"Right." Caldwell looked at the screen. Paul had recruited him because of his background at West Point in information technology. It had helped during his Ranger tour as well. He knew the basics of writing code, but this stuff went well beyond his limits.

The young woman was the designated Russian expert. She had been born Russian, spoke Russian, and thought Russian, but outwardly she was pure Boston and had been a quick study at MIT. Her move to America from Russia had come while she was in diapers, so she only had as much Russian in her as she cared to display.

"It's good," she said, as if saluting a talented adversary.

"We run the credit cards for most of America and several other countries," the ITD guide said. He looked like the big brother of the pair in the room. Caldwell knew him to be their manager, their boss and, more importantly, their biggest cheerleader.

"How much in all, approximately?"

"Well over a trillion a year."

"If Russia or China breaks into this vault," the guide said, "the free world's in deep trouble. God forbid if Bureau One-twenty-one does it."

"One-twenty-one?" Caldwell should have known the reference.

"Our buddies in Pyongyang," the woman told him.

Caldwell noticed that they had all chewed their fingernails to the quick. They seemed on edge, but energized. No surprise. Their desks were littered with Red Bull cans. Like good chess players, they were tasked with trying to anticipate not only their opponent's next move, but one or two more moves after that.

"We have zero tolerance here," said the host. ITD handled everyone's Visa bill, so their work was scrutinized daily by millions of eyes when the cardholder opened his statement. And it was the highest level of scrutiny. An overcharge for that dinner at the pizza place of even a dollar set off alarms. So, there was no tolerance for mistakes.

"Not anymore," she said.

The man gave her a frosty glare.

Caldwell knew what she was referring to and why he was there.

"Who?" That's what he had to report back. "That's what I want to know."

He didn't realize that his boss already had the answer.

Chapter 10

The Frozen Triangle of the Yukon

"Today we get out of here."

"Okay." Karen lifted her head from deep inside the sleeping bag, so close to him that her skin scraped against the two days of stubble on his cheeks.

"It's finally warming up." Will pulled himself out of the bag, quickly dressed in his clothes, parka, pulled on his mucks, and did it all much quicker than the last time so that his hands would still function when he put on his gloves. He knelt at the edge of the sleeping bags. The log fire was down again to smoldering embers. Its smoky smell gave the sense of warmth despite the fact that it had stopped putting out any heat some time ago.

The smoke reminded both of food and the lack of it. Hunger was starting to set in.

"To what?" She had shivered throughout the night and only gotten sleep in short bursts. The cold crept through the bottom of the two sleeping bags. The hips and the shoulders would compress the bag where the body weight would push down. And it was in those spots where the cold would attack first. They would turn over, trying to protect what little warmth there was and then fall asleep again. The cycle of movement did not happen in unison, which meant that a bout of cold or the other's movement might wake both parties up at any time.

"Well," he said. "Still subzero. Let me see your nose." He held her head like a doctor examining a patient. He took his glove off and felt it with his warm hand. "Frostbite can move quick. Where's your backpack?"

"Here." She had moved it during the night to serve as a brace between herself, the sleeping bags, and the outcropping.

Will opened it up and looked through it.

"Aha," he said. "I thought you might have it." He pulled out a banana and taped it on a nearby rock. It was frozen solid despite being in the pack. He pulled the peel from it and cut off a square with a knife. He held the piece of skin close to the smoldering embers until it regained some warmth.

"Hold this on your nose."

The peel started to warm her skin gradually. It served as an extra layer of heated skin.

"It smells like a banana."

He laughed. "That's because it is."

It reminded her again, however, that they hadn't eaten now for more than forty-eight hours except for the Snickers bar.

"I'm hungry."

The banana was of no help. It was as solid as a brick. He tried to heat it up and it fell apart in the process.

"Here." He pulled another candy bar from his pack. It was as solid as the last one. "It's all I got."

She clumsily pulled the wrapper off with her gloved hand. Finally, in frustration, she used her teeth to pull back the plastic.

"Just let it melt in your mouth." The sugar would be slowly absorbed as the ninety-eight-degree temperature of her body broke it down. Will smiled. "It reminds me of Fentanyl."

The opioid medication used by medics came in lollipop form so it could be absorbed directly into the membrane of the mouth and the bloodstream. Will recalled the pain of his wounds fading quickly away in a sleepy haze. He hadn't liked it. Neither did the medic. Another man with his leg shattered by an explosive device and screaming in pain would crush the lollipop in his mouth. More than one man had to be pulled back from the rush of the powerful narcotic, which was more than eighty times stronger than an injection of morphine.

"What?"

"Nothing."

He could feel the bitter cold air as he inhaled it through his nose. It still caused a burning sensation. As he exhaled through his mouth, fog projected again into the air.

The sun had started to climb over the hill mass to the east. He didn't need to see a clock to know that it had to be well into the morning for the light to start to break through the forest canopy. The air remained clear, cold, and painful.

"The wolves got close last night." He stood and kicked the fire with his boot. "The pack doesn't seem to be infected yet." In fact, their behavior seemed perfectly normal. The pack acted with patient and deliberate hesitation, much like a good Marine Raider patrol studying a target and plotting their point of attack.

"If they eat the flesh of something infected it won't be long." She looked out over the lake.

"Think your fox made it?" He remembered the direction it had taken from the lake—back toward Snag.

"Not likely, especially given the—"

Her voice stopped as they heard the deep bass sound of a radial engine. It was unmistakable. Each piston, in a circle, firing with a combined force of energy moving to the center, turning the propeller. It sounded like the bass track of a classic rock song.

An Otter came low across the lake. Like his, the bold, bright yellow stood out in sharp contrast to the white, green, and blue above.

Will ran out to the center and fired his rifle.

The search was over.

It turned, waggled its wings, then lined up against what little wind there was. The Otter lumbered across the small ice lake and extended its flight path before turning back to land. With his flaps down, the pilot gently guided the aircraft just above the tops of the trees on the far end and floated down until its skids struck the surface.

Will carried Karen to the airplane, as the relentless cold and lack of food had made it difficult for her to walk. He lifted her up into a seat in the cargo hold and felt the warmth of the cabin as he sat her down. It was probably no more than a few degrees above freezing inside, but it felt like a heated sauna. He shook the pilot's hand, ran back up to the lean-to, and grabbed their gear while the Otter's engine kept running. His legs were stiff and he hobbled as he moved back toward the airplane. They had survived the worst that the Yukon could throw at them.

Will took one last glance at the shelter that they had made. It was solid and would probably last for several more winters. It had, however, served its purpose for them. The wolf pack would pass through it shortly after man's machine left and silence returned to the woods. The leader would sniff the candy wrapper, taste it with his tongue, and then head off into the forest, perhaps following the trail of a lost, sick arctic fox.

By the time they found it, Karen and he would be back in Anchorage.

Chapter 11

Near Dulles, Virginia

"So, what am I doing here, sir?" Caldwell was on a secure line at ITD. On the other end was his employer, Alexander Paul. The encrypted phone served to keep the conversation only between the two.

Caldwell had a general base of knowledge about the information technology world, but only the basics compared to the operators at ITD. He had graduated from the Point with the special major of electronic and IT systems, training in web development and, more importantly, network security. But two years in the Rangers had pulled him completely out of the fast-moving IT field. Technology didn't wait for Caldwell's private career to begin.

At this point, he was still trying to get a handle on what was going on at ITD.

"We have an idea as to who's behind the hack," said A.P. Then, lowering his voice, "The first wave hit just after ITD announced its contract with me."

Even though they were speaking on a secure line, it seemed to Caldwell that his boss was holding something back.

For his part, Caldwell stood in a soundproof room deep within the ITD campus. Thick brown acoustic foam covered the walls, much as it had in the operation center he'd visited earlier. The smothering silence in the room swallowed any spoken word as it left his lips. The space had the silence of a church sanctuary in the middle of the week.

"Okay…." Caldwell wasn't sure what to make of A.P.'s remark. His boss seemed to be saying was that the ITD hacking attack was actually subtly directed toward Alexander Paul himself. And A.P. *seemed* to know who the attacker was.

Caldwell felt the warmth of the phone against his ear and realized that, unconsciously, he was pressing it hard against his head, as if to let out the stress of receiving insufficient information about his mission.

"I need you to follow a lead."

"Yes, sir."

"There was a team of three working on a project in a cyber school that closely resembles this hack. Two of them were Marines in training for their military cyber specialty. The other was an independent who worked for Baker."

"What school?"

"It's at the University of Maryland. It is the training ground for high-level computer operations. NSA and CIA use it for all of their entry-level IT training."

"What were they working on?"

"We know that one, for sure, was trying to break the code on the deep web."

"I didn't think it could be done."

"Yeah, correct."

"Oh, shit." Caldwell knew that if one could break open darknets or even deep nets, it would be an earth-shattering event. All of the criminals on the globe seemed to agree that the one place the law couldn't look into was the deep web. The index of a .onion dark web gave one a quick understanding of what the web was used for. Lists included how to purchase illegal automatic guns, drugs, and contact hired killers.

Only 4 percent of the internet is what the public sees. Ninety-six percent is in the deep web and within the deep web is another world: the dark web. Both forms of the internet are undecipherable and untraceable. But it is in the deep web that everything evil lurks. Heroin bought on the deep web was shipped out of Bulgaria as if it were candy. Tunisia sold sex slaves, some of which were white Europeans who made the mistake of backpacking through North Africa. And the virtual private networks allowed no trace of who sent what or received anything.

The flow of money for drugs, terrorism, and other sinister activities passed through the deep web. Child pornography worked through the deep web. Heroin could be FedEx'd by an order on the unbreakable network. The director of the FBI had made a pronouncement some time ago that they had cracked the dark web, but no one in the IT community believed him. It remained too complex. It was like a safe that changed its combination every time the dials were turned. No path was repeated.

The deep web and the dark web were overlay networks that used the internet system, but enabled users to make contact point-to-point, one person to another in a way that made their conversations untraceable.

"The brains of the group left the country some time ago." Paul didn't say the name, but clearly knew it. More was not being said. The man worked for DIA. He was a cyber operator and, seemingly, one of exceptional talent. More than that, he quickly rose to being the IT advisor to the director of DIA. He had direct access to everything—or, at least, what most thought was everything.

The cyber operator saw things that no one else was supposed to see. And then one night he saw something not meant for even his eyes. Before the offices opened up the next morning, he was gone like smoke blown away by a gust of wind. The disappearance of the cyber operator was more than a breach of national security.

The FBI wanted to know why he left so abruptly. What did he know? What had he seen? The Senate Committee on Intelligence made an inquiry that seemed to go nowhere. There were no answers. But the disappearance revealed a sloppy cybersecurity system at the director's office. And this resulted in the director losing his job. Or at least, that was what the wolves in Washington used as the excuse to fire Alexander Paul. It wasn't difficult for Paul to have a list of enemies waiting for his head to be on the chopping block.

And then the cyber technician suddenly showed up in Moscow. A close aide who unexpectedly disappears, and resurfaces in Moscow, coupled with a lax cyber system at the director's office, caused considerable embarrassment to the director and his boss, the president.

If Alexander Paul were driven, as some of his critics claimed, by vengeance, then the man who cost him the leadership of DIA would be the number-one name on his list. Losing his DIA post had blocked Paul's rising star and broken his trust and favor with the president. And the current president was not one to forgive.

Caldwell listened to the few words said. He immediately knew that he needed to retain a memory of everything that was spoken.

"What about the other two?"

"That's part of it."

"Yes, sir."

"I'll brief you in more detail when you get back here." Paul hung up before Caldwell could say good-bye.

The flight back to Washington was a red-eye that carried him across the country in the dark. He rarely drank, but two scotches with soda helped him nod off for a brief nap. The benefit of Paul and the private sector meant that Caldwell enjoyed all of his flights up front. The billion-dollar client didn't care or notice the first-class transportation required. For his part, Alexander Paul took it to another level, using a private jet whenever his presence was required.

And it didn't matter.

Caldwell knew that the problem ITD was facing could be catastrophic. If ITD had any hint that their new hacking threat was directed against the man they had hired to be their security consultant, the first-class seats, private jets, and millions of dollars would stop as fast as an unplugged computer. Viewed from that perspective, Caldwell could see why A.P. was holding the secret so closely.

But if Caldwell knew anything from an Army career spent fighting terrorism, it was this: There's always more to be revealed.

Chapter 12

Anchorage

The rescue Otter taxied up to Land and Sea Aviation at Merrill Field in Anchorage. Built in 1930, the small airport lay to the south of Elmendorf Air Force base and served as a home base to many of Alaska's bush pilots. Merrill was the first airport for Anchorage and served as the portal of aviation into the vast territory. The fixed-base operator had an ambulance waiting for Karen and Will by the time the aircraft's engine stopped spinning.

"They'll take you to the hospital to be checked out." Will helped her out of the aircraft. She could stand but was somewhat wobbly.

"I'm okay." Karen had gotten back much of her energy. The Otter had a thermos full of hot coffee loaded with sugar that she'd sipped from an aluminum cup on the flight back to Anchorage. Soon the thermos was drained.

"Sure, just let them check out some of those red spots on your nose and ears." He was sure that the frostbite had been stopped early enough, but wanted to make sure there was no permanent damage. "I'm sure CDC wants to make sure their doctor came back in one piece."

"I smell like a banana."

"It worked, didn't it?" He knew she was regaining her energy.

Will gave a nod to the man standing next to the open doors of the ambulance. He wore a parka that had the monogram of the CDC on it and had a large, pleasant smile, clearly happy to see that the missing scientist had returned from the wilderness.

"You know how cold it got?" the CDC man asked, referring to Snag.

"No."

"You set a record out there. Eighty-seven degrees below zero yesterday. As best as we can tell, the coldest spot on the North American continent."

"It wasn't that bad." Karen smiled shyly and unconsciously touched her healing nose. The color was quickly returning.

"I'm going to my cabin for a bit, but I'll check on you soon." Will stood at eye level with Karen as they put her on the stretcher and into the ambulance.

"Thank you," she said, "but I'll be fine."

"Hey, I'm the one that crashed the plane."

"No," she said with a smile. "You landed the plane."

* * * *

As the ambulance pulled away, Will turned to the pilot of the Otter.

"Can you do me a favor and fly me up to my cabin?"

"For a fifth of Jack Black," the pilot said, "I'll do about anything. No prob."

As members of the brotherhood of bush pilots, both men knew that such favors tended to be repaid several times over in the Arctic. It was a brotherhood that no one wanted to upset.

Will agreed. Actually, he was tempted to send a half gallon, but that would be like tipping a hundred-dollar bill at a hamburger joint. A fifth would do as well, plus Will would be sure that the FBO topped off the pilot's tanks on Will's account.

His cabin stood on a rise above the Susitna River and well to the north of Anchorage. It had its own airstrip and near the end of the strip, just below the trees, was a hangar that appeared unusually large for a private compound. His ranch had another feature that was unique. Most of the airfields in the backcountry had, at best, dirt runways. Will's little airfield had a concrete airstrip designed to endure the extreme cold. It was too short to accommodate a big jet, but it worked fine for the kind of aircraft that Alaskan pilots tended to fly. The concrete was scored so as to give better traction and drainage. He even had a plow that cleared it when the snowfall built up.

"Thanks again." Will took off his glove and shook the man's hand.

"No problem."

The rule in Alaska was that if a pilot diverted from another job, the cost of the rescue included the money lost from what other job was missed. Many a hapless hunter found out the hard way that when another guide had to divert to do a rescue, the bill was significant. Guided hunts ran for thousands and thousands of dollars. However, the rule did not apply to a downed aircraft and especially not for Will Parker. The other bush pilots knew that if there was another downed aircraft, he would be one of the first in the sky for the search.

Nevertheless, Will was grateful.

"How bad was the solar flare?"

"It shut down a lot."

"Well, I owe you one."

The man just smiled.

Will's pilot dropped him off near the hangar, then turned around, taxied a short distance, and lifted off. Will watched as the other Otter climbed out over the trees and banked to the east and north. The guttural, raspy sound soon disappeared and silence reigned supreme.

Will threw his backpack over his shoulder with the rifle and headed first to the hangar. The doors didn't need locks this far away from the world. The dark green building stood out in the winter months, but would have been barely noticeable in the summer. It had been built with heavy foam-insulated walls that kept the interior above the freezing mark.

He turned on the lights that filled the vast space with a fluorescent glow. Instantly revealed was the empty space where his missing Otter was normally kept. Next to it was a small white and black HondaJet HA-420 jet aircraft. With the tail number of N883CS, the jet went by the call sign Coyote Six. It was a new-era aircraft that topped out at close to five hundred miles an hour and cost a mint. The US government had been kind to Parker. At least it had recognized, if reluctantly, what it owed him. For his efforts in taking out one of the most dangerous scientists in North Korea, Will Parker had received money under the RJP program that ensured his financial independence for life. The feds had a short list of those whose capture or killing warranted a payout of twenty-five million. Abu Bakr al-Baghdadi had been on that exclusive list, along with the North Korean scientist that Will brought to his end. The United States government had a short list of those it wanted so bad that the bounty was in the millions. The Rewards for Justice program rarely paid out but when it did bad men were removed.

"I'll get the fellows at Whitehorse to help get her out," he mumbled to himself, thinking of his downed Otter. He knew that as long as the ice held, there would be no rush in retrieving the airplane from the lake. And with temperatures hitting more than eighty-below, the ice would stay stable for some time.

Will turned off the light, closed up, and headed for the cabin. Although it was only 4:00 p.m., the day had turned dark and cold, night descending even more quickly than in Snag, because Will's cabin was well north of Anchorage. The porch held a stack of cut firewood for the winter. It wouldn't take long for a fire to heat up the cabin.

Soon it was pitch-black in the woods surrounding his property. Will got some comfort in the isolation. He heard the pack of wolves that he knew were his neighbors howling in a chorus. One would call to another, who would answer, and they would go on, back and forth, for some time. The wind began to pick up.

"When will rabies hit them?" he asked the crackling logs in the fireplace, thinking of the resident pack that crossed through his woods on a regular basis. He used an iron poker to push the logs and, as he did, they would flare up and light the room. Snag was far to the east and south, well into the interior and beyond the coastal mountain range. The cold triangle, as it was called, was not on a coastline. It was known as the place where temperatures would reach low. There was one in Siberia that also was famous for records. In the cold triangles, far from the warmth of the oceans, winters lasted a long time. And the triangle where Snag was located remained a deep freeze throughout the winter. But warmth would come, and during those higher temps, the infestation would again move north.

Karen would go back to Snag as soon as she possibly could. Of that, Will had no doubt. She would overcome any fear and complete her mission. That was another thing he liked about Dr. Stewart.

Chapter 13

The Hidden Casa on the Eastern Baja Coast

"Good god." Todd's mouth was dry when he woke up on his bed, still locked to the chains. This time they had doubled the locks and added one around his neck. Escape was hopeless. He could barely reach his hand to his face and feel the caked blood. Everything was sore, especially where they had hit him on his shins with some small club. He had, however, become used to the horrific smell of his cave, his senses having adapted to the days of captivity. But his thirst overwhelmed him.

They had left a small metal cup of water on the floor near the bed. He could only reach it by stretching his cuffed hand as far as the chain would go, and then the cup barely touched the tip of his fingers. It was a sophisticated form of torture. He concentrated on the cup, slowly stretching his arm against the restraint, pushing against the burning chain that cut into his wrist until he was able to nudge it close enough to get the cup in his grip.

The water was warm and it burned his cut lips, but it was exquisite. He couldn't remember the last time he'd taken a drink. This cup barely satisfied his thirst.

In all of his interrogation sessions so far, Todd hadn't told his captors anything, not because he was particularly brave, but because he didn't know anything. At least nothing new.

Back when CNN had reported that a cyber technician from the Defense Intelligence Agency had shown up in Moscow, Todd was brought into the commanding officer's office at MarForCyBer.

"You were in class with Ridges?"

"Yes, sir."

"If you hear from him, you need to let us know."

"Yes, sir." Todd paused. "Sir? What happened?"

"No idea." Todd's commanding officer was rarely so brief.

After leaving the office, he called his classmate on his cell. She was still in the DC area. They met for a beer after duty.

"Any idea?"

"Not a one."

They tried something very dangerous. With a computer borrowed from another Marine. they reached out to Ridges through the dark web. The only response was a cryptic *Beware!*

He pondered what Ridges knew that could be so dangerous. For that matter, what could Todd himself know or have done to cause these men to chain his friend and him to bunks in the cell of a Mexican cartel's hacienda somewhere deep in the Baja.

Todd thought back to boot camp. It didn't have anything to do with Ridges, but everything to do with his survival. His father hadn't thought he'd make it through, and he'd made it clear that the Marines was the wrong choice. The colonel had told Todd in no uncertain terms that a kid who spent most of his life in a dark room playing video games would never make it. In boot camp, his drill instructor had quickly dubbed Todd "Private Geek." But the boot-camp brass and his drill instructors knew how Todd's enlistment scores had tested out; his designated military specialty had been set in stone before he first put his foot down on the famous markers at San Diego. Footprints were painted on the asphalt in a perfect formation so that the only thing the new recruit had to do was put his feet on the prints. Like basic primary colors for a kindergartner, it was the first introduction to military life. He would be a cyber operator. The drill instructors knew that the Marines needed 0651s, and while they offered no special treatment to Todd, they also didn't want to lose him.

Todd Newton also had something else working for him. He wasn't going to let his father win.

Boot camp taught him one thing: He had more inside him than he had ever realized. He excelled at the run, which caused the drill instructors to lighten up. It was a physical talent that he hadn't expected to possess. While several recruits could barely make it to the finish line of a three-mile run, Todd gained respect when he crossed it at just under eighteen minutes. After that, he became progressively better during boot camp and came close to breaking seventeen minutes in the physical fitness test. He loved the runs that took place every day before sunup. The ones where they took off without waiting for the remainder of the platoon. Those runs gave him a brief sense of freedom from the rigors of the days of training. From the start, Todd quickly left most of the others behind with his fast pace; only a few weeks into the training, he ran alone in the front. He would feel the cold sweat on his face, his steps becoming lighter as he built up his endurance. And in the final test for the Eagle, Globe, and Anchor, Todd Newton surprised everyone. He handled the three days of exercise, lack of sleep, forced marches, and hunger with a resilience that caused his two drill instructors to shake his hand with sincere, meaningful grips. He held in his hand the small badge that signified he had become a Marine – a small black globe with its anchor and eagle.

"I can handle this." He spoke the words aloud to himself despite the fact that two of his front teeth had been knocked out. The memory of those brutal runs gave him a barometer to gauge his pain. It hurt, but it was endurable. Todd glanced at the other side of the room.

"We've got this." He stared into the darkness and repeated the line that his drill instructor used repeatedly. It took his eyes a minute or two to decipher the fact that there was no shape in the small bed where his fellow Marine had been. He was talking to no one.

The screams resumed upstairs.

"Bastards!" He pulled the chains, but to no avail.

He heard the same thuds of something hitting flesh, followed by a woman's whimper. It seemed to go on endlessly.

And finally, there was silence.

Todd heard words spoken in what seemed to be Spanish. The thick walls muffled the sounds, but it was clear that the two men were shouting at each other. They seemed to be throwing the blame back and forth.

Todd heard a door open and the two struggling to drag a heavy weight across the upper floor. The men were still cussing, each blaming the other for what had happened. But there was no sound of remorse. Although Todd didn't understand the Spanish, he did understand the inflection of the words. They were upset not by what they'd done, but by the prospect of explaining to their boss what had happened. The deeper voice belonged to the big man, Todd could tell that much. His words sounded much less remorseful.

The upstairs door closed with a slam and was followed by silence. It remained that way well into the night.

Chapter 14

Sleep overcame Will Parker as he sat in his chair before the fireplace. The warmth was a change from what they had endured for several nights. He heard a noise—what seemed like an engine—well off in the distance. Will swallowed some of his coffee from a cup. It had turned cold as a consequence of his dozing off, but the drink had as much cognac in it as coffee, and it burned as he swallowed.

The engine noise returned, coming closer. This was out of place for the cabin. Will lived well off of any road that might have been plowed. A vehicle that braved the ten or so miles of unplowed roadway that connected the cabin to civilization, and in the dark, was being driven by someone with a purpose. Will listened to the sound that could only be connected to man. Nature's sounds tended to be softer and irregular. This rumble sounded like a vehicle well fitted for the backcountry and plowing through drifts of snow.

Will leaned forward in his chair. As he did, he felt the increased warmth of the fire as he got closer to the flames. He had an automatic pistol on a small table next to his chair. The HK VP40 felt cold in his grip as he picked it up. He pulled back the slide to see the brass round chambered. It was one of thirteen 180-grain Winchester PDX1 Defender brass bullets in the gun, the other twelve stored in the magazine. He knew these details, because it had long been his livelihood and job to know such things. Much like the military, living in the wilderness required a man to know his weapons down to the precise number of rounds left in the firearm. More than one warrior's life had come to an end because he lost count of what remained in the magazine.

As he sat up with the automatic pistol in his hand, lights crossed the wall through a crack in the shutters. At that same moment he heard a vehicle's tires crush the snow and ice and come to a stop. Will crossed the room and stood to one side of the door behind a thick beam that formed the door's jamb. The wood would stop any projectile. It would also give him that brief moment he needed in order to learn where the shot was coming from and aim and shoot back.

A truck door slammed shut. Will leaned near a window, careful to only glance through the edge. A motion-detector light shined on the dark shape of a vehicle and its former occupant. The truck had oversized snow tires and a winch on the front grille—made to handle the outback of Alaska. Will lifted the HK to his chest. It was an instinct that he had learned long ago. A well-aimed shot came from consistency. The pistol or rifle needed to be ready to move to the target with as little wasted motion as possible.

The man had his parka hood pulled up over his head. The rabbit-fur ruff all but sealed the face from view. He was large, easily over six feet tall, and moved slowly, like someone who spent his entire life sitting in a chair. He had on white rubber boots made for the extreme cold. He held his hands in his pockets, causing Will to tighten his grip on the HK. If a weapon came out of that pocket, the stranger would hear the door swing open and be dead before a second step had been taken.

The man seemed startled by the motion-detector light, but didn't seem lost or out of place. He acted as if he knew where he was going and as if he had been here before. It wasn't likely that one who made the trek down the road to this cabin was a wanderer. No one wandered in this wilderness in the winter in the dark and lived.

"Only one door," Will murmured as he assessed the situation. Others could be approaching from the wings, but he was prepared to take it one step at a time. His cabin had limited access, a thick door to the front and one to the rear, near the kitchen. Both were well bolted and the windows were shuttered with aged hardwood, almost as if Will had known that an assault would come one day.

The sound of steps came from just beyond the door. But for the stranger's noise, the woods remained silent.

Will loosened the grip on his pistol. An intruder with ill intent would not abandon the element of surprise. But the cabin was at least ten miles off of any paved road and the gravel road, although much improved for this part of the world, had not been plowed in weeks. A four-wheel SUV could make it through the snow, as the road was flat and it followed the ridgeline particularly if he kept the gas pedal down, but the driver would have to be extremely determined in order to complete the journey.

This man was.

Chapter 15

Northern Virginia

Virginia stopped at the entrance to her building and fumbled with the satchel she carried over her shoulder as the morning rush of people moved past her.

"Damn it." She turned around, moving against the traffic of people, heading back to her car for her ID card. She kept it under the floor mat, handy for work but unseen by the passersby who might otherwise have seen her photo, name, title (intelligence research specialist), and the Department of Treasury FinCEN logo. The Financial Crimes Enforcement Network, or FinCEN, worked with agencies from all ends of the globe for one purpose.

While the public might not recognize her job, anyone in finance would know exactly what she did for a living: Virginia followed the money. Like criminals caught because they bragged about their crimes in some late-night drunk in a bar, the flow of funds was the trail that often led back to the scene of the crime. Money was better than a trail of blood. It was an active source of intelligence. Criminals always went back to the money. And the Treasury's Financial Center, or FinCEN, chased the trail of money.

First, she found her car, an easy-to-spot Volvo with its University of Pennsylvania decal on the back window and dirty exterior that had not been washed since it rolled out of the dealership several years before. Virginia considered auto care an unnecessary distraction and depended on East Coast rainstorms to keep her automobile clean. Crushed and empty Starbucks coffee cups littered the rear and passengers' areas, but her ID card was exactly where she'd left it.

"I've got to get a life," she grumbled as she slammed the door and hit her clicker. This was supposed to be a short-term gig. She would use her accounting degree and Wharton MBA to get a job with Treasury, and in three years her student loans would be repaid. But now, in her fifth year on the job, she still worked sixteen-hour days. She had fallen in love with the hunt. Dates became infrequent, then nonexistent, as her never-ending pursuit of ill-gotten money became increasingly obsessive. Her friends had given up trying.

Currently, she was following the trail of hawala money, an informal but elaborate and widespread method for transferring funds in the Muslim world. Chasing hawala was the ultimate challenge. The funds circulated around the world like a fog that tantalizingly appeared, only to dissipate and suddenly vanish.

Virginia ran into the building, through security, and up the stairs to the conference room. She was early for the meeting, as she tried to be for such sessions. Virginia was compulsive about being in her seat well before anyone else walked into the room. Her compulsivity showed in her frame and dress. Her roommate at Penn had called her neurotic. She was tall and lanky and one might have guessed correctly that she'd played center on her high school basketball team. She kept her brown, unusually straight hair pulled back most days in a ponytail. She never wore jewelry and always sought help from her friends with regard to dress and makeup when the office held its compulsory Christmas dinner.

"Okay," Virginia said when the meeting began, "I think this is just like the one reported in SAR in 2010."

Her computer projected a flowchart onto a large screen in the conference room. Darrel Byrd and his assistant were the only attendees. The Suspicious Activity Report for the second half of 2010 contained data on the case of a hawala dealer. The money would flow from one country to another, eventually surfacing in the form of wire transfers carefully limited to amounts like $9,750 or $8,590, sums that never exceeded $10,000.

The Bank Security Act of 1970 was a tool used by FinCEN that required banks to cooperate with the flow of money suspected in criminal dealings. The banks were not always crazy about the BSA, but it had long ago become a necessary tool.

To their bottom line, the banks could make a profit on dirty money just as easily as any other. A million dollars could turn interest no matter who owned it. But the BSA meant that the banks had to carry additional staff to monitor the sources. And this took away from the budget. One accountant for BSA meant one less salesperson pulling in the investment dollars.

And the hawala dealer Virginia was chasing had used the profits to purchase land, shopping malls, and several Mercedes. With hawala, there would be a small handling fee, and then the dealer would also pay the exchange rates from country to country. Both a legitimate exchange and a useful tool for money launderers, hawala had existed in western Asia for as long as there had been currency of any type. It always beat the bank rates and was based upon an honor system. A hawala dealer received cash in Doha and, with his partner in New York, made an exchange. A small fee would be charged and virtually no records would be kept. The money flew across borders while remaining out of sight.

"They're using the deep web to run this." Virginia flashed another screen that showed the relationship of .onion sites. "The flow involves the Exchequer Bank in the Caymans and a sister bank in the UAE."

"Nice job." Her boss gave Virginia a high five. "What size are we talking about?"

"Easily a hundred million, perhaps more." She closed the cover of her laptop computer. "If only we could get into the DW," she said, referring to the deep web.

"The FBI says they're close, but I don't believe it," said her boss. "I'll share this with the Agency and see what their thoughts are."

Virginia's boss met regularly with the CIA, as well as the other intelligence organizations. In a world run by digital money, the small and mostly unknown Financial Operation Center had grown greatly in importance.

"I'll let you know what I find out. You do the same," he said.

"Yes, sir."

Chapter 16

Parker's Cabin in Alaska

"William Parker." The man had pulled down his hood. His hair was much longer and grayer than Will remembered. He had put on weight and lost that sharp edge that the two Marine Corps lieutenants had shared when they passed through the Basic School at Quantico.

"Yeah." Will hesitated for a second as he took another look and confirmed his initial reaction, then slid the HK down to the table near the door. "Wade Newton?"

"That's me."

"What are you doing here?"

"Can I come in?"

"Sure."

Newton knocked the snow off of his parka and boots. The wind had been blowing into the porch, so when the door closed the cabin's temperature immediately rose several degrees. At the same time, the timer on the spotlight went out, and everything became dark—both the outside as they closed the door and inside, where the only light came from the fireplace.

"I know you weren't expecting me." Newton's voice was humble. "In fact, I guess I wouldn't be on your invite list anytime."

Will didn't say anything.

Newton was close to the truth. They had been assigned roommates at the Basic School, which served as the first school for Marine officers in the Corps. New officers would spend six months learning the necessary ropes. It was the beginning of their Marine career. Uniforms were fitted and salutes were learned, along with the myriad military abbreviations used in the Corps. Roommates were assigned randomly. N for Newton and P for Parker landed up together. Newton was aviation and wanted to be on track to fly jet fighters. Parker was on the ground track, expecting to end up somewhere in one of the military occupational specialties of infantry or special operations. Parker finished first in the class, which had rankled Newton, who thought of himself as being smarter.

It wasn't the only thing between them.

A young lieutenant had fallen on the obstacle course and struck his head on one of the posts. Will had stopped to give the man first-aid assistance, trying to keep him alive. He told Newton to get the medic, but Newton's lack of speed cost the young Marine his life.

"What can I do for you?" Will closed the front door.

"I need your help."

"Okay." He pointed to a coat hook on the wall near the front door. "Something to drink?"

"Yeah." Wade Newton looked worn-out.

"Take that chair near the fire."

"Thanks." He mumbled the words. It didn't seem to be the same fighter pilot.

As he took a chair near the fireplace, he seemed the epitome of a man beaten down by life.

Will poured cognac into a fresh cup of coffee and handed it over. "I heard you were with FedEx." He knew that once the F/A18 ride was over, jet pilots moved on to other occupations that involved flying. The transition typically went from fighter jets to either cargo carriers or passenger carriers. It was a long way from a single seater that moved at nearly 1200 miles an hour, but it kept the man in the air.

They didn't always make the best pilots in the transition. A jet jockey could thread his aircraft through a needle. But Delta wanted a calm—if anything, boring—trip. A cargo transport gave someone like Newton a little more room to push the aircraft through its numbers.

"Yeah, big haul from New York to Europe."

"You picked up oh-six?" Will was referencing the promotion to colonel.

"I ended up with the C-130 squadron in New York." Newton was talking about the turboprop cargo ships of VMGR-452 (the Marine designation for heavier than air, Marine, General Refueling squadron). It all translated to a four-engine cargo ship that had been the mainstay of the US military since the first Hercules flew in 1954.

"What do you need?" Will asked as they settled in front of the fire. He sipped his drink as the fire flickered.

"I understand you're the go-to guy for Marines in desperate straits."

"Not sure what you mean."

"My gunny at 452 told me about you and what you've been doing." Wade Newton's gunnery sergeant at his squadron no doubt knew another particular gunny. Will made a mental note to talk to a certain Marine gunnery sergeant who was painting houses back in Georgia. Although Will's missions into North Korea, Somalia, and Afghanistan were to be kept top-secret by the government and military, he had always assumed that something would get out.

"Oh? And what did Moncrief tell your gunny, exactly?"

"It's not like anyone was broadcasting it," Newton explained quickly, then sat back, took a swig from his laced coffee, and buried his head in his hands.

Will decided that Kevin Moncrief needed to get back to painting houses, Moncrief's civilian job, but he couldn't ignore the pain wracking the man in front of him. "So, what's the deal?" he asked.

"It's bad, Will." Newton looked up, tears glistening in his eyes. "I killed my son."

Chapter 17

A Dacha on the Istrinskoye Reservoir West of Moscow

"Does he ever go to sleep?"

The Russian huddled outside the guardhouse at the dacha deep in the woods north of Moscow was looking in the direction of the main building. His collar was pulled up and his head was stuffed well into his *ushanka* fur trapper hat. The all-white uniforms of the guards matched the snowdrifts that surrounded the cabin. He pulled a final drag from his cigarette and took a swallow directly from the bottle. The label was missing from the vodka bottle, but it didn't matter. Russians bought the liquor by price, not name. The cheapest vodka was the favorite of the day.

"Mmm." The other guard barely made a sound. It required too much effort in the subzero temperatures. He also glanced over his shoulder toward the dacha.

"Fucking light stays on all night." He took another swig while glancing over his shoulder.

A green light glowed through the blinds of an upstairs window. It was well past midnight. The snowstorm had covered all of the tracks of the vehicles on the road that led up to the cabin. The main highway, P-111, although no more than two lanes, was plowed regularly during the winter, but it lay a quarter of a mile away. The dacha stood on an isolated site, which was precisely the point.

"The fucker has a better life than us," the guard said of the man who lived in the dacha. He drank from the bottle and lit a new cigarette.

He was right.

The dacha stood on eleven hectares of land and by the shore of the Istrinskoye reservoir. Food was brought in on a weekly basis. The main cabin did not stand out from the others on the lake because of its size—it had only two bedrooms upstairs and a downstairs cigar room that had been turned into a computer room. Although relatively near Moscow, it still lay more than five miles from the nearest village.

"Stop talking." The other guard flapped his arms to keep warm. The guardhouse had a small wood stove, but it went through kindling too quickly to be useful. They always ran out well before the end of their twelve-hour shift.

"You think his girl will come back?"

Michael Ridge's girlfriend had left some time earlier, returning to the United States.

"*Nyet.*"

"Not bad-looking." The guard shared the usual male analysis of the female guest with his fellow soldier.

"Did you hear their fight last week?" The guard danced in his boots, trying to keep his legs warm.

"*Da.*"

"If Alina said that shit to me…."

"You'd take it. I've seen Alina." The other guard laughed at his joke. "Give me that."

They exchanged the bottle. The second man took a long draw of the vodka and let out a huge belch. It was the wrong thing to do in Russian society, but in a guardhouse, in the middle of a frigid winter—after most of the bottle was gone—it all fell on deaf ears.

"When will they let us kill this fuck?" The first guard slid his AK-47 around as if preparing to use it.

"Why, you want to go to Syria?"

The talkative one suddenly got silent. But not for long.

"They say this guy is important." The talkative one was also the taller of the two. He stood more than a foot taller than the other.

"The American?"

"*Da.*"

"Maybe this week."

"What?"

"The FSB comes." He tossed the empty bottle into the woods behind the guard shack. "And takes him away."

Chapter 18

A Government Facility In Anchorage

NCEZID had a small sign above the entrance to its lab in Anchorage not far from the Ted Stevens International Airport. NCEZID, the Center for Disease Control's office of the National Center for Emerging and Zoonotic Infectious Diseases, was the watchdog for any disease coming to Alaska. The quarantine lab stopped and seized anything suspicious that came through Alaska's ports and airports. It was also home to a branch that had a more ominous name: the Division of High-Consequence Pathogens and Pathology. And this led to the sub-office of Poxvirus and Rabies, and to Dr. Karen Stewart's desk.

Will hit the button on the door.

"Parker for Dr. Stewart." The CDC staff all knew Parker and they knew who he was visiting.

"Hold on." The security guard called up to Stewart's office. "Dr. Stewart, you've got a visitor."

"Okay."

The guard buzzed the door and the lock clicked.

"Hey, Will." The security guard was armed. It was not a casual job. Much of what came through those doors and the loading dock were marked *Extremely Dangerous*. They always started first with treating the animal or plant as if it could do great harm. And with good reason. The fire ant had come through a US port. Killer bees, after escaping from swarms quarantined in Brazil, also came across the border like illegal immigrants, after working their way across South America and Central America. The job done at the ports in keeping dangerous creatures or plants out was both important and vital.

"What's up, George?" Will knew the guard well. He had served with 3/1 in the second Gulf War, a Marine battalion that was well respected for the fight it had taken to the enemy in the Gulf.

"Heard about your crash."

"Landing."

"Yeah, landing." The guard smiled at his fellow Marine. "She said the same thing."

"She did?"

"Yeah, she corrected me too." The guard continued to smile. "I was in one of those landings in a CH-forty-six near Bridgeport."

"No one hurt?"

"No, but the landing cost the Corps about twenty million."

"Okay, I get it."

Dr. Stewart came around the corner. Although she had on the scientist's white lab coat, her typical work attire underneath was blue jeans and a pair of Nikes.

A moment of awkward hesitation transpired between Will and her.

"How about a quick cup of coffee?" he asked.

Karen hadn't seen him since their return from the wilderness. He could sense her hesitation, but she smiled.

"Sure."

The break room was in the basement. There, a small Starbucks concession kept the scientists awake on long days looking down their microscopes. The two got their coffees and took a table near the back of the room.

"When are you going back up?" Will asked as soon as they sat down.

"Hopefully tomorrow."

He waited for more, but she fell silent.

"Sounds like there's something more to it." He sensed she had something else to say, but was hesitant.

"This is a very virulent strain of the virus."

"So, the foxes are screwed?"

"It's more than that."

"What?"

"Well," she began, "like I said back at the lake, animals can catch the virus from eating infected flesh. They don't necessarily have to be bitten."

He nodded, picturing the wolves in Snag and near his cabin.

"Think about the Yukon. It may be the last place in the world where the people are so connected to their food." She took a sip of the coffee and sat it back down on the table. Then Karen did something unusual:

She looked off in space as if considering the weight of her words. "They live off of the land."

"So?"

"So, if an Inuit kills a diseased animal and then eats it, he's got rabies."

"Oh, shit!"

He was impressed how seriously she took her work.

"I can fly you up there." Will expected a *no* and he got it.

"No, the CDC helicopter's going to run me up. I have some traps I need to carry, and they can load them up here at Stevens."

"I had a visitor last night."

"Really?"

"Someone I knew in the Marines."

"A friend?"

"Not really." Will paused. It wasn't the time or place to go into Newton's history. "He may have lost his son and he blames himself."

"Can you help?"

"I don't know if there's much I can do." Will wasn't expecting to get involved. As the father told it, he assumed his son was dead. At the very least, Todd Newton was absent without leave and probably would face charges when he resurfaced. The Marines had told his father that Todd was last known to have been talking to another woman Marine about a computer conference. They had been ordered not to go. Todd's car had been found not far from the location of the convention, his computer notebook still in the backseat. Both Marines held top-secret clearances, which may or may not have had something to do with their sudden disappearance.

"Oh."

"He got the idea from Moncrief that I could be of help."

Karen shook her head and smiled despite herself. She knew Kevin Moncrief as a member of Will's team that had rescued her from captivity in Somalia. "With friends like that...huh?"

"Apparently, the gunny has me as the go-to guy for hopeless missions." Will said it with a grin, but he really did intend to have a talk with the retired gunnery sergeant.

Will's cell phone rang. "I need to take this." It was, of all things, a call from Kevin Moncrief.

She nodded. "No problem. I'm going to get back to my work. I'll be in Snag starting tomorrow," she told Will as he turned to leave. "For some time."

* * * *

"Gunny?"

"Can you talk?"

"Hold on." He strode quickly through the halls, past the guard, and out of the CDC complex to his truck. "What's up?"

"Did you talk to Newton?"

"Yeah." He didn't want to criticize Moncrief for siccing Newton on him. At least not right now. Better to tell his old friend in person. "I told him I couldn't help."

"How'd he take it?" asked Moncrief.

"Not well, but he knows I'm no miracle worker."

In truth, Wade Newton had been devastated. Clearly, he had viewed Will Parker as his son's last chance.

"Well, there's something he may not have told you."

"Oh, yeah? How do you know?"

"Because otherwise you might have said yes."

Will held the phone away from his face and stared at it for a second. "What didn't he tell me?"

"That Lance Corporal Todd Newton has a friend from his MOS school who's hot on the national radar."

"In what way?"

"Did you follow the news story a year or so ago about Michael Ridges?"

"The computer guy that worked for the Defense Intelligence Agency?" Will leaned against the tailgate of his pickup. The weather had cleared and suddenly Alaska was going into a warm spell. It wouldn't last, of course. Moreover, a "warm period" in Alaska meant the mercury might climb slightly above zero degrees.

"That's the one. Apparently, the two missing Marines may have kept in contact with Ridges after he defected."

"Meaning what, exactly?"

"I don't know, but you can bet they're in deeper trouble than just 'missing'."

Moncrief was right, but for the wrong reasons.

Chapter 19

The Casa on the Coast

The sound of feet on the steps alone had become enough to make Todd Newton nauseated. A harbinger of what was to come.

The larger man came through the door, walked up to Todd huddled on the bed, and grabbed him by his blood-soaked shirt. The slap came down hard on the side of Todd's head. It caused a louder ringing than usual in his ears. Stars flashed in front of his eyes as he tried to pull away from the blow.

"Time's running out," the man said in his now-familiar Hispanic accent.

The other man joined him and unlocked the chains, and they proceeded to drag Todd upstairs to the room with the bright lights. Todd tried to hold back, but the nauseous feeling overcame him. He started to throw up blood, gagging as he gasped for air, made difficult by the repeated bludgeoning that had crushed his nose. He gasped for air in short bursts through his mouth, sounding like a waterboarded prisoner.

"*Mierda!*" The man dropped Newton as the spit-up blood covered his boots.

As Todd lay helpless on the floor next to the chair, he realized that the cold tile floor had a black, sticky substance covering it.

They dragged him up and into the chair.

Todd could barely hold his head upright.

"You've talked to Ridges. We know this." The big man hovered over Newton.

"No." One of Todd's eyes was now completely shut. With the other, he looked at his captor.

"Your friend said the same thing." Todd noted the killer's use of the past tense. "But you both were in VPN networks."

"We just did that. Nothing to do with Ridges." Todd babbled the words. He had played with the virtual private networks such as Tor, but never really connected with Ridges. That was not what he wanted to hear.

Whatever Ridges had done with the whole deep web system, he'd left his two classmates out of it. The problem was, Todd's captors didn't believe him when he said it.

"We don't know! Please believe me." Todd's efforts were more a plea than a confession. He gasped for air between the words and tried to make himself intelligible to the two men.

"Your friend said the same thing."

Todd knew then that she was gone. He slumped down and fell into himself. It mattered little what his captors thought. He couldn't give them what didn't exist. He'd be following his friend shortly.

"Fuck you!" he spat at the man.

The blow came instantly and sent him reeling over the chair and into pitch-black darkness.

Chapter 20

Virginia Peoples had the answer.

"I need to print this out." She pushed the *print* button and waited while the machine spit out the paper. She grabbed the hard copy and headed upstairs. Her boss worked two floors above, though he spent most of his days in meetings. It was one reason that she didn't want a promotion. She enjoyed being in the trenches. It was the puzzle needing to be solved, not the administration of paperwork, which she enjoyed.

Virginia sat outside the boss's closed office door, waiting for the chance to grab him for just a second. She played with her cell phone while waiting.

Need some cat food, she thought. She pulled up the Safeway app on her phone and looked at her notes. With the cut-and-paste feature, Virginia was able to list everything she needed and have it delivered to her apartment in Arlington by the time she got back from work later that night.

Just gotta get home in time.

Last week she'd arrived home after the grocery delivery, which had been left with her neighbor. Her neighbor, in turn, had locked the groceries away and she hadn't been able to get them until the next morning. And there was no supper in her refrigerator tonight. The neighbor meant well, but not everything was refrigerated.

She was working her way through *dairy* when she heard the door open. Several analysts were leaving his office. She knew them all.

"Hey," she said to each until the last one left, then turned to her still-seated boss. Darrel Byrd was not the boss she had wanted. He wore starched button-down shirts with sharp creases in his khaki pants. And his personality was just as rigid. She would watch him make efforts with anyone who was perceived to help his career and the others were to be ignored. She was to be ignored.

"You got a minute?" She could tell from his facial expression that the next answer would be a lie.

"Sure." He didn't sound very excited.

"This Cayman bank is dirty." She put the printout on his desk in front of him.

"Why?"

"The flow of money goes to the UAE, but it also goes elsewhere."

"Okay. So?"

She knew that this wouldn't be a surprise to him. It always goes elsewhere. And it invariably led to evil.

"They're using the deep web, but the screen sizes match someone I ran across months ago."

Communications and transactions on the deep web could not be broken into, but they did leave certain traces or tracks that could give hunters insight in who was communicating. The tracks were certain varieties of data, and these could be collected and compared to data relating to other communications. Commonalities between data could, in theory, give Virginia clues as to who was using the deep web to make the deposits and withdrawals in question.

One such datum was the screen size of the inputting computer. Comparing such small clues required a lot of legwork, but sometimes they led to big discoveries.

"Let me run this by the other agencies."

"Thanks."

"We'll see what we turn up."

Neither Virginia nor her boss realized that what they turned up would be more than they wanted to know.

Chapter 21

Off of the East Coast of Baja

Despite the season, the waters of Bahia Agua Verde were both warm and calm. The bay was a part of the Gulf of California, or Sea of Cortez as some called it, that separated Baja California from the mainland of Mexico.

The fishing vessel *El Volante* worked its way north up the inner coastline from La Paz. To the east, the Baja coast remained dark at night, with only a few houses dotting the remote, desert coastline. The full moon lit the water as if it were midday.

"What's that?" The captain pointed to a white object that glowed on the surface of the water just off of the port bow.

"It's not moving." The first mate grabbed a hook.

The *El Volante* slowed as it approached the object. It bobbed up and down in the water as the fishing boat's wake passed by the slowing object and overtook it.

"Slow down." The first mate stuck his pole out over the gunwales and felt the hook stick into the object. From a distance, it felt a little like the remains of a sea mammal. He began pulling the object in.

"What is it?" the captain hollered down to the main deck.

The first hand was on his knees, on the deck, throwing up.

* * * *

"Can you tell with the photograph?" The detective from the La Paz police department looked at the photo.

"Yeah." The photographer held the computer up and pressed the enlargement key. The photograph filled out the screen.

"So, what do we know?"

"Female, Caucasian, probably in her twenties, but no head, no hands."

"Probably CJNG. I understand they've been moving to the north."

The detective wasn't surprised. The violence had been increasing in the Baja for years now. It was, at one time, the sleepy desert where Americans would go to pitch their tents or set up their RVs and eat lobsters for three bucks. The Jalisco cartel, known as CJING, was a result of the merger of the remains of several other cartels that had lost their leadership in several bloody battles over the splits. It had grown from a small operation in the Mexican states of Jalisco and Colima to other states and even found its way into Mexico City. They were most famous for gunning down the politicians that had the nerve to run on any platform calling for the elimination of the cartels.

"Look at this." The photographer had enlarged the upper back of the torso.

"A bull?"

"The words… I can barely make them out."

"Thundering Third?"

"What does that mean?"

"I don't know." The detective hit the *expand* button again. "But I know what *that* means." Another part of the tattoo came into focus.

* * * *

Wade Newton caught the news article on his Bing cell phone summary while waiting for the final unloading clearance of his FedEx Boeing 777 at JFK. His aircraft had just returned from a run to Moscow and Wade was ready for a few days off. The trip to Alaska had been a waste of time and he was exhausted.

Body found in Sea of Cortez. He hit the button to expand the story. The police theorized the body was of a woman in her early to mid-twenties. Newton went into the crew office of FedEx and started making some phone calls. The FedEx network of pilots reached deep into Mexico, as well as around the world.

La Paz had three FedEx offices and a small crew at the airport. Shortly, he was on the phone with the detective. He was lucky. The detective's brother worked for FedEx in La Paz. Newton needed a lucky break and finally got one. Because the police were willing to follow any leads, Newton received the photograph of the tattoo in a matter of minutes.

Newton also knew what the Thundering Third meant. He placed another call to a retired Marine gunnery sergeant. It didn't take a Marine to know what the other tattoo said with the letters *USMC* imprinted on the body, but both together said who the woman on the slab was.

"I need his help."

"I'll see what I can do." Gunny Moncrief wasn't going to make any promises. He knew when Will Parker chose a course, it was hard to steer him in any other direction. It required a good reason. He caught Karen Stewart just as she was getting ready to return to the Yukon, packing her gear for another long stay in Snag.

"Is he going with you?"

"Not on this one," she said.

This was key information for the gunny. It meant that Will would have no excuse when he was pushed to help.

His next call caught Will Parker at the Whitehorse airport, setting up the retrieval of the crashed Otter.

"They found a body in Mexico."

Will didn't immediately react.

"Newton called." Moncrief waited for a reaction. He knew that Will and Newton had some history, but not enough to trump the man's son being in danger.

"Okay, so was it Newton's son?"

"No, it was a WM. She had tats with 3/1. It has to be the lance corporal with Newton." The 3d Battalion of the 1st Regiment was the same unit that Will and Moncrief had supported with air and artillery fire in the Storm.

"Not sure it changes anything."

"Well, her other tat was the Eagle, Globe, and Anchor. There was no head or hands."

The head and hands missing was brutal but also practical—it made it much more difficult to trace the body. Except for one thing: Her killer had stupidly left intact the one identifying trait that ensured an immediate identification with the right people.

"If the boy is alive," said Will, "he will need some help."

The gunny smiled. Will was in.

Chapter 22

Dulles, Virginia

"I need you to check on something." Alexander Paul hadn't talked to Caldwell since he had returned from ITD headquarters on the West Coast. "Get in."

"Yes, sir." Caldwell climbed into Paul's black Escalade as it pulled out of the garage. The vehicle had been custom-built, perhaps a carryover from Paul's days as director of the DIA: The chassis, window, and tires were bulletproof, and the backseats were separated from the front by a soundproof panel. The oversized 6.2-liter V8 engine effectively transformed the armored SUV into the equivalent of a speedy tank.

"Two Marines have been missing from Camp Pendleton for a couple of days," said Paul. He wore an Augusta green polo shirt, tan slacks, and a blue blazer over the polo shirt. He rarely looked so casual, but it was a Palm Beach–relaxed look. He had that smell of an expensive aftershave that would cost someone like Caldwell a day's wages for the bottle.

Caldwell nodded and waited for him to continue.

"The Marines worked with an IT man that was my assistant when I was at DIA."

"Ridges?" Caldwell knew about the incident that had destroyed Alexander Paul's DIA career. And he suspected that he was striking very close to a nerve by even speaking the name.

"That's right." Paul didn't seem to care to comment about Ridges, the ghost from his past who would never go away. "You're well informed."

"Yes, sir." It might have been a mistake for Frank to answer so quickly. He was learning that Paul needed to be the one who filled up the pause in conversations.

"My assistant will text you the information on the two. I want you to go to Camp Pendleton and see what you can find out."

"I'll take the flight out tomorrow."

"There's one to San Diego tonight."

Paul seemed to be testing Caldwell's loyalty, as if he knew that the man had another kids' soccer game that evening.

If so, he was correct. And the soccer game was the first in the playoffs that would end his son's season at Witter. There would be the postgame pizza party. His child would be the only one absent a father.

"Yes, sir." Caldwell knew one thing regarding the Alexander Pauls of the world: Any answer other than "yes, sir" would be a mistake. Better to submit his resignation than plead for a delayed order.

Caldwell also knew that when he went home to pack, his wife and he would discuss what he was going to do next. A bad reference from Paul would end it for Caldwell in DC, but perhaps the successful completion of this mission would provide him the opportunity to move jobs.

"Got it."

"Good."

* * * *

The armored Escalade let Frank Caldwell out near his vehicle then headed in the direction of Dulles Airport.

Paul opened the small window in the partition between his driver and him: "Jet aviation at Dulles."

The aircraft would arrive a few minutes after his SUV pulled up to the FBO on the far side of Dulles Airport. The private jet was one of several owned by the company Paul's firm was consulting for. The 737-model Boeing Business Jet came with a conference room and a chef's kitchen that could keep the company's board members entertained wherever.

"This could be it," Paul had told his wife of twenty years the night before. She was his second wife and had been his secretary when he rose to brigadier general in the Army. She had become an asset in his move up the ladder after he'd initially earned his first star. It was a different game when one achieved flag rank. Flag rank, a nickname for generals and admirals, took its name from the flag and star embroidered on the uniform. Paul's first wife had raised the children. His second wife had helped him climb the ladder of power. And now the opportunity had arisen to take the next step.

The invitation he'd received was for the retirement dinner of Herman Worth, who was retiring from the Baker Alexander board after reaching the mandatory age of seventy. As per tradition, Worth was invited to select any place in the world to hold his retirement dinner. Since Worth was from New Orleans, he'd chosen the French restaurant Galatoire's. And while the wine cellar at Galatoire's carried more than a thousand bottles of high-quality wine, Worth's favorites were being brought in from France. More important, Worth was granted the power to invite the individual he thought should replace him on the board. Alexander Paul had received an invitation to the dinner, which meant that—at least theoretically—he was being considered as Worth's replacement. Tonight's dinner would be a job interview that came with the reward of being admitted to the most exclusive club in America: a board of directors of a major company.

Finally getting past that shit with Ridges.

Paul would never be allowed to completely forget his past at the DIA, but at least his insubordinate assistant's conduct seemed to be fading into the mists of time.

Paul glanced at his watch as the big SUV approached Dulles. All he needed now was for his wife to show up in time with his Oxxford tuxedo.

Chapter 23

The office of the Naval Criminal Investigative Service resident agency was marked with a sign just off De Luz Road on Camp Pendleton. It was a part of the Marine Corps west coast field office. Will Parker knew his Marine identification card would get him at least through the front door and hoped that it might get him more.

"I served in the Marines and am looking for the agent that was handling the AWOL case of Lance Corporal Todd Newton."

The agent in the dark blue polo shirt who had front-door duty looked up from a desk piled with manila folders. His shirt was monogrammed with the badge of NCIS.

"Newton?" The agent didn't hesitate, which caused Will to take note. The agent picked up his telephone and asked the person on the other end to come up front. A densely built man, also in a dark blue polo shirt, 5.11 khaki trousers, and black tactical boots came out to the front. His Glock was attached to his web belt.

"Can I help you?"

"Yes, sir, I'm Will Parker." Will showed him his retired identification card. The agent took it, looked at it carefully, and invited him to come into his back office.

When Will had taken a seat, the investigator said, "You're the second one this week."

"Sorry?" Will leaned on the arm of the chair.

"A former Army Ranger was just here."

"Really?"

"He was connected to some high-end government computer-consulting firm."

Will wanted to know a lot more, but made a point of hesitating. He wanted the agent to give what he would willingly.

"And what's your tie to these Marines?" the agent asked.

"I'm helping Newton's father. He's a retired Marine as well."

"Yeah, he was here last week as well." The agent rolled a pencil in his hand. "The man was torn up."

"Nice to see someone still uses one of those things." Will pointed to the pencil, the suggestion being that the agent was old-school. He got the reaction he hoped he would get: a smile and a chuckle.

"I came through here on a tour with First Recon Battalion and First ANGLICO," said Will. He'd spent time, at Pendleton and in the Gulf, with both units.

"I've heard of you." The agent was clearly warming up to him. "You were at Khafji."

"Yeah."

"I was just behind you. Part of the follow-on."

The follow-on units had secured the area after the battle and seen firsthand the destruction. The burned-out shells of vehicles, with the corpses still huddled in them, covered the battlefield. The investigator didn't say more about the battle of Khafji or the Marines' first engagement with the Iraqi army, but Will now knew the man was a Marine as well.

"Well, how can I help?"

"Who was the Army Ranger that came for a visit?"

"Here's his business card."

Will studied the card with the name of Caldwell and Alexander Paul's company.

"You mind?" Will held up a cell phone he had.

"No problem."

He used the phone to snap a picture of the card.

"I understand a body's been found down in Mexico."

"We don't know much about it yet. I know that the torso had a tattoo of 3/1, but there hasn't been any positive DNA identification. You know both hands and the head were missing...."

"Someone didn't want the identification to be too easy."

"Yeah. Stupid, wasn't it?" he said, referring to the identifying tattoos that remained on the body. "I guess they were hoping the sharks would finish the job."

"Any idea as to where?"

"No, we're talking about over a thousand miles of coastline. And there's the mainland on the other side of the Gulf as well. My guess is the Baja."

"Why?" Will only knew of the Baja by word of mouth.

"The Baja's gotten much worse over the years. The First Marine Division's issued several warnings about not going down there, particularly to the east shore. Not much law there."

Will detected an undercurrent of disapproval from the man, who had clearly grown tired of young Marines spending long weekends in the Baja and running into trouble. The agent also didn't seem convinced that the female Marine's murder hadn't been anything more than the result of unwise behavior on the part of two stupid, young Marines.

"Here's my card." He wrote on the back of the card with his pencil. "And my cell, if you need any help, twenty-four-seven."

"Thanks."

"They did find Newton's car. His computer was still in the backseat."

"Oh? Did you get in it?" Will wondered if the computer left any clues.

"No, pretty sophisticated security." The agent put the pencil down. "They don't think they can."

"He knew what he was doing." Will was learning about Todd Newton with every fact.

"Might mean a lot more than two AWOLs." The agent seemed willing to at least consider that this might have been more.

"Sure."

"But the command wasn't crazy about where they found the car."

"Why?"

"They'd clearly gone to Hackfest in the Bay Area. Basically, a DARPA-run convention for hackers. Which meant they'd disobeyed a direct order."

"I see." Will started to get out of the chair.

"Oh, the Army Ranger, Caldwell…he mentioned something in passing. Not sure if it means anything, but the two were tied somehow to Michael Ridges. They came up through the same cyber schooling together."

"Do you mind if I stop by Newton's barracks?"

"No." The agent picked up the telephone on his desk. "In fact, I'll call the CO and let him know you're coming."

* * * *

The barracks stood in the middle of the Pendleton base near the beach. It was called Area 41 or Las Flores. Will traveled the long road that wound through the center of the installation. Pendleton covered some of the most expensive, undeveloped land in the United States. But for the occasional convoy of brown vehicles and the separate camps, the area remained untouched. He passed Las Pulgas, with its artillery pieces lined up on the tarmac behind heavy military trucks. Will had taken his ANGLICO team to Las Pulgas in preparation for deploying to the Gulf. 1st ANGLICO had also been stationed at Las Flores. ANGLICO, or Air Naval Gunfire Liaison Company, teams were dropped in well behind the enemy's lines and called in artillery and air fire on the unsuspecting enemy. It was on this field that he'd first gotten to know Kevin Moncrief. Marines who were sent here went on to receive several purple hearts.

Right there. Will looked at the building where he was called one day to meet with the senior enlisted man of the 11th Marines. The first sergeant pulled him into the office at Las Pulgas.

"Sir, I am assigning Moncrief to you. He's like a puppy. Treat him right and he'll follow you anywhere." The first sergeant had enjoyed a reputation for being gruff and to the point, but also with a touch of humor. "Also, he knows his stuff. It would be best for you to listen."

Will had followed the advice and never regretted it.

Las Pulgas took him somewhat out of the way, but Will quickly turned back onto Las Pulgas road toward Area 41.

The barracks was a new structure that looked more like a hotel than the old Quonset huts that still dotted some areas of the base. Solar panels covered the roofs. As he pulled into the parking lot, Will noticed yellow tape across a door to one of the rooms. He didn't need to go inside. He had seen a Marine's barracks room a million times. There were two bunks, each made up with a tight hospital fold in case the first sergeant did a walk-around inspection, and a load of electronics. The local exchange store kept the young enlisted men fully equipped with the best Game Boys, computers, and devices.

Will put his hand on the door and imagined the last day Lance Corporal Newton walked through it. It felt odd to think that only some short time ago the young man had passed through this same space. Another Marine walked by in his utilities—ordinary brown desert camouflage, but perfectly starched and shaped in the essential Marine style. His hat tilted down, almost covering his eyes. His arms bulged out of the sleeves. He'd clearly spent many an hour in the gym pressing the iron.

"Sir, can I help?"

"Thanks, no, just a friend of the family and a prior Marine."

"Squirt was good."

"What?"

"Oh, sorry, sir. Just a nickname. Not a very big guy, but he would do anything for you. He was the guy that could fix all of our shit. Sorry, sir. I was his roommate until this hit."

"Really?"

"Yes, sir. They put me on the ground floor with Squirt while I rehabbed my leg. Bad jump from a CH-53." He was noting a parachute drop that ended poorly after he jumped out of the back of a Super Stallion helicopter. It was the largest and heaviest in the Marine Corps inventory and often used for jumps by the special operations teams.

"Squirt?"

The Marine smiled and shrugged shyly.

The name probably fit the kid's image, Will thought. And his ability to "fix" stuff matched up with what Todd's father had told him.

"Did he hit the gym a lot?"

"Not once. Newton liked the run, but bitched about the rest of the PFT."

"Really?"

"He could go sub eighteen minutes on that run. Left us in the dirt, but the rest of the physical fitness test was shit."

The best score on the Marine run was eighteen minutes for three miles. It also included crunches, or a version of sit-ups, and pull-ups.

"How did he score?"

"Third class. Good guy, but he's an Xbox Marine. Sir."

"How about the WM?" Will was using the short vernacular for woman Marine.

"She was assigned to 3/1. She was a geek too, but not like Newton. She could max the PFT, but they both were into IT. When they were together, it was like they were talking German or French."

"Thanks, Marine."

Will Parker had become convinced of one thing: Newton and his fellow Marine hadn't intended to be absent without leave. They might have gone to Hackfest despite orders, but there was no way they'd intended to miss roll call that following Monday.

* * * *

After leaving Las Flores, Will headed north on Interstate 5. He hadn't stayed at the San Clemente Inn since he'd left for the Gulf years before. After Operation Enduring Freedom, he spent time at Bethesda and after Bethesda, his active duty had ended. He pulled into the inn and paid cash for a room. That rattled the desk clerk a bit, but soon he had a key and confirmed checkout for the one-night stay. It was close to the same beach where Will had run every day before shipping out to the Gulf. After dressing down, he headed out on Avenida Califia, which took him toward the beach. There, he crossed under the Amtrak rails through a tunnel and headed to the water's edge, where the sand was firm. He headed to the pier and then reversed directions to the south. As he sped down the beach, the occasional wave would reach his feet and break across his shins. Starting to feel the burn, he headed further south for San Onofre Beach and the nuclear power plant. Surfers lined up offshore waited their turn to catch the perfect wave home.

The sun was blinding as its rays reflected off of the waters of the Pacific.

The run gave him a much-needed chance to think. After putting in ten miles, he walked back north on the beach and made a call on a burner phone he'd brought on the trip.

"Wade?"

"Hey, Will. I really want to thank you for looking into this."

Wade Newton had become a humble man. Will might never forgive him for what happened at the Basic School, but the man was missing his son.

"He didn't go AWOL."

"I appreciate that."

Though it gave the father less than full comfort, Will could tell that Newton had hoped to hear this from a fellow Marine.

"Have you ever heard from a man named Frank Caldwell?" Will thought he knew the answer before asking the question.

"No. Should I have?"

"Maybe."

"I found something in an email he sent me," said Newton, raising an issue he had not mentioned before. "Todd said if he ever got into some kind of trouble I needed to talk to the female Marine and Michael Ridges—you know, that guy in Russia." The woman Marine was out of play, so that left one possibility.

Everything seemed to be pointing toward Michael Ridges. Will remembered the gunny's conversation regarding both Ridges and the DIA.

"Now I have only one choice, and I don't know how to get in touch with Ridges." Every turn that the father made seemed to lead to a dead end.

"I have some thoughts. We need to meet."

"Anywhere, any time."

"All right," said Will. "Make it Memphis, tomorrow night."

* * * *

Will Parker had another suspicion. Back at the motel lobby, he Googled the company listed on the Army Ranger Caldwell's card. What he found convinced him that there was much more to the disappearance of Todd Newton than a pair of Marines on a dangerous lark.

The business that Caldwell worked for was a Baker Alexander–type of defense contract that worked in the IT field. It was too close to be purely incidental.

The name Alexander Paul surfaced as Caldwell's employer. Moncrief had told Will about Ridges's connection with DIA; a bit more Googling yielded news articles and op-ed pieces published at the time of Paul's resignation that all pointed to Ridges as the cause of Paul's fall from grace.

He called the NCIS agent and asked for a favor.

"Can you call the Ranger and let him know another inquiry was made?"

"Sounds like you're baiting some kind of hook, eh?"

Will sensed a smile on the other end of the call.

"Just let him know that I inquired about the lance corporal."

Will had a feeling. Perhaps it came from his days working as a district attorney, but a company representing Alexander Paul sending a man to Pendleton without ever talking to the father of the missing Marine seemed odd to the prosecutor that still lived inside Will Parker's head.

"That's it?"

"Yeah, that should do it."

Chapter 24

"What's up?"

Normally, Virginia Peoples arrived earliest to work and was the one who turned on the lights to her office. Not this time. She was a multitasker and had several computer terminals and monitors arrayed around her desk that looked almost like the walls protecting a city under siege. She had no chairs for visitors; even if someone had sat across from her at her desk, they wouldn't have been able to see her past the shield of flat-screen monitors. And she came to work every day to blank screens that had to be turned on after the lights.

This morning, however, her boss was sitting in her chair, with all the terminals all on; standing next to him was a man she didn't recognize.

"Hey, Virginia." Byrd looked up from the terminals. He didn't seem disturbed about the circumstances. In fact, he was acting as if this were normal office procedure. "This is Mr. Smith. He's from another government agency."

Virginia had had enough exposure to government-speak to know how to translate what she'd heard. The man's name was not Smith, and there was only one agency that described itself as just "another government agency."

She wanted to shout, "What is Langley's problem?" but knew better.

"We need to shut down the project you've been working on with the Caymans bank and the one in the UAE." Her boss wasn't asking. He was directing. "Can you do me a favor and delete what you have?'

"Sure." Virginia was stunned.

He stood and let her take her seat.

It took Virginia about five minutes to delete the last two years of work from her computers. It didn't require her Wharton MBA to read between the lines.

"Is that it?"

"Okay, Mr. Smith?" Byrd asked the stranger.

"Thank you." The stranger didn't seem to need more than her verbal confirmation that their efforts on the Exchange Bank of the Caymans had stopped. He wore a button-down white shirt, dark sports jacket, brown pants, with contrasting light brown shoes and a slim dark tie. If she had to guess, she would have thought the man was a graduate of the University of Pennsylvania like herself. He was, however, only the messenger.

"Virginia, I could use your help on being in charge of our new exchange program." Her boss was throwing her a bone. The FinCEN exchange was no demotion. It was the new brainchild of the director and would link a cross section of agencies to monitor the movement of money. The message sent was that she hadn't done anything wrong, but needed to move on to this next project.

"Thanks," she said as graciously as she could manage, given the circumstances.

Byrd and Mr. Smith left her to tend to her computer. All her work on the Exchange Bank was gone, as well as the flow of money and the list of the IP addresses that were found. The only thing left was her suspicions. It was clear who owned the Exchange Bank. She opened the lower drawer, opened a book with the interior center cut in a small square, and pulled out of the space a flash drive marked with a strip of labeling tape. It said only *Dups*.

It made her both nervous and excited holding it in her hand. The book's title was *Six Days of the Condor*.

Chapter 25

The Anchorage Airport

Karen Stewart's traps and cages filled the Bell 212 helicopter, along with her supplies that were intended to last several days in the Yukon. The chopper had been dispatched from Merrill Field and traveled over to Stevens International Airport to pick up the load.

This time, the flight to Snag took several hours to cover the nearly six hundred miles. The refuel stops burned up some time as well.

"You got everything?"

The crew chief had helped her unload and carry most of the gear up to the shack near the end of the runway. It was humble, one room, with a potbelly stove, left over from the days when the airfield was used by the Royal Canadian Air Force to train pilots for the war in Europe. During the war, the field had been home to Avro 621 biplanes used to teach cadets the basics of flying. Now, Snag displayed none of its glorious past; since the war, it had largely been overgrown by spruce and pines.

"Yeah, thanks." She slung her Winchester .30-30 over her shoulder. Once the helicopter left, the Yukon would take over. Except for the call of the wolves, Snag would return to its blanket of silence.

The helicopter's blades spun up and with it, the dusting of flying ice particles stung her face. She pulled the hood down and felt the tickle of the fur on her face. The chopper quickly disappeared over the tree line.

"I've got at least two hours of daylight," she told herself as she checked the time. "I can still get some of these cages set up."

After two winters in Snag, Karen had a good idea of the path that the animals took. She set out two cages on the other side of the airfield and then worked her way back to the cabin. The snow had drifted in some areas, but her Atlas snowshoes helped her cross the drifts. The snow was a light powder created by the extreme temperature. It flew up like powdered sugar with each step.

She stopped near the end of the airfield. A path of tracks, some zigzagging, led into the woods. Yellow mucus stained the snow in spots. Karen took the rifle off of her shoulder and chambered a round with the lever action.

God, that mucus does not look good. In fact, the yellow snow was a veritable factory for the neurotropic virus. It did not live long, however, outside of the body.

"Where are you?" She knelt and waited for a sound. Only heard silence. A wind kicked up out of the north and started to blow a dusting of snow. Karen kept her hood pulled back so that she could hear any sound. The chill seemed to burn the tips of her ears, but it was just as important that every sound could be heard. There was a killer in the wilderness.

The sun was setting already.

Better get out of these woods before darkness settles in.

Slowly, Karen backed up until she was clear of the tree line. If the animal attacked, she wanted to have the chance of seeing it before it was on top of her. She held the Winchester .30-30 with one arm. She pulled off one of her gloves in case she needed to get a quickly aimed bullet downrange. The wood stock was cold on her fingers, but not nearly as bad as the metal. Bare skin could stick to the cold steel. Karen made sure to touch the wooden stock only. The gun was beaten up by years of use—she'd borrowed it from another scientist at the CDC office—but had proved itself reliable. The action never failed and the bullet hit its target with enough force that it would knock the animal down even if the bullet only struck a leg. The blunt force of the bullet was what was needed to slow down the deranged creature.

"One well-aimed shot is better than a magazine emptied," Will had often said. He had shared his Marine marksmanship-training pearls of wisdom. In the spring, he'd taken her to a target range he'd set up near his cabin. There, she'd become comfortable with the lever action and learned to shoot more by instinct than using a scope, or glass, as he would call it. Karen wouldn't have time to focus through a scope if a rabid animal was making its charge. Better to concentrate on the target and not the sights. Karen heard Will's familiar voice, telling her to "put the rifle in the same spot." She knew he meant holding the weapon consistently: butt pressed to shoulder, face alongside the stock. Only then could you concentrate on the target. "Don't shoot the quarter, shoot Washington's nose," was another of Will's gems, meaning: Concentrate on your target as you never have before. The brain would do the rest.

The thing was, it all worked. So well, in fact, that she had been shooting plastic balls he had hung on strings from a tree limb. The ball would flip over the tree limb when she hit the target perfectly in the center of mass. Before the first snow came, she had been flipping the balls regularly.

"Breathe," he told her again and again. "You'll always have time to take a breath before anything gets too close."

"Are you sure?"

"Yes," he said without hesitation. "You never need more than two well-aimed shots."

Karen moved backward slowly until she had gained enough space between herself and the woods. She got onto the runway and walked down its center. It gave her excellent footing, even with the snowshoes. After hiking the airstrip for more than half of its 3000-foot length, her heart rate started to slow.

"I need to mark that spot." She turned and looked at her tracks, seeing where they went into the wood line. She noted a particularly tall pine tree that stood out from the rest. Her tracks had passed just below it.

As she looked back at her tracks, she followed the trail of yellow mucus with her eyes.

He's not long for this world.

Unfortunately, the demise of the animal would mean danger for others. As its carcass became food for other wildlife, the rabies virus would spread. Karen hadn't seen any scavenging birds, but they too could contract the disease. Like dominoes, the chain of animals could topple under the spread of the virus.

Karen made the short trek back to the cabin. It had a tin roof and had been built out of sawed timber by the Royal Air Force back during the war. The timber had come from trees in the nearby forest. A single, old-growth giant could have supplied all that was needed to create the cabin, plus provide years' worth of firewood in addition. Even now, several of the trees near the cabin had large girths, some wider than a large dining-room table. Karen imagined what such giants had seen during their lifetime: Native Americans passing by, Royal Canadian aircraft flying over. And now, a rabies epidemic.

Despite the quality construction, the old cabin had gaps in its walls, most likely from the structure settling over time. Some prior occupant had stuffed the holes with rags. They gave the cabin a stale smell that could only be overcome by the fire in the small stove. She was not the first scientist from the CDC to stay there. It had been used for more than a decade as a remote location to gather observations on the wildlife. But the room was small, extremely close quarters, and the potbelly stove heated it up quickly.

A sleeping bag was made more comfortable by a cot that she had left in the cabin during a previous trip. She knew that the first few nights would use up the fresh food supplies. She'd brought a well-used iron skillet. The eggs warmed her so much so that she had to crack a window, which was placed above the cabin's only door. The glass to the window was still intact after almost three-quarters of a century's use. It had a thick green tint and was in a frame that would fold in. The frigid incoming air quickly reached a balance between the heat of the stove and the outside subzero temperature.

Karen had brought an Iridium satellite phone along with her on this trip, the crash having convinced her superior at the CDC office that it was a necessary precaution. "You need to check in once a day," her boss in Anchorage had told her. In fact, he had made it a condition of her return to Snag alone. "I'm not too crazy about this," he'd said before granting her request, "but keep in mind we don't have anyone who can go out after you in the next several weeks."

She'd simply shrugged, saying, "I need to capture this data now." Karen could be a strong advocate of her own work when necessary. "I know these animals and their patterns. I can handle this."

She still felt confident and secure, but it did feel a little riskier, now that she was out in the bush.

As she started to drift off to sleep, the wolves called out of the darkness.

Chapter 26

Paul's Corporate Headquarters

"We may have a problem." Caldwell had asked for the meeting with Alexander Paul.

"What?" Paul looked up from his computer on the mahogany table that served as his desk. It was an antique that his secretary said he had carried with him since his days as a general.

The sun was setting on Washington and Caldwell could see the jets, well off in the distance, lining up for a landing at Dulles. Their lights were arrayed in a nearly perfect row, like a string of Christmas lights ready to decorate a home in December. A.P.'s office had glass windows from the floor to ceiling. But for the furniture in the space, one might have felt like they were falling off the twenty-sixth story of the building.

"There's been an inquiry made at Pendleton. In addition to ours," said Caldwell, watching for his boss's reaction.

"Well, given the interest of their family members, that shouldn't be unexpected." Despite his calm, relaxed demeanor, Paul's face showed strain.

It wasn't lost on Caldwell that his boss hadn't asked him to sit while briefing him.

"Well," Caldwell said, "this may be different. A fellow named Parker, William Parker, was asking NCIS at Pendleton about the lance corporal."

"And?"

"He has some background."

Paul simply stared, waiting.

Caldwell shifted his weight from one foot to the other as he continued. "He served in the Marines but has done work for the Agency." Caldwell watched his boss's eyes wander back to the PC on his desk. He seemed unable to keep Paul's attention.

"How do you know this?" Paul asked while still looking at his monitor.

"I spoke with someone in the Agency who's been there a while." Caldwell had worked with the CIA on more than one Ranger mission in Afghanistan. He had made it a point to keep in touch with the Agency operators after leaving the Army. He even visited Langley every now and then.

"What did he say?"

"Nothing."

Paul looked at Caldwell as if he were some kind of fool.

"What?"

"He said Parker was known to the Agency."

"And?"

"Well," Caldwell said, in case it wasn't self-evident, "that says a lot."

"Thanks, Frank," said Paul, sounding less grateful than inconvenienced. "I'll look into this. Tell me if you find out anything else."

His boss didn't have to say the word for Caldwell to know that he'd been dismissed.

* * * *

After Caldwell left, Alexander Paul turned back to his computer and went to his deep web account. He still had plenty of contacts at DIA who would tell him everything he needed to know. Several held their current positions because of Alexander Paul. They weren't going to let their old boss down on something so simple as giving the background of a once-served Marine, even if he had worked with the Agency.

He got only so far.

It was no problem, especially given his contacts, to access Parker's military records. The OQR, or officer qualification record, was thick despite some pages marked *Removed for Security Reasons—Top Secret/Need to Know Clearance Required to Access*. The man had served with distinction and also gotten into a fight with a general over the lack of artillery support in a combat operation that had cost the lives of several Marines. The Army one-star had made an apparent error in judgment: He'd wanted confirmation that no civilians were in the area before ordering in the supporting fire. As it turned out, a band of well-armed Taliban terrorists had been there, not civilians. Pleas were made over the radio and Parker's team on the other end of the valley could only watch as their fellow Marines pleaded for their lives. The delay ended up sending six Marines to Arlington National Cemetery.

Parker's record showed an unusual, resourceful, and dangerous warrior. He was also fluent in multiple languages and had been involved in three other classified operations. Paul couldn't get any details on two of them, but was able to open the file regarding Somalia. There, Parker had saved the life of a Dr. Karen Stewart, who worked with Doctors Without Borders. After that, Parker had essentially disappeared. DIA's last report had Parker flying as a bush pilot in Alaska.

Paul did a quick cross-check and found Dr. Stewart researching in the Yukon.

Right.

He sat back in his chair, stretched expansively, and cracked his knuckles one by one. He had it. He had found Parker's weak spot.

Paul returned to the deep web and opened his Tor server to access the dark web. There, he pulled up a familiar address.

He typed: *What is the status of our guest?*

He knew the reply wouldn't come for a day or two.

Closing that tab, Paul opened another in the deep web. The Exchequer Bank of the Caymans had a board of directors that was not publicly listed. As a member of the board, he was accorded complete access to the flow of money coming through the bank.

Paul went back to the open internet and checked on the price of the stock of ITD and Baker Alexander. ITD was trading well over ninety a share. He felt a sense of inordinate power while looking at the number.

"If they knew what I knew, it would drop to the floor," he spoke to the computer screen. He could short the stock and make millions in a matter of a day. However, the transaction needed to be handled carefully. It might require the order being placed by the connected bank in the UAE. He called an international number and placed the order.

He scanned down to his other stock of interest. Baker was trading just below its fifty-two-week high. If he were admitted to the Baker board, he'd receive stock options that would immediately turn a profit.

"We're going to need someone to go to Alaska," he told the empty office. He also realized that he needed to talk to William Parker.

He picked up his cell phone and selected the number from his contacts.

"Caldwell?"

"Yes, sir."

Paul had no doubt caught him on the way to another soccer game.

"I need something."

"Yes, sir."

"That agent with NCIS. Did he get Parker's number?"

"I don't know, sir, but I can easily find out."

Chapter 27

Memphis

The HondaJet started its descent into the landing pattern at KMEM, Memphis International Airport. The HA-420 twin-engine light aircraft flew like the sports car it was meant to be. Will was the sole occupant of the airplane. With a tailwind, it had crossed the United States from San Diego to Memphis with a ground speed of more than 650 miles per hour.

The jet was fully computerized with the newest avionics. The Garmin G3000 flight deck plotted the route and the autopilot steered the aircraft across the country. A refuel stop near Dallas took more time on descent and climb out, but the aircraft was able to pick the right altitude for the best winds.

His aircraft, with the call sign of N883CS, was soon on its final leg to the landing at Memphis International Airport. Will slowed the plane down, went through the landing checklist, lowered the flaps and, near the outer marker, dropped his landing gear. The airport was lit up like the Las Vegas strip, but only in white. Will tilted his wing to see the world hub of FedEx. There, under the lights, stood an air force of white, jumbo cargo-carrying aircraft with the familiar blue tail lined up for what seemed like miles of tarmac. Boeing 767s, 777s, and other heavy airplanes were parked, liked NASCAR race cars in the pits, in line receiving their load of cargo and before departing on voyages to places around the country and the world. Being relatively close to the center of continental America had made Memphis a perfect choice for the original hub of FedEx.

The HondaJet's wheels screeched as the aircraft settled down on the runway.

"November-eight-eight-three-Charlie Sierra request taxiing instructions to the FBO," Will radioed after he pulled off of the active runway.

"Yes, sir, which one?"

"Wilson?"

He taxied the jet to the far end of the airport and pulled up beneath the cover of a large metal canopy.

"I won't be long. Please refuel the aircraft. Here's the number to call for funds."

The man looked at him with a puzzled look.

"Call this number?"

"Yes, sir."

A call on the number went directly to a particular bank's main operations center and would then be transferred to a senior vice president on duty, whose job was to greenlight any funds Will Parker needed at a moment's notice. The bank also offered twenty-four-hour access to the transfer of Will's money when and wherever it was required.

The grounds man made the call as requested. After speaking with the person on the other end of the line for a moment, he put a hand over the phone and waved Will over: "They asked if you want fuel for a jet or to buy one."

"Just the gas," said Will. "Thanks. I'll be leaving in a half hour."

He still had several other destinations tonight and too short a time.

* * * *

"Let me finish this." Will was using one of the burn phones he carried with him. The person he'd called would meet him in Washington, DC, in the morning. He made a special request, then thanked the person and clicked off.

He turned to Wade Newton, who was wearing his FedEx captain's uniform. "Let's go in the back."

They headed to a quiet spot behind the rest area for visiting pilots, and Will sat across from him at a small table.

"Thank you for this." Newton looked even worse than he had a few days earlier in Alaska. "I don't expect much."

The body found in the Sea of Cortez was, in all likelihood, the woman Marine who had been traveling with Newton's son. Because of this, Wade Newton could only assume that the authorities would soon find the other body and return his son home for burial. A shallow grave in the desert of the Baja was a cold end that neither man could imagine.

Will Parker, however, was offering him hope. And hope was a dangerous thing.

"You might not want to do what I need you to do."

"I'll do it, don't worry."

Will nodded. "If you do, you'll have to follow the exact timeline. You have to be at this exact spot at this time. And with these things."

Newton looked at the sheet of paper on which Will had diagrammed the plan. Despite the details, it didn't tell the whole story; it only showed the role that Wade Newton would play.

Wade looked up from the paper. "If this leads to whoever did this, I don't give a damn what may come."

"Okay," said Will. "I'll see you soon." Thousands of miles were involved before what would happen next.

"Let me say this," Newton added quickly. "I'm really sorry for what happened in Quantico." Newton didn't need to say it, but his speaking it helped. "I should have done more."

A long silence unspooled between them.

"Let's find out what happened to your son." Will Parker shook the hand of a man who, one week before, he had never expected to see again.

* * * *

The HondaJet took off from Memphis as soon as it had been fueled. Will steered it to the southeast, heading for an airfield that had no designator. The flight from Memphis to Will Parker's farm in southern Georgia caught a tailwind and took only slightly more than an hour. The airfield, like the one in Anchorage, had an unusually improved runway with lights and a hangar hidden in the pine trees at the far end.

Will saw the familiar figure of a man waiting outside the building as the aircraft taxied up and came to a stop. The man knew N883CS well. He pulled open the hatch after the airplane came to a stop.

"Gunny, I have a special mission for you."

"Yes, sir."

"You did get me into this mess," Will said, not unkindly. He now needed Kevin Moncrief to do something most important. Like a good chess player, Will was thinking not about the next move, but two to three steps after that.

"I need some special equipment for Coyote Six, and you need to go north." Will had a list of equipment he needed loaded on the jet and gave Moncrief the coordinates of his mission. The supplies for Coyote Six were all available at his cabin in Georgia. It wouldn't take long.

The main cabin was on a ridge above the valley that held the airstrip. Moncrief's truck took less than fifteen minutes to make the journey and was back with everything shortly thereafter. Will stayed with the aircraft, checking his aviation sectional charts and recording all of the frequencies on the avionics.

Will told Moncrief about his part of the mission as the gunny listened carefully.

"You need to be there no later than tomorrow night," Parker said. "After that, things will start moving fast."

* * * *

The jet lifted off from the small airstrip, turned to the north and, with the turn, started to lose some of the tailwinds that had carried it so far. Every pilot knew that winds could be fickle. And every trip was at the mercy of the wind gods. A hard headwind could slow an aircraft down to a crawl, just as a tailwind could provide a push. In between, a crosswind might help or hurt, but never to the same degree.

Will had landed at the next airfield a few times before and felt fairly familiar with it. VKX was barely on the maps. Potomac Airfield was a single strip just to the east of Fort Washington and a few miles outside of DC's Capital Beltway. The owner had provided more than one favor over the years. He had served in the Marines and also happened to know personally the man who had put the general down with a punch. The Marine Corps was small enough that many knew most things that happened—on and off the battlefield. And all but a few had come down on Parker's side regarding the lack of timely fire support that had resulted in the Marine team being overrun.

Will Parker didn't have a problem with Potomac Airfield. Its strip was short by jet standards, but his skill with the HondaJet let it do more than what other pilots could do. Experience in the bush had taught him how to get in and out of tight places.

In addition to the safe landing, he needed an overnight hangar for Coyote Six, and even if it meant moving another plane out under the stars for an evening. It wasn't protecting his plane that concerned Will; it was keeping it out of sight. The HondaJet was a hot rod that would cause other pilots to come by to kick the tires and take a look. The aircraft had a unique over-wing mount of its engines, and the jet motors looked like they were attached to pedestals. The design caused the aircraft less drag and created more space inside. But it was all too obvious, too singular. And Will was, after all, trying to keep as low a profile as possible.

"Potomac approach, this is November-eight-eight-three Charlie Sierra for a full stop landing." Will had lined up the aircraft for a landing on runway 24. It had just under 3000 feet of asphalt to work with. The HondaJet's short-field capabilities made it work, plus the jet was light, with no passengers and little luggage, far less fuel than full tanks, so it could both land and take off in much less space than even a full HondaJet could have done. Nevertheless, it was a tight fit.

The airplane touched down just as the sun was coming up. The entire area seemed to be asleep, except for the few that ran the airfield. The problem was that those few who saw the HondaJet would speak of it.

"Don't refuel it. I need to be light." Will gave the instructions to the man who had slid the hangar door open and was pulling a smaller Cessna out to make room.

"Nice airplane." The grounds man studied the lines of the jet as he hooked the HondaJet to a tow and backed it into the hangar.

His jet in place, Parker began the next step of his journey: to a five-sided building just across the Potomac. Time to set up the next piece of his plan.

Chapter 28

A Small Airfield in Maryland

Potomac Aviation had a nondescript, 1992 Oldsmobile Cutlass crew car that served as a courtesy car for pilots and crews that needed to do business away from the airport. The car's odometer showed more than 150,000 miles and the vehicle clearly hadn't seen the inside of a car wash in at least a decade. The free rental was ugly but convenient, and it also served another purpose for Will Parker: He'd leave less and less of a trail. The car would not be traceable to its driver, and no paperwork was involved in its use.

Similarly, he would not be using a registered cell phone or any credit cards. If all worked to plan, the tired former Marine in the Cutlass would officially never have driven on Indian Head Highway north toward Washington.

He checked his watch to ensure he was on time for the meeting, as he parked the car at the Pentagon City Mall public parking lot and crossed through the pedestrian tunnel. He wore a black baseball cap and sunglasses and kept his coat collar up, hands in his pockets. It wasn't likely that the hundreds of cameras throughout the area would be used to search for him, but he preferred to remain as invisible as possible.

He crossed the grass to an area just below Arlington National Cemetery and not far from where the Pentagon's helicopter pad had been located before September 11. The entrance to the memorial for those lost on that day was a short walk away. The sun lit up the area and its bright light reflected off of the stainless-steel cantilevered benches that marked each life lost the day American Airlines Flight 77 slammed into the structure immediately to his right. Will stopped at the first bench and read the name of three-year-old Dana Falkenberg, the youngest passenger on the aircraft. He stared at her name for a minute before moving on. The child had done nothing to incur the cruelty of the world. She, her sister, and her mother and father had been leaving for Australia when their plane had been hijacked.

Their fate reminded Will of another family that had boarded an ill-fated passenger jet on a trip that had been planned for years. Will glanced across the highway to Arlington, which hosted an unusual monument that few ever visited. He was one of the few. The Lockerbie Cairn, a short, circular tower made of Scottish red sandstone, had 270 blocks marking the 270 lives lost in the terrorist bombing of Pan Am Flight 103. Its place in Arlington marked one of the first acts of brutalism that would soon be known as terrorism. Two of the blocks in the monument were for Will's own mother and father.

A woman dressed in a Marine Corps uniform was sitting on another bench not too far from the child's memorial. She had a short haircut with some salt-and-pepper hair just below her cover and four rows of colored ribbons that told of more than one tour overseas. One of the medals was a Bronze Star with a V for valor. Below the decorations hung the Marine expert rifle badge and sharpshooter pistol badge.

Will looked up at the Pentagon. It had taken only sixteen months to build, despite the construction happening in the middle of World War II. Roosevelt hadn't wanted it to stand higher than any building across the river. Today, 16,000 workers called it home.

Will joined the woman on the bench. "How's your job?"

He had known Gail Ritchie since Basic School.

"Marine Corps Director of Intelligence? Good days and bad ones." She understated the job. As the senior colonel, she ran the office for the two-star that held the top post.

"Still running marathons?" Will had had her on his shoulder in more than one race.

She smiled. "Maybe next time you come through here we can see what you've got."

Will pointed at the seat she'd chosen. "It's Chic Burlingame's bench." Will stood next to her as she rose and straightened out her uniform.

"You knew him?"

"Yeah. F-four pilot and Academy grad. We crossed paths several years ago." Will looked at the bench, remembering the man who finished first in his class at Top Gun. He had served in the Pentagon briefly with Will.

"Wasn't he the pilot of Flight 77?"

"Yep. He'd retired from the Navy as a reservist and was waiting for his retirement to kick in."

Gail sighed and looked at the bench with respect.

"All those years of danger and it ended like this." She looked down to her hands as if they held the answer.

Will knew how she felt and he shared her anger. It wasn't as if the nearly two decades had made much of a difference in the evil that still circled the world.

The particular pain caused by terrorism had struck him well before September 11. To this day, he lived with the memory of the telephone call. Every day something reminded him of it. The call had come from his mother; she'd said they were leaving London that evening and would be back in Georgia the next day.

"Still having trouble on the trigger pull with the pistol?" Will eyed the sharpshooter badge on her uniform. A sharpshooter was not a bad shot, but he knew she could do better.

"Yeah." She said it with sarcasm, as if she were a student who still failed the test. "You're right."

A repeated fault of many was to anticipate the kick of the pistol just before it discharged. In anticipation, one would pull the trigger before the gun discharged. It tended to cause the shot to go down and to the left. Will had helped Gail on the range at Quantico more than once. She started out shooting so poorly that even the marksmanship badge seemed like a reach. It was a problem. Failure to qualify as a marksman meant disqualification as an officer until he or she got it right. Every Marine had to know how to shoot. The fundamental core of the Corps had always been each Marine's ability to act as an infantryman or woman, first and foremost. So, failure on the firing range meant days and days of returning to it until one got it right. Failure also said that the extra time spent on the range put one further behind on other training, when everyone else had moved on. The embarrassment didn't help. But Will, a natural shot, had taken her aside and with his help, she had qualified on time. Range officers didn't let another young officer help a fellow lieutenant, but Lt. Parker had done things on that range that helped establish his reputation early on as an unusual officer. His max scores and accuracy qualified him to stay on at Quantico and be on the Marine firing team, but what he'd really wanted was to get out into the fleet so he could be shipped to the frontline fighting force.

Ultimately, his assistance had done more than help Gail Ritchie avoid getting a "toilet seat," as Marines called the square marksmanship badge with a circle target in it, instead earning the sharpshooter badge. His training had also helped get Gail earn the Bronze Star when her convoy was overrun near Lashkar Gah in the Helmand province of Afghanistan.

He was also there for her during the divorce. She had made the mistake of marrying another Marine who liked hanging around the officer's club when drinks were only a dollar. Her husband had one too many DUIs at a time when just one would derail a career. He didn't handle the civilian world well. And Will helped her through the bad times. But she wasn't smart—she was brilliant. The Marine Corps knew how important she was and made sure her career survived.

Will's demeanor turned serious as he turned to his reason for meeting there.

He had already called her, so Col. Gail Ritchie knew what the mission was. She also knew Wade Newton. The man wasn't on her favorite list either, but the loss of two young Marines meant much more than any personal likes or dislikes. Gail was one of only a few people who could deliver what Parker needed.

"I had to call in some IOUs to make this work," she said. "It seems the woman Marine is likely dead."

He nodded. "What were you able to do?"

"You're going from here to New York. At CNN, you'll check in with their bureau and they'll handle what you need. You have the credentials as a freelance reporter working on a story about Michael Ridges. It usually takes a lot more time, but a friend has managed to get you an appointment with our expatriate hacker friend." Gail Richie gave him the names of several people. "I got this from someone upriver." She handed him a packet. The only agency upriver from the Pentagon was one known by its three initials.

He looked inside and saw a passport and other documents.

"They all match what we gave CNN. The photo's a little old, but they blurred it enough that it should work."

"Thanks." Will looked at his cell phone, calculating timetables. "You got this done since just last night." He was impressed. There was, however, no other option.

"If you hadn't worked for Langley before, it would have been much harder."

"Yeah." Will recognized that there was some benefit from having a history.

"I don't want to know anything else. Officially, I'll be forgetting all of this once you step on that airplane."

Col. Ritchie was saying this was a one-way street. He nodded his understanding.

"Still up on your Russian?"

"Yeah. I guess we'll see."

She nodded. "Good hunting."

It was better than saying *good luck*.

* * * *

The crew car was parked back in the same spot near the FBO. He left the key under the floor mat. It was a middle of the weekday, which was perfect for the little airport. Much of its business was from the Cessna 172 single-engine pilot who was working on his hours to get his instrument rating. Some of the younger ones were working toward the dream of flying for one of the airlines. Most of the pilots using Potomac Airfield were still at their day jobs at this hour, so when the HondaJet taxied out later, the field should still be vacant.

A taxi was waiting for him at a nearby gas station. Will hiked the mile to the station to gain more separation from any would-be trackers. He climbed in and gave the driver his instructions.

"Run me up to Reagan." From Reagan, he would take the subway to Union Station. If anyone were on his trail, he would at least make it more difficult. He handed the man a hundred-dollar bill, which would more than cover the fare.

"Yes, sir."

When he got to Union Station, he stopped and used one of his burner phones to call back to the small airfield. He had a request to the chief flight instructor, whom he had known for years.

"Take the HondaJet for a trip." Will knew more about the flight instructor when he made the offer than many of his student pilots. The man's logbook went easily over 10,000 hours, much of which included several tours in the Gulf flying the F-15E Strike Eagle. Will wasn't entrusting his bird with a pilot who didn't know how to handle a twin-engine jet aircraft.

The instructor's eagerness to fly the hot rod came through in his single-word response: "Okay?"

"Don't do any Panther tricks." Will was referencing the name of the man's squadron. The 494th, or Panthers, were known for coming in low and fast.

"I got it."

"I need you to fly VFR to Atlantic City and refuel. From there, file IFR in the air to JFK. The FBO has instructions about the aircraft. Under the pilot's seat is an envelope that should cover everything."

No one would notice the slight change made to the aircraft. Its tail number had been slightly modified so tracking it would be impossible.

"And one other thing."

"You got it."

"In the envelope are instructions about buying a ticket. Details on a passport and a credit card under that name should work. You can do it all by phone from the New York FBO."

The pilot would call Air France once he landed and place the order for a round-trip ticket on Flight 007 connecting in Paris to 1044 into Sheremetyevo under the name that matched the passport. The same credit card also cleared the express Russian entry visa, but under the name of Will Parker's passport—a different name than Will Parker. His placing the order from New York gave Will some further cover should anyone be on his trail.

When Will offered the man cash, he refused. "Hell, just for the chance to fly a HondaJet," said the instructor, "I'd do it for free." Every pilot liked to expand his repertoire of airplanes he has flown.

Will insisted on at least paying for the man's shuttle flight home. He was glad the instructor would enjoy himself along the way.

* * * *

The next morning the jet taxied to the very end of the runway and set up for a short-field takeoff. It required the pilot's holding the brake pedals on until the very last second while the two jet engines spun up to maximum power. The aircraft rocked as the energy surged through it. When he released the brakes, the airplane's roll pushed him back into his seat. In a few yards, he pulled up on the yoke to lighten the weight on the nose. Slightly beyond the halfway point, he felt the aircraft free contact with the ground. The HondaJet stayed at a low profile to build up speed after it broke from the friction of the tires on the asphalt and then, just before the pine trees at the end of the runway started to fill up his view in the window, the pilot pulled back on the yoke, and the jet took off like the race car it was meant to be. He banked left, away from Washington, headed to the New Jersey coastline below 18,000 feet, on a visual flight rule journey that kept it off of the records, and was soon down on the runway in Atlantic City. Touching down, he took on fuel, took off again, opened an instrument flight plan, and made his way to JFK.

The HondaJet made good time into JFK. There, the pilot taxied the small plane to the general aviation terminal where Sheltair JFK was waiting.

"You should have a hangar reservation for it," the pilot said.

"Yes, sir. November-eight-eight-three-Charlie Sierra will be in hangar six." The man with the tow truck pulled the aircraft away from the FBO.

"Shouldn't need much, but top off the tanks." He gave the man the credit card information.

The flight instructor made the call from the pilot's lounge to Air France, locked down the ticket and visa, left the FBO, took a cab to LaGuardia, and was on the Delta shuttle within an hour.

The only problem was that the aircraft was not N883CS.

* * * *

Will looked at his cell phone for the time. The Amtrak Acela Express from Washington's Union Station was early. It had taken less than three hours to make the journey to Penn Station. He took the subway to the Time Warner Center at Columbus Circle. The woman at the desk had a package waiting for the freelance reporter working on a follow-up story about the famous hacker who had sought sanctuary in Russia. Under the new administration, CNN had assigned more reporters to the Russian beat. Consequently, his going to Moscow didn't raise any eyebrows in New York.

The ticket on the Air France flight was in business class. Will had suspected that it would attract less attention if he were simply another businessman flying to Moscow. And it gave him the chance to eat and catch up on his sleep for the first time since returning from Snag.

The Airbus A380 flew through the night, landing in Paris at just after dawn. Will made his way to the Air France lounge, where he used a computer to log into an email-provider website that resided on the deep web. This way, he could communicate with the gunny in secret. He had a Mac with him, but it was intended both to fit his cover and contain fabricated articles that supported his journalistic credentials. The computers here could be trusted; in Moscow, the FSB had eyes on everything and everyone. If he failed to remember that, it would end badly.

"You have a bride waiting for you. Alina." Moncrief's email seemed comical, but was far from it. He sent her name, her photo, and the other details. She was the contact who would supply what was needed on the other end. "You have four nights reserved at the Arbat Six near Arbatskiy Pereulok."

Will knew the area on the west side of the center of Moscow. He exchanged several thousand dollars into rubles. Using local currency would help him fade into the background. He looked through the shop at de Gaulle, trying to find the most nondescript clothing available, pulling a plain gray sweatshirt from a rack, along with prefaded blue jeans. He also bought a pair of black sneakers that had labels not recognizable as American. Muscovites thought of themselves as being stylish and liked Western fashions, but they rarely wore clothes with recognizable Western logos. Nike sightings were rare in the city of twelve and a half million people. A black Lomaiyi parka finished the outfit.

The short layover allowed him to buy two burner phones equipped with Russian SIM cards. The flight arrived in Moscow late in the afternoon. In customs, officials studied his two phones for a while.

"One for family and one for business," he said, as if it mattered. The phones were both registered with the SORM eavesdropping system that the FSB used, a semantic archive that followed every electronic device entering Russia. He had planned on it.

And not only electronics surveillance. Will was followed as soon as he waved a taxi down at the airport entrance.

"*CNN bureau 7/4 kopnyc 1in Kutuzovsky.*" He thought it best to check in with the CNN bureau as soon as he arrived.

"Yes." The taxi driver was probably an FSB agent; at the very least, all conversations in the car would be overheard and taped. Reporters always drew some level of attention when they entered Russia.

Will reported to the bureau, arriving just before they closed the door.

"Not aware of you much." The clerk was American and, after years of being in Russia, had clearly become wary of those she didn't recognize.

He noticed that she was wearing a puffy down vest over a thick sweater.

"Don't they pay the heat bill?"

"Of course they don't." She smiled. "What work have you done?"

"Mostly freelance."

"You got some time with Ridges?"

"Yes."

"How'd you pull that off?"

"Just hit it at the right time," he deflected. She wouldn't have believed him if he told her it came courtesy of Col. Gail Ritchie's extensive contacts.

"Okay. Do you need lodging?"

"No. Doing a quick human-interest story, then I'm out of here. My Air France leaves at three ten on Saturday." He needed to plant the idea in her mind should any inquiry be made.

* * * *

Will checked into a hotel on the west side of Moscow. He put both phones down in the room, as well as the used PowerBook with the dummy stories he'd pounded out during the flight over. Most were human interest stories about the bright computer technician from Nowhere, Ohio, who'd brought down the director of the Defense Intelligence Agency. He thought it was the right hook for the FSB to believe. It imparted the proper tone—namely, that his upcoming article would only serve to embarrass both the DIA director and the US president.

Odds were that the FSB agents would let Ridges take a look at his stories. Will was guessing that Michael Ridges might like the story as well. A small-town, but brilliant, computer geek takes down a key member of the new cabinet. It seemed clear that he wanted to embarrass Alexander Paul, though it was still very unclear as to why. Will mumbled aloud to himself for the benefit of any hidden microphones as he left the PowerBook open and on the table. It was probably a little too apparent that he was making it accessible; still, it was vital that he appear to be an open book to the Russians, thus providing them with no reason to delay the visit with Ridges.

He found a small café near the hotel, drank some shots of vodka, ate a supper of beef stroganoff and boiled potatoes, and went back to his hotel and bed. As he walked back into the hotel, it was snowing and dark. He glanced in the reflection of the glass at the two men in the car across the street.

Poor guys, trailing a boring American while freezing in a Lada. He wanted to knock on their window and invite them in for some vodka, but he imagined that the car was probably already well-stocked.

Sorry, boys. It's gonna be a cold one. His mercy stopped short. He knew if they had any inkling as to who he really was, the blows would be brutal.

Will took in the dark, frigid winter night in Moscow as he walked the final block to his hotel. The snow had stopped for a short time, but the cold air hung close to the ground. The streetlights let out a glow that reflected off of the new snow's surface.

"Goddamn freezing," he mumbled to himself as he stopped at the front desk. The clerk was a middle-aged man, with large, yellow, crooked teeth, a balding pate, and a pleasant smile.

"What's the weather going to do?" He said it in slow, all-too-clear English, as if he was someone who wouldn't even try to learn the local language.

"A bad storm is coming."

"Where can I buy some gloves?"

All his life, Will had possessed a talent that followed him through his military career. He was a perfect linguist, able to speak languages from six continents, and he could speak Russian with a few different local accents, when required. Here, he didn't even try his Russian.

The phone rang while he was standing there. The clerk answered the call and spoke with an FSB agent asking about the status of the new guest. The clerk, thinking the American had no idea, gave the agent a clear description of the man standing in front of him. He finally hung up the phone.

"Busy night?" Will asked.

The clerk didn't answer that question.

"Bershka...but it's a long way." The man seemed to ponder the right store for the American, as if to judge the size of his pocketbook. Almost certainly, he already had been briefed by the FSB as to why the guest was there. Another American here to make Russia look bad.

Will thanked the man.

He stopped as he turned away and then turned around.

"I am expecting a visitor in the morning."

The clerk put on his reading glasses to look at the piece of paper that Will handed him from his pocket. It had the name of a woman.

"Mmm. Is she coming here?"

"I believe so." It was the name of the Russian bride that Moncrief had given him. She was more than a Russian bride. And her help was vital.

Chapter 29

Paul's Headquarters Near Dulles, Virginia

"He's disappeared," Caldwell told his boss.

Retired Marine and self-appointed investigator William Parker was nowhere to be found.

"I've checked with several sources. He was seen in Memphis. We know his airplane went from there to his farm in Georgia and then landed at a small airfield in Maryland."

"What airfield?" Alexander Paul snapped. His usual air of calm seemed to be evaporating.

"Potomac Airfield."

"Never heard of it."

"It's about ten miles from here."

Paul gave him the look that usually was followed with a flood of cusswords. "Planes don't disappear. Check it out." He clearly didn't like the idea that Parker was somewhere in the area of the capital and no one had any idea as to why.

"Yes, sir."

"What about Stewart?" He knew that the doctor was somewhere in Alaska.

"I'll get on it."

"Any number for him?"

Caldwell shook his head.

"There's got to be another way to get in touch with him."

"I may have an idea." Caldwell gave Paul a curt nod and turned for the door. "I'll report back as soon as I have something."

* * * *

Caldwell drove the thirty miles to Potomac Airfield. Traffic slowed him down as it was near the end of the day. The airstrip had a line of small, single-engine airplanes, a hangar that looked like a tin building from the forties, and what looked like a small office near the hangar.

"Hello." Caldwell walked through the door to see a man in his mid-thirties sitting behind a desk covered with paper, and several shelves behind the man with models of a variety of small and large aircraft. It was immediately apparent to Caldwell that this airport was a work of passion for flying, as compared to a business looking for substantial profits.

"Can I help you?" The man at the desk didn't get up. In the background, the radio chirped with calls from pilots flying in the area. The sound of aircraft engines spinning up for takeoff filled the room with noise.

"A friend of mine came through here yesterday. A Mr. Parker. The record showed his aircraft landed here."

"Oh, the little jet?"

"I think so."

"Our airfield was too short for him. He had to divert at the last minute."

Caldwell blinked, waited a beat. "Well, I can't find a record of him landing anywhere."

"Who knows? You might want to try Ocean City. I think he diverted to there."

Caldwell nodded. Visual-flight-rule landings required no record. Jets rarely did VFR flights, which were at low altitudes. It was a line, but Caldwell knew that there would be no help here. "Thanks and sorry to bother you."

Well-played, he thought.

Will Parker had friends and he was clearly up to something. To have any chance of finding out what, Caldwell knew he'd need to speak to Kevin Moncrief or find Dr. Stewart.

Chapter 30

Whitehorse, Yukon

The four-wheel-drive pickup truck that Kevin Moncrief rented from K&K was ready for the hardship of a Yukon winter. The tires were well knobbed and the radiator had a heating plug-in for severe drops in temperature. Moncrief pulled out of the airport at Whitehorse and went half a mile to Hougen's Sports Lodge, one of the largest hunting-supply stores in the western Yukon.

"Hello." Moncrief was a descendant of the Apache tribe, so folks in the Yukon might easily have thought he came from one of the local indigenous communities.

"Yes, sir." The clerk didn't know that the perfect customer had just come through the door.

"I'm heading out into the wilderness and need to get some supplies." Moncrief looked around the space. "Nice moose," he said, nodding at the large mount that looked over the store.

"What type of supplies are you talking about?"

"I'm backpacking into a remote location."

"This time of year?"

"Yeah." He looked at the guns that lined the wall. "Let's start with a rifle."

"What are you thinking about?"

"How about the Marlin?"

"Okay." The clerk's interest grew visibly as he realized he had a guy who knew his weapons. "You planning on stopping a bear?"

"In a .45-70 with a shoulder strap. Hopefully, the wrong time of year for a bear." Kevin deflected the comment.

"Lucky bear. What else?"

* * * *

Moncrief's silver pickup pulled out of Hougen's and headed north on the Alaska Highway. He looked at the map and calculated that he could spend the night at Beaver Creek and then hike the miles it took to get to Snag. With no airplanes or anything to trace him by, he would disappear into the backcountry and leave little or no trail.

He hadn't seen Dr. Stewart in some time. He smiled at the surprise that would cross her face when this stranger came out of the woods.

What he really needed, though, was a computer terminal.

Will would be trying to reach him via the deep web from Moscow. Even if anyone read their communications, it would still stump them—even the FSB—because Moncrief and Will could opt to write in Ndee or Apache. It was the one speech that Moncrief had to teach his friend. But it also was one of the most difficult languages to learn. Marines in the South Pacific in World War II learned quickly that it was the one dialect that the Japanese could never break.

His cell phone rang just as he pulled out on the highway heading north. It was from a number that he didn't recognize and on a cell phone that Kevin rarely gave out.

"Yep?"

"Gunnery Sergeant?"

No one used that as an introduction, and no one used the full pronunciation of the rank unless he was a stranger and, likely, not a Marine. A Marine would have said "Gunny."

"Who is this?"

"My name's Frank Caldwell. I'm trying to reach your man."

Chapter 31

The Yukon

So, you've gotten popular all of a sudden, Moncrief emailed Parker through the deep web from a computer in the back of a gas station just off of the highway in Koidern, a few miles south of Beaver Creek. The clerk had no idea that the funny man in the back with the brand-new parka was talking to a man in Moscow. It took a hundred-dollar bill for Moncrief to have access to the computer, download the Tor browser, and open up communication with Will.

You want the guy's number? He knows you aren't in Alaska.

Yes.

Both men knew the call confirmed that Coyote Six was being followed.

Moncrief took a sip from a hot cup of coffee as he sat in the plastic chair. His bulky clothes made it a tight fit.

So, they know you're in Alaska. The two assumed that the call from Caldwell to Moncrief had been traced, revealing the gunny's location.

Moncrief looked outside at the gloomy weather; another snowstorm seemed to be coming in.

Roger that.

This also meant that Karen Stewart was at higher risk. If they knew Moncrief was in the Yukon and near Snag, they probably knew that she was nearby.

I need for you to do something, Will wrote. *Let the CO of 1st Raiders Battalion know that the body found in Mexico was that of a Marine. And that the other Marine, one of his, is likely being kept somewhere on the east side of the Baja Peninsula.*

Got it.

And tell him it isn't a case of AWOL.

Moncrief nodded to himself, knowing where Will was going with this. The 1st Raiders Battalion had been doing a lot of joint training with the Mexican Marines. The Infantería de Marina's special force, known as FES, was well-trained, well-equipped, and capable of reaching out to any place in the Baja with great speed. Between the US Marines and the FES, if there was anyone else left alive, it was the only chance they had. It had to be a bolt of lightning. And it couldn't be the normal police. Any police officer in that part of the Baja would likely make a second call as soon as he received the first. Only the FES could be trusted. The Mexican Marines had gained the reputation of taking down cartels and drawing the unwanted attention of the drug lords. On more than one occasion, the cartel had kidnapped a Mexican Marine, killed him on videotape, and then killed his family. Such attacks only made the FES stronger and more determined.

The problem with rescuing Todd Newton, if he still lived, was that the US Marines couldn't make an incursion into Baja California without someone from Mexico being involved. And the only ones who could be trusted would be the Mexican Marines. But too early a call had too high a risk of a leak.

"Tell him that as soon as I know more, I'll let him know. Get me his cell number."

Chapter 32

FinCEN Headquarters

Virginia Peoples hadn't slept since the FinCEN project on the Cayman Islands bank had been quashed. Consequently, she had been coming to work even earlier than usual. As always, the building was dark when she went through security. Once again, she was the one who turned on the lights in the offices.

At her desk, she played with some research. She didn't use the flash drive for fear that it would be caught up in the scan that her computers were most likely to be under. She did do some open-ended research. The Cayman Islands bank had subsidiaries in the Isle of Man as well as the UAE. It bragged on its website about leading the industry in anti-laundering processes. She laughed at the comment.

Virginia crossed over to some independent research with the Egmont Group. Created in 1995, the organization had taken on the role of the international monitor of the movement of money. Her working group had a contact there whom she had relied upon often in the past.

She lifted her fingers from her keyboard. An email wouldn't be smart, given that she'd been ordered to drop the investigation. She looked at the clock. It was too early to call Egmont.

She sighed, pushing her keyboard away. As little as she liked it, she would wait, and then call.

* * * *

At one minute past seven, Virginia was knocking on Darrel Byrd's door. It was open a crack already; inside, she saw that he hadn't even had a chance to open his computer.

"Hey," she said. "I was just checking in with you on the Caymans."

"I thought we were dropping that."

"Do you know who Alexander Paul is?"

"Wasn't he DIA?"

She nodded.

"Virginia, you do good work," he said in his most patronizing tone. She hated it when he did that. If she didn't interrupt, he'd go on to say that the project had been closed down and she needed to move on.

"I bet he's in that bank. Maybe it's to follow the trail of money going through there...but maybe something else is going on."

"Would that be so bad?"

"You mean that the CIA and DIA own a bank in the Caymans?"

"I didn't say that. All I am saying is that we've been ordered to leave it alone."

"Let me ask this: What if someone used that as an opportunity to steal? Who would catch him?"

"Not sure, but presently, it's not our problem." His voice rose. "I'll say it one more time: Leave it alone."

She nodded, turned, and left his office, stunned but more determined than ever. The Cayman Islands bank had been given a get-out-of-jail-free card unlike any other.

* * * *

When Virginia left work that night, her Volvo with the University of Pennsylvania Wharton School window decal was not difficult for someone to follow.

As she fought traffic, Virginia checked the time. It had been a long day at work. Or rather, she'd made it a long day.

I need to learn to let things go. She heard her mother's voice in her head, like a passenger who wasn't there. Virginia also knew what Mom would say next. That particular admonition was always followed by, *Or else you'll never find a husband.*

Virginia was tired and decided to stop at her small grocery store just around the corner from her apartment. They had premade salads that were unusually good. When the kitchen was bare, the store provided an easy fix. They had a north Indian–style rice salad that ranked high as a favorite.

"Hello, Mr. Patel." She had come in there often enough that she knew him and he knew the young professionals by their dress when they worked for the government. Those who worked with the computer contractors who had government contracts wore just about anything. And those who worked with the government had a professional look that would work in a courtroom.

"Fresh tuna today," he said cheerily from behind the counter.

"Thank you." She sorted through the trays of premade salad, picked one, checked its date, and turned down the aisle to the counter. As she looked up, she saw the man holding his pistol at Mr. Patel, just before bright red blood sprayed the rack of cigarettes that was just behind the counter. She didn't hear a gunshot. The suppressor silenced the .22 caliber bullet to virtually nothing. The man had a black mask, black gloves, and a gray hoodie that covered much of the upper part of his body.

"Oh," was her last word.

Like the professional he was, the killer needed only one shot to drop her. As she turned to retreat, the bullet went through the back of her skull at an angle. The salad fell from her hands and slid across the floor.

Chapter 33

Moscow

The phone rang in Will Parker's room at the Arbat Six. The room was so small that he had to turn sideways to get around the bed. The ringer was loud and the sound seemed to echo off of the walls. The room had the smell of one too many cigarettes. Russia cared little with the health issues that worried much of America. More than a third of Russians smoked.

"Hello." He made a point of answering in English.

"Yes, I am here to meet you." She had a young voice and seemed to be struggling with her English.

"Oh, I'll be there. " He started to leave, but stopped as he was closing the door. He went back into the room and grabbed a small, black backpack that he had purchased in Sheremetyevo at a RegStaer duty-free shop.

Downstairs, the woman's striking blond hair under her fur hat had clearly caught the eye of the now-smiling desk clerk. She had nearly perfect features, with a cream-colored complexion and a ruby red shade of lipstick that only made her facial features more striking.

She approached Will, standing only chest-high in her heavy parka and thick wool gloves. She took off her gloves, stood up on tiptoes, and kissed his cheek.

"It is so nice to meet you." Her English seemed to have improved since the call upstairs. There was only the hint of an accent.

"Alina, I have been looking forward to this for some time." Will gave her a long hug.

"Would you like to get some coffee?" She put her gloves back on. "Perhaps for us to get to know each other a little better."

"Yes, good idea."

Will pulled up his parka and they headed out the door.

The snow had stopped and it was a bright day with an azure-blue sky. The Lada had not moved from its spot across the street. Will noticed some movement inside the auto as they turned and walked in the opposite direction. Both the car's roof and hood were deep in snow. The passengers might have moved, but the Lada had remained in the same place for some time.

"It is a walk, but let's take the Arbatsko number three." She had on tall black boots, but cut across the street as if she had a pair of running shoes on. The metro was some distance away.

"Who did you talk to?"

"Your Moncrief." She said it over her shoulder without stopping.

"What did he say?"

"He told me he was an American Indian? Is that true? Like your movies?"

Certain he was with the correct person now, Will switched to fluent Russian.

"So, you are to be my bride?"

"Nice, huh? Perhaps you take me back with you." She laughed at the thought.

They cut through a back alley, walked through a market, and kept moving at the same pace.

"Why?" He asked the obvious question. It wasn't *why* as in *Why would you go back with me?* but *Why are you helping?*

"Why would I help an American?" She didn't even look back. "You are not supposed to ask that question."

"You don't need to answer it."

"I support Navalny." A dissident following the only man who'd had the guts to run against Putin in recent years.

They reached an entrance with a large red sign that read *Mockobcknn Metpononnteh* or Moscow Metro. Will was familiar with the system. She took a long stairway down to the subway, bought tickets for both of them, and took the next train to the east. They were crammed in tightly against each other and, as the train went into the dark, she exchanged her backpack with him. The backpack he gave her was light. It contained only a few items, of which the most important one was the number of a Swiss bank account. The pack she gave Will contained the supplies he needed that would never have made it through customs.

"They'll want to search it when you get back, so you need to leave it in a locker at the last stop. It's a train station and they have storage."

He knew the plan. And he knew cameras would be everywhere. It all was about risk. They took another train to another station and then went to a coffee shop.

"Do you know this stop?"

He looked at the sign. It had significance.

"This is Leningradsky?"

"Yes."

Leningradsky was the oldest train station in Moscow. It also was the train station to Tver, a small town just outside of the city. The tracks were mainline, meaning that the fast-international trains would pass through Leningradsky, with some going to St. Petersburg and others to the border and Helsinki.

"We will go back to your room and make love."

Will looked at her.

"You think the FSB would believe otherwise?"

He knew she was right. Their little game required that all the chips be on the table.

"Plus, you will be my first American." She laughed again.

Afterward, she would be heard making a date for Saturday morning with her future husband. He would talk about changing his flight so that they could visit the American Embassy when it opened on Monday. When the FSB came, she would be in tears, cursing the cruel American who'd gotten her hopes up.

As she left his room that night, she whispered in Will's ear: "Like I said before, do you think the FSB would have believed us otherwise?"

Chapter 34

Parker's Hotel on the East Side of Moscow

The phone rang just as Will returned from seeing Alina out of the hotel. He felt his pulse go up. He looked out the window while listening on the phone. The Lada was gone. Perhaps another shift of guards would take over.

"Sir?"

"Yes?"

"You will be picked up today at ten." The agent from FSB was the coordinator for his upcoming visit with Michael Ridges. His flat voice had little inflection.

"Okay."

Will went downstairs and had a coffee with sugar and cream. He sat near the window and watched as the two agents returned in their car. They walked around the vehicle, stretching as if they were back on watch after a long, cold night, watching the entrance to the hotel.

At least they'd been busy at one point. He assumed that Alina had done a good job losing them.

Will looked at his cell phone and went back to his room. There, he used one of the burn phones to call Air France and move up his reservation a day. He also bought a second ticket under an alias of a male name.

He used the second phone to call the Russian rail service to inquire about two seats on the Tolstoy train to Helsinki. He didn't buy any tickets. That would be done later.

The FSB agent was waiting outside of the hotel at 9:30.

Will walked out, with his Russian coat on and the hood pulled up around his head, and walked directly to the car. He had his computer bag over his shoulder.

The ride took less than thirty minutes. During the last fifteen, he was required to wear a blindfold. The computer, however, had a program buried deep inside of it that tracked the journey via GPS.

Will closed his eyes, even under the blindfold, to feel every mile of the journey, constructing in his mind the exact path of the vehicle. It had made three turns from the highway. One road was smoother than the next, indicating a snowplowed highway. After another turn, the Lada started to hit bump after bump. Potholes. The third road curved back and forth several times as if it were winding along a watercourse. He held his hand out the window while blindfolded, feeling the shift of the wind and the warmth of the sun. He could tell when the vehicle passed through thick woods because the sunlight vanished and his hand turned cold. When the car came to a stop, Will's memory had recorded every move, stop, and turn.

When they removed his hood, Parker saw that they had come to a small cabin overlooking a frozen lake covered in snow. His car had been pulled up to a front porch that guarded a dark, thick oak door. He looked over his shoulder and saw a small white guardhouse through the trees. A man dressed in all-white with an AK-47 stood guard.

"Hello," Will greeted a guard who opened the door. He was in winter whites with a white fur cap marked by a metal red and gold star in the center of his hat.

The guard frisked him and looked at the computer in the bag.

"We will take this." The FSB guard spoke clear English. It made sense that someone assigned to guard an American would be able to hear and understand anything that was said.

"Sure. At some point, I would like it back so I can take notes for the interview," Will protested, but only mildly.

Will Parker walked into the main room of the small cabin. A fire was burning and a short-statured, pale man with glasses stood up. He looked like a college student, perhaps one working on his master's, dressed in a red-and-black–striped flannel shirt, baggy blue jeans, and Clarks boots. He wore a small, cheap watch and his fingernails were short, as if the wear of the last few years had taken a toll on his nerves.

"You're from CNN." Ridges looked Will directly in the eyes.

"Yes." Will waited as the FSB agent left the room.

"This is my third interview this month."

"Really?"

"Let's sit by the fire. Do you want some tea?"

"Thank you." It gave Will the chance to see all of the players in the cabin, but there were clearly no servants. Michael Ridges went to the kitchen and came back with two cups. It appeared that the guards only rarely entered the cabin.

"Cream? Sugar?"

"Yes, thanks."

Ridges pulled up a chair near the fireplace and reached for a pad and pen on a table. He wrote furiously on it. He removed the page quietly, folded it, and handed it to Will. It was likely that both microphones and cameras were studying the two.

"The tea is from London," Ridges said, clearly trying to fill what would otherwise be suspicious silence while Will read his note.

THEY HEAR ALL AND SEE US. WHAT DO YOU WANT?

"It's good," said Will as he read it, then tossed the note into the fire. He took the thick marker from Ridges like a school buddy passing notes.

"Do they get you whatever you want?" he asked.

"You mean food?"

"Yeah."

"They're very good to me."

Will wrote down three names.

RIDGES, NEWTON, O'HARA: ONE IS DEAD.

O'Hara was the woman whose mangled corpse now rested on a cold steel table in La Paz.

Ridges read it once, read it again, and began to shake.

* * * *

YOU CARED ABOUT HER. Will wrote the next note, which was read and then tossed into the fire.

"So, you want to know why I did it? Everyone does." Ridges held his teacup with both hands. He was keeping the conversation going. "Am I right?"

"Sure, if you're comfortable telling me."

Will looked around the small room. It was a cottage with a kitchen just off the sitting room. The windows had shutters, but they were all open. The fireplace gave the place warmth and a smoky smell. It didn't seem that the fire drafted well. A pair of French doors were on the opposite side from the kitchen and led to a small porch, covered, and just to the bottom of the door, Will could see the edge of a well-stocked woodpile within easy reach. Being an experienced operative, Will knew the details were important. They gave one insight and were stored in one's memory in case of need later. There were no ashtrays. There was a vase on a table near the kitchen door with some dead flowers in it. It seemed that a woman had been here.

Will's research had confirmed that Ridges had met another woman since his days at Maryland and she had visited him often in Russia, but her absence was reflected in the rest of the relatively bare cabin.

He assumed that everything was being recorded. And cameras would probably have recorded the writings, but the guards seemed to have gotten lazy with the many visitors their guest had had. They weren't in the room and left the two alone.

Nevertheless, he imagined that the guards would be most interested in the notes in the fire. They would see them use the pad and try to look over their shoulders to see what was being written. Ridges covered the pad as he wrote and used one sheet to cover the printed page. Will followed suit. He assumed that when Ridges went out for exercise, an FSB agent would gather up the ashes with the hope of finding something.

"So, tell me why you left?" Will kept the conversation going.

"There was a man that was corrupt and vengeful."

Will had a good guess as to who that person was.

"I was onto something that if he found out, it would have been bad."

"So not much choice about where to hide."

YOU'RE NOT SAFE HERE, Will wrote.

EVEN HERE? Ridges wrote back.

YES.

The notes went back and forth. Ridges seemed easily enough convinced, almost as if he had secretly been wanting to leave Russia.

Will suspected that Alexander Paul's reach could extend into Russia if needed, but not strongly enough to stop Putin's desire to hold onto the bargaining chip that was Michael Ridges. At any moment, though, the bigger situation could change, and it would be over for Ridges. And if his fellow ex-trainees were being abducted and murdered, things were indeed changing.

I'VE A WAY OUT.

Michael Ridges looked up from the last note, then wrote his response: *I'VE BEEN WORKING ON SOMETHING THAT NEEDS TO GET OUT.*

"Do you miss America?"

"Some things, yeah, but like I said, they've been good to me." Ridges played along with the game.

A man came into the room. Ridges stared at the FSB guard. His boots had tracked in snow, which was melting on the rug.

"What do you want?" He seemed to have no problem letting it be known that he didn't appreciate the interruption.

"The time is done," the guard said, shifting his weight from foot to foot. He seemed uncomfortable about the change in the normal routine caused by Will's visit. It appeared that there was a nervous tension caused by the passing of notes.

"Leave us alone a little longer."

Will was mildly surprised that Ridges seemed to be granted some control over his situation.

Like a scolded child, the guard turned abruptly, almost petulantly, and went back outside. Will's last note ran longer than the others. It was the most important one.

USE TIPPENHAUER, GUARDS WILL BE GONE AT MIDNIGHT. BE ON MAIN ROAD, FIVE MINUTES.

Ridges would know of Tippenhauer—a scientific paper published several years earlier that had outraged law enforcement when it hit the press.

Ridges wadded the note up in his hand but held it for what seemed like an eternity.

Will stood. "Perhaps we can communicate by email so I can flesh out this interview?"

"Sure. This is my email." Ridges rose to get a piece of paper and pencil.

Will stopped him and touched the other man's hand for a short moment. Ridges seemed hesitant at first, but after another moment dropped the ball of paper into Will's palm. Will tossed it into the fireplace, then used a poker to stir the ashes. He slipped Ridges's email address into his pocket.

At the door, the guard stopped him and frisked him. He took the slip of paper from Will's pocket, looked at it, and then stuck it in his own pocket. He pointed with a nod of his head toward the Lada. Once again, Will submitted to being blindfolded and sat back for the journey to his hotel.

Chapter 35

Paul's Headquarters Near Dulles, Virginia

Frank Caldwell was skimming through news stories on his phone when he noticed two articles that stood out. The first covered the robbery of a small grocery store that his wife often used. It was only a couple of blocks from their small-town house in Arlington. Two people were dead.

"The first murder this year," the police chief said in the online interview. "Anyone who knows anything, please call." Arlington was a safe city and homicides rare. Suicides were more likely in the highly stressed city of government employees and contractors.

It was the final comment that caught Caldwell's eye.

"The cameras were all destroyed and the killer used a small-caliber weapon." The chief's observations telegraphed a professional hit to Caldwell. True, any random robber might use a small-caliber pistol, but destroying the store's cameras displayed the kind of tradecraft used by special operators behind the enemy's lines. He made a mental note to find out who the victims were.

The second story caused him to sit up. It came from an American newspaper's Moscow bureau and concerned Michael Ridges.

Caldwell looked up from his phone and stared into the middle distance.

So that's *where Parker is.*

Caldwell already knew about the connection between the two Marines and Ridges. He also knew that Parker had gotten onto that same trail and then disappeared from public sight. There was something else he remembered in the Will Parker file with the Agency: The man had an unusual talent for languages, in particular Russian.

His phone rang and the conversation was short.

Since the line was not secure, it only took one word.
"Moscow."

* * * *

Alexander Paul hit the red button to end the call. Caldwell may have served a useful purpose after all. He turned to his computer and opened the Tor browser. It had been some time since Alexander Paul had used the deep web address of his friend in Russia's FSB. Suddenly, having a contact in the Russian intelligence bureau seemed like a godsend. If William Parker were in Moscow, then Paul's FSB friend would be delighted to follow up on an uninvited foreign agent in his country.

Chapter 36

The Hideout in Mexico

The fever had started the day before. Todd Newton's clothes were soaked, and the dampness had him shivering in his cell. It had been more than twenty-four hours since he had received anything to drink. He was fighting the thought of giving in.

Maybe she knew something.

Todd remembered that at one time Lucy O'Hara and Ridges had been a thing, but it hadn't lasted long. Ridges had mentioned his new girlfriend in the few emails they'd exchanged before he defected. He had started the relationship with the new woman while working in Washington. It had sounded serious at the time.

"If only they'd told me," Todd pleaded to the wall.

If his captors wanted something that Ridges and O'Hara knew, it might save his life to know it. He would have gladly given up anything—anything at all—in order to stop this nightmare.

The door swung open.

The two men covered his head with a black bag and dragged him up the stairs. He felt, for the first time in days, a cool breeze coming off of the water. It had the taste of salt air. He felt his feet drag on gravel and smelled dust, its sterility and chalky taste signaling that nothing green grew anywhere near this place. The taste of salt air was soon replaced by the taste of dust in his mouth as he inhaled. The broken nose made it a struggle to breathe, but his sensation of taste had not been affected by the beatings.

The van had a metal floor. He moaned from the pain as his elbows and knees struck the van's bed. As soon as he did, a hand slapped the bag hard, causing his ears to ring again.

They accelerated from the parking spot with the tires spinning gravel. Deep ruts in the road bounced the vehicle up and down and to the side, tossing Todd from one wall to the other inside the cargo area. With each jolt, he painfully banged his elbow or knee or head on steel. The journey seemed endless, and Todd was expecting to lose consciousness at any moment, when the van finally slammed to a stop, banging his head once more against steel.

The doors swung open and one man grabbed him by his chained feet and dragged him to the edge of the van. There, another threw him across his shoulder like a bag of potatoes and proceeded up a stairway.

The nightmare repeated itself as Todd's hood was removed, only to reveal another dark basement, a small metal cot, and this time a metal lug sunk into the floor that was used to padlock his chains.

"Water?" Todd tried to speak. "Please."

It seemed he still needed to be kept alive. The giant with the big black eyebrows said something to the smaller man. Shortly, the other one returned with a plastic bucket full of water. It had the logo of Ace Hardware with the words *La Paz* below it.

For the first time in days, Todd could fully quench his thirst. The water was lukewarm, but it didn't matter. He had no guess as to why they had moved him—his conditions had not changed in any meaningful way. Except for the water.

It seemed he would live another day, but the clock was still ticking loudly.

The two men left, and with the water and his craving satisfied, Newton collapsed on the cot and fell into a deep, feverish sleep.

Chapter 37

Moscow

The phone rang again in Will Parker's room.

He was lying on his bed, working his way through the night's plans.

"Yes?"

It was a woman's voice. It only said one word. He recognized it immediately.

"*Deeya*!"

"You must have a wrong number." His message was intended to slow down the guards that were listening, but he knew exactly what it meant. *Deeya* was Apache and could only come from one person.

He hung up the phone, went to the window, and peered through a crack in the blinds. The two FSB agents were standing outside of their Lada, looking down the street as two cars approached. One stopped short of the other, and a tall man got out from the front passenger seat.

His hair was gray but full enough that even in the frigid air he wasn't wearing a cap.

Spetsgruppa commander.

Simply by looking at the man's face and the insignia on his uniform, Will knew much. This was a seasoned combat veteran who probably rose through the ranks in Afghanistan. He had been transferred to the Federalnaya Sluzhba Beszopasnosti because he was smart. An officer of the FSB, particularly one stationed in Moscow, always made for a capable opponent.

Will gathered his parka, gloves, and the bag that held his computer. He stopped at the phone and wrote down on a pad *Bolshoy Deviatinsky Pereulok No.8*. He then ripped the pad paper off, leaving only the ghostly, written impression on the page underneath. The address to the US Embassy might cause his watchers some hesitation. At least, it would pull their attention and some number of troops to another location. At best, it would buy him a little time.

He quietly opened the door to see the hallway empty, then ran to the bathroom, turned on the shower, and locked the bathroom door from the outside. Again, it gave him the chance of buying a few seconds. His experience had taught him that every bought second paid a dividend. If they hesitated in the room waiting for the shower to stop, it bought time. If they took the pad and analyzed it for the address, that bought time. If the embassy address misled them, then the extra time could be significant.

Will slipped out the door, went to the back stairs, walked up two flights, and walked down the hallway until he found a room that faced the back of the hotel. He quietly knocked, hoping for no response, and heard nothing. He then pushed his shoulder into the door. A crunch of wood and then it forced open.

The room was dark and empty. Will closed the door, slipped to the window, opened it, and slid out onto a ledge connected to an adjoining building. He crossed to the roofline of the next building, then traversed several more, passing across most of the block. One building had a fire escape a floor below that descended into an alley. Will slid down a pole to the landing and was in the alley in a matter of seconds.

He went in the direction opposite of the American Embassy, worked his way to the metro, and then went deeper into the center of Moscow. At one stop he went to a mall and purchased a new parka, a long-tailed sweater, a hat, and a new pair of sunglasses. In the store restroom, he changed his outfit and put the used clothes in the plastic shopping bag he'd just received with his purchase.

An old man was sitting on the floor with his back up against the wall near the entrance to the subway. The smell of vodka was soaked into his clothing.

"Here, old man." Will said it in perfect Russian with a Moscow accent.

The man's eyes were bright blue, and his face looked like well-worn leather. He glanced into the bag and smiled. If the man chose to change into the clothing, it might cause another useful distraction.

Moscow would turn dark soon. Will stopped in a restaurant, took a table in the back, and ordered in perfect Russian, albeit with a southern accent, making him sound as if he'd just come in from Belarus. The waiter teased him about his accent, precisely as Will had intended. For one thing, it was meant to put the man at ease. In addition, if pushed, the man would later remember a stranger, but deny that he could have been an American. Clearly, the customer was from Belarus.

Will had a hot bowl of borscht and a cold beer. He ate the black bread that came with the soup, unsure when his next meal would be.

Alina knew they were coming and had called Will just in time. It meant that while the FSB were watching him, Alina's group was watching the FSB. He was impressed, including by her use of the Apache word for *escape*. Moncrief had taught her well. It would take the FSB some time to figure it out.

The snow started again as he headed out the door.

Who told them I was here? He thought back on his last twenty-four hours. He recalled the conversation with Kevin Moncrief involving the man named Caldwell. That seemed a likely link, especially since he worked for Alexander Paul. Will remembered the business card of Frank Caldwell at Camp Pendleton.

He pulled out his Mac and quickly went on the Wi-Fi. A site called Beeline opened up. Beeline provided Wi-Fi service in Moscow and was easily picked up by Will. It was the third largest wireless operator in the country and covered the city. It was all in Russian, which was no problem for him. He quickly did a search of Caldwell, who he worked for, and the connection of Alexander Paul with Michael Ridges. The man he hoped to meet in the next few hours and lead out of Russia worked for the men who called Kevin Moncrief. And once the call from Caldwell came, the FSB showed up at Will's hotel.

Alexander Paul. Will studied the dated photograph of the former director of the Defense Intelligence Agency. He read the follow-up stories of his outrage at the media and his fall from power. In his divorce from his first wife, her attorney described him as ruthless, obsessed with the advancement of his career, and vengeful. It appeared that he could not keep the ire of his wife out of the divorce.

Sounds like a man who could make two Marines disappear, Will thought. And someone who had a direct line to the FSB and didn't mind using it.

Now it seemed that Paul and his compatriots wanted another former Marine to disappear.

Best move fast, he told himself as he strode into the night.

Chapter 38

"He's on the second floor in room two-oh-three." The officer had just come back from talking to the hotel's desk clerk.

"Is he still there?" Boris Mikhailov, lieutenant colonel of the Alfa Group, was taller than the others. He had a scar that ran from above his left eye, across the eye, and down his cheek. Somehow the IED on the road just outside of Kabul had spared his eyesight. But Mikhailov lived with pain that only let him sleep for two or three hours at a time. Before leaving Afghanistan, he had reaped his revenge on anything that moved.

"The clerk says he hasn't left, sir."

"You think?" Mikhailov laughed.

A call from above had come, announcing that an operative for the CIA was working in Moscow. The caller had also told Mikhailov that word about the operative had come from a source in the United States. If the American were a true operative, then he wouldn't be waiting for the FSB to knock down his door. If, however, he was some dumb American who had made his boss angry for some unknown reason, then the man would likely be found in bed with a Russian woman. A knock on the door from the FSB would be embarrassing to the man, but a waste of time for Mikhailov. They'd take the American in, keep him for a week or two, and then release him.

"Let's see. Circle the building."

Another car showed up; now the building had armed soldiers on every corner. They went inside the lobby and Mikhailov followed his men upstairs to room 203. They heard a shower on. A knock prompted no response. The clerk used his master key to open the door, revealing a reasonably neat room, a tightly-made bed, and the shower still running.

"A military man." Mikhailov recognized the hospital folds as something one learned in a Marine boot camp. He had been assigned to a Marine unit at a school in Oberammergau, Germany years ago, before the winds changed. Russia was not a member of NATO, but had enjoyed a "friends of NATO" status for a few years during the thaw in which the Americans, Europeans, and Russians had shared intel and training. Schools previously restricted opened to the Russians. A few training exercises were conducted with the joint forces. And then Putin came into power.

"He received a call just before we got here."

"Of course." Mikhailov knew that it would be untraceable. "What was said?"

"We don't know the word."

"I do." It didn't require translation for Mikhailov to understand it could only mean "get out!" He didn't know Apache, but knew an alarm when he heard it.

"Open the door to the bathroom."

The guard used his shoulder to push the door open. It was, as Mikhailov expected, empty. The room was filled with steam, but the towels hung perfectly straight.

Another soldier came downstairs to report that a door on a floor above had been broken in and foot tracks through the snow had crossed over the tops of several buildings before descending into an alley.

"What do you want us to do?" the soldier asked, proud to be relaying the information to the colonel. He had a young face, pimples still covering his cheeks, and pitch-black eyebrows, much like the boy soldiers Mikhailov remembered from Kabul.

"Nothing for now." The lieutenant colonel knew that the man was long gone. He would resurface, but in a city of over twelve million people, if he were good, it would take a while. If he were bad, it would be quick. "I'm going back to headquarters. I need to find out from our source why they think he's here."

The Lada took its passenger to the old KGB headquarters on Lubyanka Square, deep in the heart of Moscow. A side entrance brought the vehicle down a ramp into a dark garage. It dropped off its passenger at a guarded door. It was the same door that doomed prisoners of the state had been ushered through by the thousands for decades.

The operation center was well-lit. A sense of energy suffused the air, as if the assembled officers had finally found something real to do for the first time in weeks.

"Okay, lads, stay alert." The lieutenant colonel took his seat behind his desk and reached for the telephone to speak with the source of information. The voice on the other end mentioned a name they were both familiar with.

"Ridges?" Mikhailov lit up a cigarette and took a long drag as he listened to his boss. He laughed. "If they want Ridges that bad, why not just give him back? Perhaps a trade for some oil rights?" His joke fell on deaf ears. It was well known that Putin didn't know what to do with the man. Perhaps the best solution would be for him to die in a gunfight with a proven CIA operative.

"I'll double the guard at his cabin. I'm going to get something to eat at my bathhouse." He looked at his watch. With the chase on, the American agent would almost surely seek a hole to hide in, like a spider caught in bright lights. "Nothing's going to happen tonight."

Boris Mikhailov guessed wrong.

Chapter 39

The Snag Outpost

The sick fox had become a danger. Karen's traps had failed to capture him, the same animal she'd followed into the woods. The bait had failed. It was losing its appetite. Soon the creature would collapse somewhere in the forest and disappear in the snow. Then it would only be a matter of time before a pack of wolves found the carcass. They would feast on the easy game, but the virus would quickly spread to the pack.

Karen had captured one female fox in the early stages of the disease. It hissed when she came close to the cage. She had filled it up with straw that she had carried in on the helicopter. The straw gave the animal some protection from the cold. It couldn't come inside. The warmth of the potbelly stove would have been too much for a creature. It was built to last through a brutal winter, but not a warm hut. The fox was buried deep in the straw and Karen could hear her panting with each breath.

"I need to give you a name," she said to the small creature. It was a mistake. She was giving too much to an animal that had no chance of survival. Once the disease showed symptoms, the end was inevitable.

"Hope, maybe?"

Maybe this was the fox that would help them figure out how to stop the virus.

Maybe not.

Karen headed for the cabin, where she'd left the fox cage up high, above the stacked firewood; the wolves would not dare come that close. It was a false belief that wolves picked fights with man. They knew better.

A board locked the door. It was dark inside, except for a soft glow from the potbelly stove. Karen put in a few pieces of kindling, which brightened the room considerably.

Time to check in.

Karen dialed the satellite phone and got her boss's voice mail. She shrugged.

Done.

She turned to her computer. In one of the last trips she convinced the CDC to put both a satellite dish and small generator in Snag. Still, the satellite reception was intermittent at best. Her inbox was full with emails. She looked for one in particular. A note had come in some time ago from Will in Paris.

"Paris?" she said aloud, scowling. She'd expected Georgia or even California, but not Paris.

"Why Paris?" she asked herself. No one in the cabin provided an answer. She shrugged. "Hope he's safe."

Then, as perfectly timed as it could be, the howls resumed in the darkness.

"Right," she said with a sigh. "As if *any* of us are safe."

Chapter 40

The Department of Treasury FinCEN Center

FBI agent Thomas Donahue sat outside the security door to the FinCEN facility, waiting for Virginia Peoples's boss to come to the front desk. He seemed uncomfortable and looked at his watch several times. He looked up as the door was opened from the operations center.

"Can I help you?" Virginia's boss came through the door. "I'm Darrel Byrd."

"I need a moment of your time." The agent showed him his FBI field credentials. "I'm Tom Donahue."

"We are rushed, as you can imagine, with the loss of Virginia." Byrd sounded frustrated. "It's like someone just handed us a load of extra projects."

"I understand. It'll only take a moment." The visitor's pass admitted Donahue into the center. They went up a flight of stairs above an open bay of computer terminals, with numerous FinCEN agents only pausing for a second to glance at the stranger.

"I thought this was a matter for the Arlington police. A detective already interviewed me."

"Well, she was a federal officer and had a high-level clearance, so we were asked to make sure it was just a case of terrible luck. What was she working on?"

"I am not sure if I can answer that. We…ah…need to sort out what we can share."

Agent Donahue hadn't expected such evasiveness from Virginia's superior. "I understand." He proceeded to ask a few standard questions. "Anyone have a reason for wanting to hurt her?"

"Oh, no. She was smart and sweet."

"And you saw her that afternoon?"

"Of course. I can say she had just started a new project. It followed a sizable promotion."

"Oh, is that right?" said Donahue. "You know, I became an agent based on my accounting degree. Got my CPA in New Jersey."

"Yeah?" The boss fidgeted with his pen. "Perhaps we could get you transferred here?" Byrd joked.

"I wouldn't mind following money trails, to tell you the truth." Donahue watched Byrd continue to fidget with the pen. "Well, that's all I have. I'm sorry to intrude on your busy day. I'll ask my superiors if we need to go into what she was working on and how we get permission to do it."

Before the interview, Donahue had assumed that the time spent on today's FinCEN visit would be a waste. Now he wasn't so sure. At the very least, he would seek access to the woman's files, he decided.

As he headed out of the building, he dialed a number.

"Hey, I'm just leaving."

The tone of the person on the other end of the line was dismissive—an assumption that the FinCen visit was a waste of time—which is why the case had been assigned to a relatively junior agent like Donahue, after all.

Now Tom wanted to see more.

"Isn't this a waste of time?"

"No," Donahue told the senior agent. "There's something here."

Chapter 41

Near Beaver Creek in the Yukon

Kevin Moncrief pulled the pack over his shoulders, balancing himself on the two small snowshoes, and then slung the Marlin rifle over his shoulder. It had a big barrel that gave it much weight. The .45-70 caliber bullet was the size of a marble or the tip of a man's finger, and a gun with a magazine full of those big slugs weighed heavily. It was not the rifle he would have selected to carry in the mountains of Afghanistan. But it would stop anything he ran into in these woods.

His mind wandered as he pulled the hood up. There was still light for several hours. It was a good time to start out. The sun peered high over the mountain range to the west.

What *would* I carry? he asked himself. The journey was long and the only person he could speak to had the rifle slung over his shoulder. The question was an age-old debate among combat soldiers. Many would overpack, taking a long-range bolt action rifle for the long shot and an HK416 for fast, short firepower. And then they'd need to lug ammunition for both, plus perhaps a pistol and water. One soon became a pack animal.

It was no wonder the Taliban could move and shoot as they did. They carried a single weapon with only a few shots, a handful of bread from the tandoori oven, and nothing else. Body armor didn't matter, as death meant a direct trip to a blissful afterlife.

Moncrief followed the Alcan—or Alaska-to-Yukon Highway—south of Beaver Creek, where he parked the rented truck. From there he had to go overland. He followed the river to the east. It was more than seventeen miles across the rough snowbound country as the crow files, but with the bend of the river, the deep snow and the thick woods, it was more like thirty.

The hike would be slow. He didn't want to rent an airplane or helicopter, as it was important that no one would follow a trail caused by his use of some type of air transportation. Also, if he flew, there was the chance that she would tell him to just get back on the airplane and turn around. He recalled from Somalia that Karen Stewart could be best described as having a Katharine Hepburn type of personality.

He was also nowhere near any help. The terrain lost its features quickly, raising a very real risk of getting lost. And this was not the kind of backcountry in which one wanted to get lost.

"You know how cold it gets out there?" the gas-station attendant at Beaver Creek had asked as he studied Moncrief, who had the look of an Inuit, but whose clothes were clearly off the rack.

"Yeah."

"Didn't know that there was any reason to go to Snag even in the summer."

"Not much there?"

"Snag?"

A common response, he'd learned.

Moncrief hoped to leave as early as the light would let him, ideally arriving at Snag before it became dark.

"When does it get dark around here?"

"You won't be able to see your hand by three or four, this time of year."

"Really?"

"Yes, sir. And we got some wolves. I wouldn't mess with them."

"Not planning on it."

Moncrief made it to the river and followed the bends for several miles. The hours passed as he treaded through the drifts of snow. The hike took much longer than expected and it was getting dark.

Damn. A large brown object stood in his direct path. He grabbed his rifle, chambered a round, and held still while his eyes focused in the low light. A giant bull moose had sought shelter in the tree line, along the river and in the valley below the mountain range to the west. The bull snorted and his breath projected like steam from his nostrils. Moncrief didn't move for some time, waiting until the beast decided to take the first step and finally headed north. He could feel his heartbeat in his chest. Moncrief had seen a lot in more than a dozen combat tours; however, the element of surprise never got old.

I don't need to be wandering around in the dark.

It was cold in the woods, but not a brutal cold. Deep in under the trees, some warmth could be found. He used his snowshoes to clear off a small area below the protection of a large spruce tree by stomping on the snow until it packed down to a base. The EV2 tent took only a few minutes to set up, and he was soon in it and out of the cold. Between the sleeping bag and the shelter, he quickly warmed up. Moncrief laid the rifle next to his bag and used his backpack as the pillow. He pulled a Snickers out of his pack and ate it to increase the heat in his sleeping bag.

I can't be more than ten miles from the airfield.

Moncrief used his flashlight to look at a satellite photo of the area. With the short days, he didn't need to rush to move out. The sun's rays would not penetrate the forest until well into the morning. Likewise, he didn't want to arrive in darkness. A stranger suddenly appearing out of the dark in the Yukon could be shot before he could make an introduction.

"I wonder what Will's Russian bride looks like," he asked as he lay in the dark in the small tent, remembering her striking face and blond hair. Photographs didn't always tell the whole story, particularly with a Russian bride.

Kevin looked at the glow of his watch and calculated the time difference. On the other side of the world, the Russian bride was the least of his friend's worries.

Chapter 42

The Hidden Casa

It was a bad sign. Todd Newton had received nothing to eat for several days. The lack of food meant that they cared little about their captive's survival. He was losing body fat at an alarming rate. His rib cage was starting to show through.

"I have to think of something that will keep me alive." He spoke the words through his beaten and sore mouth, trying desperately to find a reason for hope. The water was now gone. Todd looked up at the open beams and the slats of wood that made up the ceiling. The wood was old, as was the hacienda, and sturdy despite its age. He looked at the logs that made up the beams and counted them one by one. It was a mind game he used to channel his thoughts. He recounted them several times.

Just like code. A rhythm. A purpose, he thought as he tried to keep his mind off of the starvation that was setting in.

He needed something to buy time.

"Hey! Hey!" He yelled out the words as best as he could.

He received only silence in return. It seemed that his captors were gone or taking a nap.

"You sons of bitches!" he yelled again. The words were barely intelligible through his damaged mouth.

Finally, he heard footsteps cross the floor above. Soon, they were coming down a stairway; then the door opened. The man he most feared came into the room. His bulkiness gave him a hunched-over look in the small space. He didn't say anything.

"I know what Ridges was working on. I know how to do it." He said the words despite the fact that now his mouth was as dry as if he had eaten a bale of cotton. The man looked at him with a puzzled look. It appeared that his English was not as strong as his partner's. He turned to the door.

Todd thought of all those spy movies in which, at this exact point, the agent would ambush and overpower the man. They didn't account for the chains and exhaustion caused by his being starved for days, having little water, little sleep, and probably several broken ribs.

The man yelled something in Spanish upstairs.

Moments later, another set of footsteps could be heard crossing the floor. The partner came down the stairs and stood so close to Todd that the smell of onions and a cheap cologne filled his nose. Todd might have expected that it would make him crave food even more, but instead, it made him sick to his stomach.

"What do you want?" The smaller man's English was broken but clear enough.

"I know what Ridges found out."

The man stood up, spoke to the other one in Spanish, and turned back to Newton with a smile.

"You hungry?"

"Yeah."

The second man brought down a small metal bucket that held two tacos. The meat was stringy like a goat's, but Newton consumed it rapidly, licking his fingers after they swept the inside of the bucket. The taste lingered in his mouth.

He knew that this was a dangerous tactic. At best, it would only buy him time. But time was a commodity like gold to a dying man.

"We talk to the man. You can tell us what to say." The little one spoke slowly, as if the words needed to be absorbed.

"Tell him that Ridges has planted back doors."

It wasn't necessarily true. It was, however, the right answer for buying time. Todd was playing the bluff that they were concerned that Ridges had access deep in their computers. A back door would be the way for Ridges, or anyone, to get in and out. If a man wanted to get in, this would be the way to do it. And if the man was afraid someone was in, the only way to stop it was to close the back door. More importantly, Todd knew that it would take some time for the message from his captors to get to whoever was running this nightmare. It would have to be sent and received. The two Mexicans could not understand the first part of what he was talking about. It would require someone with some sense to know what to ask next.

Buying time. I'm buying time, he thought as he lay back on the small bunk. Todd could only hope that his feint would mean something to the person directing his captors. He couldn't have known that his best chance of survival resided in a man more than 10,000 miles away who was being chased by the most brutal and efficient Gestapo-like service in the world.

Chapter 43

Moscow

The snow was starting to come down in thick sheets as Will walked out of the little Russian bistro. Another snowstorm was coming in. It had served him well. The cameras would all be blurred, requiring more time for those looking through the thousands of views and videos on the streets of Moscow. Even the automated facial-recognition programs would have difficulty with the blur caused by the sheets of snow. The thousands of security cameras that crossed the city meant that he had to keep moving and couldn't go into any place of business that would have cameras that might get a clear facial shot. He needed a hiding place where cameras would not exist. He had time to kill as well before his rendezvous. The rumble of a jet came from above as it landed in one of the many Moscow airports. The snow clouds muted the noise of the engines, but this one seemed a little lower than expected. He headed north on one of the side streets.

After several blocks, Will saw a white marble baroque building that occupied a triangular space between two side streets. It displayed the year 1808 and its name above the entrance. It was clear that this was an early resident of the city.

It occurred to him that this was the perfect place to buy time.

The clerk of the Turkish bath hadn't seen the man with the Belarus accent come in before. Parker knew he would sound a little like Mikhail Gorbachev, whose famous southern accent was long a joke to those from Moscow. Gorbachev had been raised not far from a fictional place that Will would suggest he was from.

"I need a bath." Will spoke with just the right accent.

"Did you know Mikhail?"

The clerk's joke caused Will to laugh out loud.

"No, but he was from Stavropol Krai, wasn't he?"

"Yeah."

"Not far. My grandfather had a farm near there." Will saw that he was winning over the man with the casual conversation.

"How about some food too?" The clerk's smile displayed one gold tooth directly in the center of his mouth.

"I just ate."

"Okay, a bath then." The man turned to the register and rang up the charge. He handed Will a key to a locker.

Will stared at an array of framed black-and-white photographs on the wall behind the desk. One showed a different building surrounded by bombed-out husks of buildings on both sides.

"How close did they get?" Will pointed to the photo of three Russian officers decked out in uniforms from World War II standing on the front steps of the bath.

"The Nazi scouts got within seven miles."

Seven miles from the center of Moscow. The Russians had a reason for fearing the world.

"We never closed." The clerk smiled with pride. "Russian officers took their baths while an invading army was at their doorstep. My father said the artillery rounds flew right above this building."

Will nodded, feigned wiping a tear from the corner of his eye, and said, "I think I'll take that bath now, thank you."

He passed through the ornate gold, white, and blue hallway to the bath's locker room, where he stripped off his clothes, put on a towel, and walked into the steam room. The long bench was empty except for one older, bent man sitting on his sheet in the corner. The steam came on and off in waves. Between the waves, Will took in a longer glance at the man, whose body seemed to have been wracked by rheumatoid arthritis. His hands, arms, and legs were bent in odd shapes. His crooked body seemed to scream out of a later life of pain. He used a small white towel to rub his face.

"Afghanistan?" The old man suddenly spoke after a period of silence.

"What?" Will turned to him.

"Afghanistan?" The man pointed to the scars on Will's body. They were from combat, but not from when Russia occupied Afghanistan.

"Yes."

"I served in the Pacific fleet on a submarine. The *Som*." The old man's pride showed in his face. Here in the bath, they were two veterans connecting, albeit from two different wars and two different sides. They sat and talked for most of an hour. Will spoke of a fictional grandfather and the man spoke of his grandchildren. His son had been lost in Afghanistan more than twenty years ago.

Soon it was time for Will to go.

"You must stay. A veteran of your war comes in here often at this time."

"Thank you, but it is snowing hard again and I have to get to the metro."

"He was also wounded in Afghanistan. You would enjoy meeting him." The old man was trying to make a connection, the main highlight of his life being the visits to the bath.

"I'm sorry that I can't meet him." Will walked over to the man and shook his crippled hand. "You take care."

"I am old with not many friends now. Soon I will see many."

"Not too soon." They laughed as they parted ways.

As he left the steam room, a man built like Will Parker passed at the doorway. They smiled at each other and said a small greeting. The man also only had a towel, his scar cut across his face. Another injury went from the bottom of his neck down across his chest.

Will thought he had seen the man somewhere before.

He showered, bundled up, paid his bill, and went back out into the snowstorm.

Time to move.

Out on the street, it occurred to Parker where he had seen the man.

Chapter 44

Cupertino, California

"There's a problem."

The young woman with the shaggy bob haircut and green highlights called her boss over to her screen. The operation center at Integral Transaction Data quickly became crammed with people. Her boss, his boss, and the chief information officer of the data company stood at the desks, looking at the displays.

"What's up?" her boss asked, looking back and forth at the several screens.

"He's tapping into all of the accounts. Now, it seems like a joke. He's adding a penny to each credit-card charge." She pushed up her Tom Ford glasses on her nose.

"So, we have a breach?" The CIO, a well-dressed, slightly older woman, studied the screens from the other side of the chair.

"Oh, yeah."

"Can they get to our data?" The CIO pointed the question to the head of the operations center.

"They have." The woman with the green bob haircut spoke out of turn. Her manager gave her a look that could have frozen a freshly boiled hot dog.

"Can we fix this?"

"Oh, yeah," her boss answered quickly.

The young operator returned him a quick look, as if to say, *Are you kidding?*

"I need to know quickly. We can't sit on this. We are *not* doing an Equifax," said the CIO, determined to get control of the situation. "We need to get general counsel and our public-relations people on standby."

She was muttering to herself as she left the operations center. Then, louder: "I need some good news, guys."

* * * *

"We have a problem." The CIO was on her cell phone with the chief executive officer of ITD in the empty hallway outside of the operations center.

"Let's get to some secure phones." He always had a calm demeanor. He was a self-made man, not with Ivy League credentials, who had worked his way up from an entry-level job to the top position after his mentor reached retirement age and nominated him for the position. The CEO might not have been an Ivy Leaguer, but he had learned the game well and learned it quickly.

"There's a breach. It's sophisticated." She gave him the download on the secure telephone.

"The board members need to know so no one will go out and make the foolish mistake of selling any shares." The CEO knew that the one way to burn both the company and the board was off-loading stock at the wrong time. ITD's shares had just hit a record high of $101. "Equifax dropped seventeen percent of its value in just the first twenty-four hours after word got out of the breach."

"Yes, sir."

"I need to call our duty expert on this to check out his sources."

The CEO's next secure call was to the man who was paid a lot to ensure that such headaches went away.

He reached Alexander Paul, who answered on the first ring.

The CEO explained the situation. "This could be from anywhere on the globe…any ideas?"

"Yes." Paul didn't say more and the CEO didn't ask. It would not benefit either man for Paul to speak what was on his mind.

* * * *

Paul hung up and made a call to the bank in the Cayman Islands. He was not a member of the ITD board of directors. He had no obligation other than ethics and professionalism, which were not about to hold him back. Or at least no problems that would be directly connected. It was insider trading, but going through the offshore bank would make it nearly impossible to follow the international trail.

"Buy a short position on ITD."

"How much?"

"One hundred million. Spread it out over several accounts."

Paul already had a good idea who was behind the hack, but he wasn't going to move too quickly in his efforts to fix it.

Chapter 45

Paul's Headquarters Near Dulles

"I understand that the FSB has a lead on Parker in Moscow." Alexander Paul sounded positively gleeful, as if all the stars were aligning for him. "He's under the name of Donnelly."

"Huh?" Caldwell's response was muted. He'd only glimpsed the screen for a second, but it was enough to conclude that Paul was on the deep web. The Tor logo with an onion was the giveaway, a symbol signifying the layers of virtual tunnels the transmissions went through to reach their intended recipients. He tried to shift his eyes quickly away, but in the same moment, Paul caught his gaze.

With a sickening sensation growing in his stomach, Caldwell knew what Paul was up to and, more dangerously for the young Ranger, Paul knew he knew, which meant that Caldwell was becoming a risk.

"Frank, do you like it here?" Paul looked directly into Caldwell's eyes.

"Yes, sir."

"You have a great future. A happy life with more money than you've ever seen."

Caldwell knew his boss was playing to his background as a kid from a lower-middle-class family who'd had several brothers and sisters. It was also a veiled reference to his wife and young son. "We need to go to Alaska." Paul turned back to his computer as he spoke the words. "It might be an insurance policy in case things get difficult in Moscow."

Caldwell nodded. Though he couldn't be 100 percent sure, it seemed as though Paul were planning for an alternate action in case the situation required it. A contingency for the unlikely eventuality that Will Parker managed to get Ridges out of Moscow—or even slipped out of Moscow alone with whatever information Paul was worried about. In that case, it wouldn't hurt for Paul to have his hands on a particular CDC doctor as a bargaining chip.

"Yes, sir."

"Where exactly is the doctor?"

"We understand she's in a remote location and the closest city is Anchorage." Caldwell didn't know exactly where Snag was, but had a sense that it would be within reach of Anchorage.

"Let's get a team up there." Paul had several men that he described as his bodyguards. They were an odd assortment of past Delta Force operators. From what he'd seen of them, Caldwell wasn't impressed. They struck him as would-be cowboys who thought their missions were above the law. Paul didn't seem to discourage that impression.

"I'll get the ball rolling," Caldwell said noncommittally.

"Tell my assistant to get the G650 ready."

The Gulfstream was the Rolls-Royce of the sky and cost infinitely more. But the crisis at ITD granted Paul license to spend even the exorbitant $25,000 per hour for aircraft rentals. Of course, the fact that the G650 could fly 8000 miles at speeds above 600 miles an hour made it an ideal choice for a mission requiring haste despite distance.

Paul's team was more than capable. An innocent call to the CDC office in Anchorage had revealed Snag as their destination. Soon, they would have supplies and helicopter support in Alaska, waiting for the arrival of the Gulfstream.

"I'll meet you at the airport in forty-five minutes." Paul looked at his watch as he spoke.

Caldwell was surprised that Paul was coming. He rarely left his corporate headquarters. But some time ago, he too had been trained as a Ranger.

"Yes, sir."

* * * *

Paul was already at the signature flight operations before the jet landed. Frank Caldwell found Paul and his team in the waiting room when he arrived.

"Gun bags?" Caldwell immediately noticed that the bodyguards had black bags with the stencil HK in red on their side. Each also carried backpacks and vests packed with magazines of ammunition.

"Oh, I guess." Paul was looking at his cell phone.

"Sir, the cold-weather gear will be at the FBO."

To Caldwell, this operation felt similar to the ones that he'd undertaken years ago with his Ranger unit. It felt strange to be back in action. Odder yet, however, was the fact that Caldwell didn't know exactly what the action would be. They were packing out for what looked like a combat mission.

"And we have a helicopter that's reserved, but the weather's gonna be dicey." And by "dicey," Caldwell meant life-threatening.

Paul looked at him blankly. "What do you mean?"

"A front's coming in, and there's a mountain range between Anchorage and Snag."

"Okay." Paul looked out the window at the run of aircraft coming and going to and from Reagan. A wisp of visible air spun up from the wings of the plane. It was overcast and the air was full of water molecules. As the wind over the wings churned the sky, the particles put on a show coming off of the surface.

"Didn't you say you talked to Parker's buddy?"

"Yes, sir. Moncrief is his name."

"What's the story on him?"

"Retired Marine gunnery sergeant. A good man. Served under Parker. Wounded. Parker saved his life."

"Oh. So, he'd take a bullet for Parker if it came to that?"

Caldwell hesitated in answering. It was an odd comment.

"Yes, sir, I believe he would."

Chapter 46

The Cabin Near Snag in the Yukon

The sun broke through Snag. Karen gathered up her gear, her backpack, and snowshoes to start the trek looking at each of the traps. She didn't forget her Winchester. Ever since the first day, when she had the encounter with the ill fox, she had been careful in keeping her eyes out for the animal.

She checked on the little fox in the cage. It was still alive, not stirring and bundled up in the straw. The fox's red-tipped ears stuck out from the cover. It had plenty of water and she had caught a mouse in a cabin trap. The dead mouse lay in the same spot on the straw. The vixen's appetite seemed to be waning.

The air was still. The potbelly stove gave the air in the cabin a smoky smell.

She had used up the last of her fresh food the evening before.

I'll miss the bananas. She always lamented the end of fresh fruit the most. It never lasted long.

Now it's MREs, she thought as she closed the door to the cabin. The meals were a benefit of working for the government. The CDC had an ample supply of meals-ready-to-eat, and she had been given a case to carry with her into the Yukon.

Chili with beans or chicken fajitas?

First, she wanted to make a call.

The satellite phone rang on Will Parker's cell phone number and then went to voice mail.

"Odd," she said into the dead line. He should have been back by now.

She walked south across the airstrip and into the forest near the river. The water was frozen now, but with the warm-ups that occasionally happen during this winter, blocks of ice covered the surface. It would be difficult to cross.

The crack of a rifle shattered the air, stunning her.

She looked to the west well beyond the airstrip. The sound was of a large-caliber weapon. It echoed off the trees. And then, a moment later, everything became eerily silent. She took her rifle off of her shoulder, pulled the lever action, and saw the bright brass color of a round in the weapon's chamber.

No reason for anyone else to be out here. She scanned the horizon. The mountain range could be seen well off in the distance. Snag wasn't the place to be for a casual visit. She turned back to her cabin, thinking that she had left the satellite phone in the cabin.

As she neared the hut, Karen noticed something move well off in the distance beyond the end of the airstrip. She stared at the figure, trying to make out what it was.

The man was walking as if on a Sunday stroll. Except, she saw now, that he was also dragging something behind him on a rope. She couldn't tell from the distance what was at the end of the line.

"Who in the hell?" Karen whispered to herself.

She chambered a round in the rifle and brought it up to her shoulder.

If the stranger was trouble, the shot would be in the center of his chest.

Chapter 47

The Northern Side of Moscow

Will Parker saw the Lada waiting outside of the Turkish bath just across the street with its engine running. He immediately recognized the vehicle. It was the same one that had been in front of his hotel earlier. Instead of turning away from it, he made a point of crossing directly to it and cutting directly in front of the car, waving to the driver in the front seat. The engine was running and the man inside looked bored. It was likely that he was drunk as well. The FSB knew that vodka was the only way to cope with the cold. It was much more than a drink.

After passing in front of the Lada, Will went back to the center of the street and walked in the tracks left by other vehicles. The snow on the sidewalk was too deep to traverse quickly. He headed in the same direction as the car. He continued on the street for several blocks before cutting to the west. The snow kept coming down in sheets, giving him the cover he so desperately needed.

On one side street, he saw what he had been looking for in a Lada Niva. It was old enough that it wouldn't stand out, its dark green visible even under the coating of the snow, and had been designed to go off-road. He tried the door and it was unlocked. Moscow was a trusting city.

Will dusted the snow off of the front and opened the hood. A spare tire and the engine were both in the engine compartment. He reached under the engine cowling and then returned to under the steering wheel. There, he pulled two wires, touched them together to cause a spark. The engine turned over. He quietly closed the hood and looked down the street to see a Christmas-card look of snow falling, streetlights glowing in the frosty night, and complete stillness all around. Not a single sign of life.

Time to go.

Will first drove across Moscow to the railroad station, where he'd left his backpack in storage. He parked on a side street, put the car in neutral, and left the engine running while he crossed the lane to the rail station. He pulled his hat down low and his parka's collar tight. In the snowstorm, he didn't stand out, so it was easy to retrieve what he'd come for. The backpack felt every bit as heavy as he recalled.

Now, the dangerous part, Will thought as he crossed the street back to the running vehicle.

The Lada's four-wheel drive was surprisingly good; he was impressed how well it handled in the new snow. Will drove back to the hotel where he'd stayed. He wasn't going in. He turned the block so that he came back past it in the same direction as when he had been picked up for his visit to Ridges. He was trying to reorient himself for the next step of the journey—this time without a blindfold.

Will also had his laptop open on the front seat. He had the map from the previous journey. Although he carried it in his bag, Will had set the computer to record the journey as a backup to his memory.

As he passed the hotel, he noticed the same Lada parked across the street.

Hoping I might come back, he thought as he glanced at the car through his peripheral vision, making a point of not looking in the direction of the two men sitting in the vehicle. At the next light, he reached into the backpack.

The cold metal of the Baikal .380 Makarov automatic pistol lay at the bottom.

Will was happy to see the Lada's gas tank was half full.

More than I should need.

And Moscow had not gone to a full lockdown. Yet. He had noticed, however, when he walked through the train station what appeared to be more men in uniform than usual.

Snowplows had cleared the highway for several miles out of downtown Moscow. The wipers were at full speed as the large flakes fell and stuck to the warm glass. It was cold, but not a brutal subzero cold.

Will closed his eyes occasionally to follow the track in his mind of the journey he had made while blindfolded. He felt as though he was on the route as he had imagined it. He anticipated the next turn before the computer showed it. He slowed and took the exit off of the main highway to a side road. It had also been plowed, but the snow was rapidly catching up to it. The snow had drifted in places; each time his front bumper blew up a drift, a heavy blast of snow came back down on the hood and windshield. The wheels wiggled a little as they lost traction for a brief moment.

Ah, Russia. It was starting to remind him of the Yukon....

No. Keep focused.

The final turn came up on the left.

Will stopped the car and turned off the lights. He left the engine running and looked around in the quiet for any movement. The last road was several miles to the cabin and the lake, but it was a single lane that went into the dark woods.

He turned into the side road, drove for several miles until he came to another side road that veered off to the right. Vehicle tracks were on both lanes despite the snow. The past trip had taken him directly down the main way, but here he headed into the side road. Again, he was playing the odds. Will had a sense that the lake went to both the right and left of the main gravel road, which meant that other cabins surrounded the lake. It also was likely that these were vacation cabins only used in the summer season. He just needed one dark cabin closed for the winter—and found it around the next bend. Off in the distance stood another dark cabin; further on, one had a light on in the window. It seemed like the perfect scenario.

"We need a little luck," he murmured to himself, thinking how foolish the whole effort seemed.

Will parked the Lada under the shed to the side of the dark cabin. Before he turned off the engine, he used the light to open the backpack and pull out the other items needed.

The two white Tyvek coverall suits would typically be used for the spraying of chemicals in a garden. They'd been easy to buy on the internet; here, the suits served as white camouflage in a snow-covered forest. He pulled the Tyvek suit over his sweater and pants. Will left his parka in the car. It was too bulky and he wasn't planning to stay out long.

Another package in the backpack had been more difficult to source. A small plastic case held an Instant Eye quadcopter and a small Q4S viewer. He put the Instant Eye back in the pack and quietly closed the door to the car. He looked around him in the snowy dark, and only after his eyes adjusted to the low light did he get a feel for his directions. Will put the backpack on and turned toward the other cabins. It was nearing midnight.

The lake was frozen and covered with snow that came up to above his ankles. He started out to the west, crossing past several dark cottages and docks until he saw the well-illuminated guardhouse through the woods. The cabin Ridges was in still had one window glowing green from an interior light. Will lay in the snow. The Tyvek did not provide any warmth, but it did keep the moisture out.

He pulled the drone from the backpack and started the quadcopter from behind one of the sheds on a dock and watched on the screen as it quickly flew up, above the tree line and over the cabin. It circled the cabin in nearly complete silence as he took in the positions of the guards. There were twice as many guards as before. One walked the premises, while the other three stood together near the guard shack. He watched as he paced out their actions and then returned the quadcopter to the shed.

The green light went out in the cabin.

"Okay, let's see if they gave him a babysitter," Will whispered to himself.

He pulled the other Tyvek suit out of the backpack and slowly crossed over the lake and up to the back edge of the cabin. Inside, a guard sat in front of the fireplace, but Ridges was nowhere to be seen.

Where are you, Mr. Ridges? Will had decided that he would give the effort no more than a minute. If Ridges hadn't figured out a way to get out of the cottage, Will would be on the Air France flight in the morning.

Chapter 48

The Mexican Hideout

The footsteps coming across the floor above shook Todd Newton from a deep sleep. He was numb with fear, exhaustion, and thirst. Todd unconsciously pulled into the fetal position, rightfully fearful that every time he heard the steps it meant another beating.

Just gotta hold on, he thought. It never had occurred to him before now that Parris Island boot camp implanted within him a certain resolve. Todd remembered the name of Staff Sgt. Virgil Williams. The six-foot-two drill instructor in his starched, crisp utility uniform cussed at him almost religiously, using words he'd never heard before.

"I'm going to beat the civilian out of you!" Williams would wake them up with the same call every morning. "This ain't no Nintendo world!" But Williams taught Todd how to survive the twenty-hour days, the backpack marches through the night, and the built-in torture of standing on the parade deck at attention in the brutally hot South Carolina summer.

I won't ever forget his name. Todd held onto the thought. Marine boot camp had pushed him beyond what he thought his limits were. Now Parris Island was paying a small dividend.

The sound of conversation came from the room above. He heard the noise of two new voices, the men arguing, and then it stopped. It seemed as if one had left.

God, please be him, Todd hoped. The big one's leaving might give some chance of his survival. But just as quickly, self-doubt started to creep in again. The man's departure could also mean the end. It had been some time since his friend had been taken away. He knew her fate.

After a long period of silence, he heard the footsteps coming down the stairs. It was more than one man. The door swung open.

Todd looked through his arms that covered his face. The little one was with two other men. They spoke to each other in Spanish. He got the drift of what was being said. It had been a mistake that he had seen their faces. It guaranteed his death sentence.

"I know more about Ridges." Todd tried to speak the words loudly, but they almost came out in a whisper. It was a plea.

"What else, my friend?" It was one of the new strangers who spoke. The man had long black hair that went down to his shirt collar, a thin mustache and chin beard, and the glittering eyes of a killer. His shirt was plaid, open at the collar for three buttons down, revealing a leather-woven necklace and a gold one with a small gold cross. He was brown-skinned with no chest hair. He wore black shooting gloves that left the fingers exposed; on his wrist were several colored glass bracelets. The glass beads looked oddly out of place on the killer's wrist. No doubt they had some brutal meaning and history. The man's fingernails were long and uncut. He had pointed black boots with heels that made him taller than the other two men.

He also held a silver semiautomatic pistol in one hand.

"I know how to find his back door into DIA." Todd was grasping at straws. He could only guess that Ridges had left a back door into his old agency, especially if he thought he might need it one day. More important, Todd's lie sounded important enough that it should get the attention of his captors. If nothing else, a back door into a US military-intelligence agency would be highly marketable.

The man with the gun turned to the others, said something in Spanish, and laughed. "Good," he said, lowering the hand with the pistol. He looked at the gun and raised it up in the air. "I wasn't going to shoot you anyway. Angel said we had to keep you alive until he called."

The suggestion of a call that would end Todd's life was another brutal form of torture. He knew he'd jump every time he heard the ring of a cell phone upstairs. By now he knew the ringtones that each man had on his phone.

The two guards spoke to each other in Spanish. Todd caught two words that stood out. They referenced Angel, who must have been the large guard. His was the call that could end Todd's life. And there was another word that didn't take any translation:

Angel was in Alaska.

Alaska? Todd thought hopelessly as he covered his head once more.

The guard took a fake swing at Todd's head, just missing, laughed, and then walked back upstairs, leaving Todd curled on the bed alone.

Chapter 49

Moscow

Lt. Col. Mikhailov knocked on the driver's window of his car, which was parked and running in front of the Sandunovskie Bani on Neglinnaya Street. The bathhouse's white marble facade looked like a cake with white icing under the snow, which was starting to pile up on Moscow's unplowed side streets.

"Did you see anyone come out?"

"What?" The driver was in a half stupor from the snow, the cold, the wait, and the vodka. The snow was coming down now in blinding sheets.

"A man, my height?" Mikhailov put his hand to his forehead, demonstrating the height comparison.

The FSB commander had put two and two together while talking to the old veteran in the bath. There was no other veteran of Afghanistan. At least, there was no other Russian veteran of Afghanistan in the bath that night. The colonel had thrown on his clothes and run out of the bath. It had to be the American that they were looking for.

"No, sir, no one." The driver looked down as he spoke.

Mikhailov had had this driver for more than a year and knew that the man had one fault: Like a child, he didn't lie well. Based on his reaction, Mikahilov decided it was likely that the driver knew the stranger had come out of the bath and probably cut directly across the guard's field of vision.

"This damn snow. Not a track in sight." Mikhailov looked around the small alleyway that joined the street in front of the bathhouse. If the man had come through here, his tracks were long gone.

So, this is my enemy, he thought. He looked up to the sky, feeling a flake hit his face, sting, and then immediately turn into a droplet of water.

Exactly as the colonel had predicted, the man had gone underground. And Moscow made for the ideal hiding place. He could be hidden but in plain sight.

"Canis lupus lupus LC," he mumbled to himself. Mikhailov had heard his grandfather speak of the gray ghosts that prowled the forest and steppes of Russia. "Call in and tell them that our target was seen in the city near the Gonduras meat market." He shouted the words to his driver as he turned to the door of the bathhouse. The meat market was less than a block or two away from the bath. It would give the searchers a known point of reference. "And tell them to keep a lookout at the American's cabin."

The colonel knocked the snow off from his fur hat and parka after going back in to the bathhouse. The carpet leading in had become fully soaked and squelched as he strode in.

"My friend, tell me of your last customer?" the colonel asked the clerk at the desk.

The man immediately pulled back, the smile vanishing from his face. An FSB officer was asking about a visitor.

"He hadn't been in here before," the man said defensively.

"I understand." The officer knew the clerk. He had been here in the same job as his father for decades. The bath was the oldest in Moscow. It had survived the czar, the revolution, and Hitler's invasion. Despite it all, the bath endured.

"I just need to know what you remember."

"He was from Belarus." The clerk smiled as if he had pulled a gem out of a mine. "Yes, he was from Belarus."

"Why do you say that?"

"He had that accent just like Mikhail."

"Gorbachev?"

"Yes, a southern one." The man paused. "I remember he was from somewhere near Minsk."

"How did he pay?"

"With rubles."

"Of course, cash." It didn't matter, as the credit card would have funds tied to a false name of a false man.

Mikhailov remembered from earlier in the day how the clerk at the hotel talked about the American. There was no mention of a southern accent, only his broken Russian. In fact, he'd painted the picture of a man who would stand out in Moscow because he was so American.

"Thank you." The officer turned, pulled his white fur *ushanka* hat on and headed toward the door.

"Sir, I will call you the moment he steps in that door!" the clerk called after him.

"No need to worry."

The American was good, very good. He would not be returning to the bath.

But he would eventually fall.

"It is only a matter of time," he murmured as he opened his door. "If only this snow would stop, we could use the drones."

Mikhailov carried all of the strength of the largest security force in the world behind him. The FSB had inherited all of the traits and talents of its former agency, the KGB. When Moscow awakened to a new day, eyes would be everywhere.

Chapter 50

Snag

"Hello!" The man shouted the words. They carried across the open snow-covered airstrip like they were spoken in a sound chamber void of other sounds. He waved his rifle above his head in what appeared to be a signal of friendship. The rifle was in one hand and the other held a rope over his shoulder that dragged some object behind him.

Some instinctive sense told Karen that the man posed no danger to her. There was even something about him that looked vaguely familiar. She loosened her grip on her rifle. Her heartbeat settled, even though dropping her guard went against everything Will had taught her.

"Always expect the unexpected," she remembered him saying whenever he took her to Snag. Once in the summer, she had let her guard down. He had carried her out to the encampment and stayed for a day. The grizzly mother made no sound. Karen didn't even see the cub. Will was with her, moved quietly to her back, grabbed her shoulder while putting his hand over her mouth so as to silence any sound. He pulled her behind him and held his rifle in a tight grip. Slowly, they moved backwards away from the creature. Later, she had realized that the cub was just beyond the bend of the path she was taking. If alone and without being aware, within twenty paces she would have been on top of the cub. It was a lesson that followed her from then on, as before she had often hiked with her head down, looking at her boots and the flora of the green Yukon summer. The failure to keep one's head up in the Yukon could mean death.

"Hello?" she called back. They headed separately in the direction of the cabin, where their paths would meet. As she got closer, she studied the man with his new parka, new backpack, and red snowshoes.

"You don't remember me." Kevin Moncrief dropped his rifle and the rope. "I was in Somalia."

She felt immediate comfort from the words. Somalia was a nightmare that had pushed her to the brink of survival until William Parker and his men had come to her rescue. If this stranger knew to mention those words, then he could only be here because of Will.

"So, where is he?"

"Right now, I'm not totally sure."

She sensed a hedge and caught a brief look of guilt flashing across the big man's expression. She suspected that he at least knew what side of the planet Will Parker was on.

"I'm Moncrief."

"The one who served with him?"

"Yep." Moncrief turned to the shape in the snow at the end of the rope. "Sorry."

"Why?"

"This morning he came at me." Moncrief pointed to the bloody carcass of a fox tied to the rope. "One of your animals?"

"Sort of." She was a scientist first and foremost. Like a rancher raising cattle, she tried to not attach herself to the creatures. Naming them was more of a method of keeping track than any deeper bond.

"One sick animal." Moncrief kept his distance. Even though the carcass was already stiff, foam around the muzzle was still visible. "Came at me like he'd OD'd on crank."

"Right." Karen knelt and studied the creature from a careful distance. The fur was white and the only color against the snow was a small streak of blood that followed the trail. "Did you touch it?"

"No, ma'am, as kids we learned quick not to touch sick animals and rattlesnakes."

"Seen something like this before?" Karen knew that rabies, while often spoken of, was rarer than strikes of lighting. Few ever came in contact with rabid creatures.

"My dad had to shoot a dog once," Moncrief said. "It was just as sick as this one. But Dad told me to stay away even if it's dead. Just like with rattlesnakes. They can still bite when they're dead."

She nodded. "So, why are you here?"

"There is a small chance that trouble might show up. Will just wanted to make sure you would be all right." Moncrief smiled. "Sorta like sending flowers."

She looked at the dead fox, then at his gun, and smiled. "Roses or lilies?"

Chapter 51

The Aircraft on Approach to Landing in Anchorage

Despite fighting a fifty-knot headwind across Canada, the Gulfstream beat the pilot's expectation of arrival by nearly an hour. The jet flew at Mach .85. A private jet wasn't supposed to be able to fly near the speed of sound, but this was the fastest general aviation aircraft in the world. It flirted with the speed of sound because, like its competitors, Gulfstream knew its customers wanted to cross continents and oceans ever-faster and higher.

The five passengers were separated into several spaces. They seemed out of place in the $80 million aircraft's tan leather lounge chairs. The dark wood and gold trim marked the cabin as a form of transportation for the chairman of a major corporate board, not special-operation types. These passengers, except for one, looked like men who'd earned most of their frequent-flier miles in the cargo hold of a C-130 military turboprop.

Frank Caldwell looked around the cabin as they started the descent into Anchorage. Alexander Paul sat in the back with his computer and the aircraft's satellite telephone, speaking with callers throughout the journey. He had a Waterford crystal old-fashioned glass half full of a scotch of some kind. A young pixie of a flight attendant with short, strawberry-blond hair kept his tumbler full. Caldwell had found Paul to be the rare type of person who didn't show his liquor. Perhaps this was because the man was already mean and short-tempered; despite the flight attendant's best efforts, he gave her the same scowl each time she came to refill his drink.

The three bodyguards who traveled with Paul sat in the front in seats that faced each other. They all had beards, which had probably been initiated during their service in the mountains of the Hindu Kush. Caldwell recognized the other signs of such veterans: heavy tattooing on block-sized arms hardened by hours in the weight room; and the almost total absence of conversation between men who were comfortable with breaking down doors and killing anyone behind them. In fact, like many twilight warriors, they used much of the flight to recharge their batteries and sleep.

Caldwell sat in another seat, alone, looking at the satellite photos of Snag. A small cabin sat at the end of a runway that was covered in snow, but remained visible due to the straight runway and absence of trees around it. One photo was recent and showed the tracks of an aircraft that had landed and marked its path with its skids.

Why the weapons? he wondered. There didn't seem to be any danger other than a fox or an eagle. Even the bears had bunked down for the season. A CDC doctor didn't seem to require anything other than asking her for some help.

He looked out through the large oval window. The aircraft was engulfed in clouds as it continued its decent.

Probably over Snag, he thought. With the speed of the aircraft, they would have started their descent from 41,000 feet on the other side of the mountain range from Anchorage. He thought of the scientist, somewhere below him, under the cloud cover, marching through the snow like some figure out of a *National Geographic* documentary, looking for her animals in the outback and not even thinking that the sound far up in the sky was an aircraft heading for a collision with her.

They'd be arriving at Snag soon enough, after they'd switched aircraft in Anch—

"Caldwell!" Paul called from the rear of the jet.

Caldwell stood and walked back to him while the aircraft jiggled in the turbulence. He didn't say anything.

"Where will we meet the chopper?"

"Ross Aviation."

"Someone is joining us." Paul seemed to indicate that another special-ops guy would meet up with them.

"Yes, sir." Caldwell didn't understand the mystery. "Do I need to get him some cold-weather gear?"

"Yeah, he's already at ANC. He can hook up with our contact there to get what he needs." Paul took another swallow from his drink.

Caldwell had given up drinking when he got off active duty, but he recognized the look and smell of a high-grade scotch. As Caldwell studied his superior, the large oval windows of the Gulfstream illuminated the cabin in cold, white light. Paul's expression looked distant and he had his chin tilted up in a way as if to ask, "You dare mess with me?" His gray hair betrayed a receding hairline, and his skin had acquired dark spots that signaled too much sun exposure over the years. Paul's deep-seated, dark eyes suggested a brooding soul and stood atop a strong nose— like that of a Roman emperor—and pointed chin. Age had camouflaged his eyebrows, turning them gray and leaving them almost an afterthought on the man's face.

As he regarded Paul in the Yukon light, Caldwell realized that he had made an error in taking the job. His friends would have dismissed such grumblings if he told them he went to work in an $80 million private aircraft, but they hadn't spent a day with Alexander Paul. West Point had taught Caldwell principles of leadership. One of the most important was number six: It's essential that a leader know his men and look out for them. Paul didn't seem to care much for that commandment.

"I'll tell the chopper pilot to be on the lookout for the guy."

"Okay."

"Anything special we need to know?"

"He'll stand out." The question was dismissed with the answer.

"The pilot told me a few minutes ago that the mountain range is still under the storm. It's clearing on the other side, but a chopper can't go over this weather."

Paul's reaction was exactly what Caldwell expected: He looked at his watch and, from his expression, made a calculation involving time zones on the other side of the planet.

"We need to get there." The order was clear. "They still haven't found him."

"Yes, sir."

There was only one answer for a man like Alexander Paul.

Chapter 52

The Treasury Department's FinCEN Center

"It took an act of Congress." FBI Special Agent Donahue's superior handed the paper to his lead investigator.

"They didn't want to cooperate?" Donahue had convinced his boss that, when talking about Virginia Peoples's death with her FinCEN boss, that the man's reaction had seemed odd.

"Hell, no."

The two agencies worked together on many cases, but the one investigative branch that Virginia had been working in seemed separate from the rest.

"Justice had to hash it out." Donahue's boss was old-school and didn't tolerate well the lack of cooperation between federal agencies.

Donahue nodded. "Good enough. I'll go back over there with this and get a download of her computer."

* * * *

"I don't know why this took a subpoena." The director of the FinCEN operations center wore thick glasses and seemed like a stick figure inside his cheap suit.

Donahue sat in a chair by the front desk of the FinCEN center with another fellow special agent who had expertise in both computers and software. They had been waiting nearly an hour for the agency to comply with the court's order.

"Anyway," said the IT man, "I won't waste any more of your time."

"I'm sorry?"

"Virginia's computer is blank."

"Blank?"

"Yeah, you can check it. The hard drive has been completely deleted."

"Are you talking about the files?"

"Everything. Even the operating system."

The two agents looked at each other.

"Is her supervisor here?"

"No, he left a message that he had to leave early for a doctor's appointment."

Donahue shrugged. "Well, we're going to have to pull the hard drive and take it to our forensic lab."

The special agent with computer expertise followed the director to Virginia's desk.

"I understand." The op-center director seemed in shock and disbelief. "I would have never thought this. I can give you whatever you need on Byrd, Virginia's boss."

"Got his home address?" The agent thought this would be a good place to start if he was, in fact, at a doctor's appointment.

"Sure." The operations-center director crossed over to a secretary's desk, opened up a screen on the computer, and hit *print*. "This is all of his contact information."

"Yes, thanks."

"First, Virginia's death and now her boss?" The director seemed shell-shocked.

"Yes, sir." Donahue suspected there was much more to it all.

"He won't be there, will he?"

"No." It was Donahue's guess, but it was a guess that would be proven right in a way.

* * * *

The agents also pulled the hard drive from Darrel Byrd's computer.

"This is probably a waste of time." The operations director didn't seem uncooperative. More than anything, he appeared to be in shock. "Both he and Virginia knew computer technology cold. If they wanted anything deleted, it's not coming back."

"Virginia was the target of a murder." Donahue decided it did little harm to let the FinCEN operations-center director know how deep this was getting.

"Oh, god." The director sank into a chair. "I thought it was a random robbery that went wrong."

A cell phone rang.

"MPD." The second agent held up his cell phone, showing an incoming call. Metro police had been alerted by the two agents and given the address where Virginia's missing supervisor lived.

"Yes?"

The agent leaned against the supervisor's desk with his cell phone up to his ear.

"Okay, we'll see you there in half an hour." He killed the call.

"Gone?" Donahue sat in the chair behind the desk, looking at the computer, but turned to his fellow officer.

The operations-center director leaned forward to listen as well.

"No, he's still there." The agent said it in a way that didn't sound quite right. "We were wrong."

"What?"

"When we guessed he'd be long gone."

"And?"

"Looks like a small-caliber bullet to his head."

The op-center director inhaled sharply and sank deeper into the chair.

The agent put the phone back in his coat pocket. "And a suicide note."

"Suicide?" The IT man spoke the word as if exhaling a breath.

No one with an FBI badge believed it.

Chapter 53

Near the Dacha West of Moscow

Will watched the Russian soldier sitting in the chair with the glow of the fire lighting his face. A dim lamp near the front door provided the only other light in the room. The man looked half asleep. Sniper school and a childhood of hunting had taught Will the self-discipline of freezing in place. He didn't stop breathing. That would be a mistake, leading to an unwanted and noisy gasp for air when his oxygen ran out. Instead, he slowed his breathing to small sips of air. In so doing, he also slowed his heart rate and could remain frozen like a buck that had heard a sound in the forest.

As he watched and waited, Will relaxed his muscles, thinking how important it was to become small…waiting for the next move.

It didn't take long.

A barely audible noise came from around the side of the cabin. Will moved only his eyes, taking a glance in the direction of the sound. A window was slowly being pulled open.

He turned his eyes back to the room and the guard, who remained motionless.

A figure was climbing out of the window, moving in an intentionally slow way. The window was at ground level and, fortunately, had only a short drop to the bank of snow below. The man stopped when his feet hit the ground, stayed motionless for a moment, and then slowly pulled a small backpack through the window. He was heading around the corner of the cabin, mistakenly toward the main road, when he stopped. A glance to the back caused him to freeze as he recognized the shape of a man who was standing almost within reach.

Will slowly raised his hand to stop Ridges. As he leaned slightly forward to speak, he glanced back through the window into the main room of the cabin.

The guard's chair was empty.

Instinctively, Will reached into the pocket of the Tyvek suit and felt for his pistol, then pulled back close to the tree. Again, he gave the hand signal to Ridges not to move. They both froze in place.

The door to the back porch opened.

The guard came out into the cold without a jacket or hat. He walked to the end of the porch and unzipped his trousers, belched, and began to urinate on the fresh snow. He had finished and was turning back to the cabin when he stopped and stared at the tree trunk where Will was standing. It was as if he were focused on a Gergely Dudás puzzle, looking for a panda in a field of snowmen, like one trying to see the missing piece directly in front of him, when it suddenly stood out.

Before the man could speak, Will was on top of him. The man was clearly strong and well-trained, but he didn't say a thing. Instead of calling for help, he smiled at Will, as if to say, *My bad…I'll handle the American.*

It was a mistake.

Will moved without a moment's hesitation. His elbow slammed into the man's rib cage, causing all of the air to come out of his lungs. Before the guard could recover, Will headbutted the bridge of the man's nose. The guard had somehow produced a knife, and he swung the blade blindly at Will, who followed with his elbow to the man's throat. A moment later, the guard was unconscious on his knees, looking like a victim of an execution, slumped and with blood coming from his ear and mouth. He was, however, still alive.

Will stood over him, waiting to see if movement came from any other direction. Everything became still again. The snow kept coming down, quickly covering the man in white powder. Will turned back to the side of the cabin.

Ridges stood against the wall, seemingly in shock, as if he'd only now realized that they had crossed the line and there was no turning back.

Will beckoned him with another hand signal: *Are you ready?*

Ridges didn't seem to understand, but he got it when Will signaled more obviously to come toward him. Ridges first looked back, around the corner of the cabin toward the sentry post, then turned to Will, nodding.

"Put this on," Will whispered, giving him the other Tyvek coveralls.

Ridges stumbled as he tried to stand on one leg, but finally he got the suit on.

"Follow me," Will whispered in his ear.

When Ridges nodded, Will pointed to his own lips, making the universal signal to be as silent as possible.

The two stepped carefully in single file through the drifts and toward the lake, opposite of the direction in which Will had come earlier. They reached the shoreline, then went out onto the ice, continuing to head away from the dock. Once they reached the dock of another cabin, he signaled his follower to climb up onto the dock. They walked the dock in the dark and, when near the end in the lake, climbed back down on the ice and headed back in the direction of the cabin where the Lada was parked. The maneuver was designed to buy them at least as much time as it cost. The searchers would follow the tracks, spreading out as they moved along, and then would have to double back to where the Lada had been stowed.

At the car, Will quietly opened the door to the passenger side. Ridges started to climb in, but then stopped.

"You're hurt." Ridges whispered the words.

Will's Tyvek was stained with blood at his forearm.

"We'll take care of that later."

Will moved the Lada back down the road with its lights out. The snow illuminated the road well enough for him to see in the night. The absence of trees along its path gave him some guidance.

As they pulled out onto the main road, Will turned on the Lada's headlights. He pulled out onto the main road and headed back toward Moscow. On the main road, three military vehicles rushed past on the other side of the highway. They were outfitted with blue lights and sirens operating at full blast.

"Well, they know." Ridges still spoke quietly, as if the risk remained that they would be overheard.

Will didn't say anything. He had a direction in mind.

The snowstorm suddenly cleared. A moonlit sky quickly became cloudless. Will pulled the Lada into a parking lot near a BP gas station.

"Can you get into the net?"

"Of course." For the first time, Ridges smiled. He opened his backpack and pulled out a small computer. In a matter of a minute, he was on the Moscow net.

"They'll be on top of us with a drone soon." Will looked up in the clear sky. "Probably a Dozor eighty five." Russia had been slow in adapting to the drone world, but it was catching up fast. The Dozor 85 was one of the newer models the FSB used for surveillance and border patrol. Kronshtadt, its manufacturer, produced a drone that could fly over Moscow at 20,000 feet or more and produce detailed video of a car's license plate.

"Yeah, that's what the FSB uses in the Moscow district." Ridges looked up from his laptop. "I did some research after you told me about Tippenhauer."

Tippenhauer was a study that had been released to the public by some overenthusiastic Swiss scientists who had diagrammed how to misdirect drones.

"Can you use it?" Will asked.

"Yeah." Ridges started to work on the problem. His computer showed only Cyrillic script. A couple of minutes later, he said, "You were right. FSB has security drones on patrol all over the city."

"Does Tippenhauer work with GLONASS?"

GLONASS was the Russian version of the United States's Global Positioning Satellite network. The Swiss scientists' paper had included instructions on how to do a spoofing attack using GPS systems.

"No." Ridges continued to type. "GLONASS is unreliable, but has cryptic access since it is military."

"Okay...."

"What I just did was better." Ridges looked up from his Alienware laptop with a smile.

"We need some time." Will pulled the Lada back onto the highway, heading to the north and west.

"I hacked the FSB computers." Ridges continued to type. "I set it up so they'll believe that we used Tippenhauer to spoof the drone."

Dr. Tippenhauer's paper was the guide to how to misdirect a drone. It would send a signal to the drone that deceived its GPS receiver into thinking it was far from where it actually was. Both the world of terrorism and the FSB were very familiar with Tippenhauer. Here, however, Ridges sent signals that convinced the drone operators into believing that the drone was wrong when it was actually right. The FSB operations center would be sending out instructions for the Dozor 85 to do a circle surveillance of the roads around the cabin. But when it seemed to not follow the commands, they would ignore the aircraft even as it flew directly over the gas station.

"You need to ditch the laptop."

"I know."

Although the laptop was made by Dell in the US, the risk was too high that the laptop had been doctored by Ridges's Russian hosts to serve as locator beacon.

"Pull up here next to the truck." Ridges pointed to a grime-covered delivery truck getting refueled at a pump. It was in a dark area of the station, out of sight of any cameras.

Will stopped the Lada near the back of the truck. Ridges got out, opened the cargo door, slipped the laptop in, and closed it back up. The transfer was like a mailman making a postal delivery to a mailbox. If the Russians were following the computer, it would take them well north of the city.

"I have this"—Ridges held up a flash drive as he slid back into the car—"from my DIA days."

Will nodded.

"If anything happens to me and you can get it out of Russia, do it." It seemed strange for Ridges to admit that the small black object held something more important than he himself was. "You'll need a password, but I'm not ready to give that out yet."

"Good idea." Will understood the hesitation. They hadn't even known each other for more than twenty-four hours. He understood why Ridges would be hesitant to bet the farm on him.

"We need to get to Leningradsky." Will took Ridges's wrist, turned it, and looked at his watch.

He explained to Ridges that the train station on the north side of the city served as the region's gateway for trains traveling to and from Finland.

"Out of Russia on a train?" Ridges looked at him in disbelief. "Are you crazy?"

"I *will* get you out of here." Will left it at that. Much like his passenger, hesitant to entrust his password to Will, it made no sense for Will to tell everything to Ridges. Not yet. And it was more than a security precaution. The details of his plan might cause doubt or even errors on Ridges's part. He just needed the young hacker to follow instructions.

Ridges nodded, looking less smug and more like his previous, shell-shocked self again.

Will patted him on the shoulder. "You can count on it."

* * * *

Will parked the car on a side street several blocks away from Leningradsky. It was the oldest of the six major train stations in Moscow. Like Ridges, the FSB would be less likely to expect Will to choose a train for their escape, which was precisely why the railroad had played a key part in the many layers of Will's plan.

"You need to fix that arm." Ridges reminded him of the wound.

The guard's blade had been sharp and, despite a glancing blow, easily cut through the Tyvek and clothes underneath. Pain was something that Will Parker had learned to distance himself from years ago. Adrenaline made it easy. When your world was on overload, pain took a backseat.

"What's in the glove compartment?"

Ridges opened it and started doing inventory.

"Not much here. Cigarettes. Pictures of a couple." He pulled out each item and put them on the dashboard.

"They're required to carry a first-aid kit." Will knew that cars registered in Moscow had to carry certain equipment, including fire extinguishers and first aid. "Let me check the back. You can get out of the coveralls."

Ridges stepped out of the small SUV and pulled off the Tyvek. They were in a dark area, well beyond the likely view of any cameras. Ridges started to throw the coveralls in the back and stopped.

"How about this?" He held up half a roll of what looked like duct tape. "Izolenta?" He described the Russian version of duct tape.

The blue electric tape had the same qualities of duct tape, but half the size. Everything in Russia was apt to break at some point, so nearly every car or truck carried a roll.

"That'll do." Will pulled off the Tyvek suit and his shirt. He wrapped the tape around the forearm laceration and put back on the parka he had shed earlier.

"Do you have a cap?"

"Just this." Ridges pulled out a ski cap from his pocket.

"Put it on, pull it down over your forehead, put your hands in your pockets, never look up, and never make eye contact unless you're confronted. If that happens, look 'em directly in the eye." Will was giving him a short lesson in tradecraft. He grabbed his heavy backpack and put the automatic pistol back in it, slung it over his parka, and headed toward the back end of the railroad yard. "I speak Russian well, so I'll be the one to engage them if we pass a guard or cop."

Ridges, clearly still a student of the language, nodded.

"Follow behind me, but close to my shoulder. When I point to a spot, you go there and stay. We need to separate occasionally and if we get separated, go to the men's room and enter the third stall. I'll come and get you."

They crossed the side street, moved up two blocks and then crossed over to the back end of the station. Will searched for an opening in the tracks and the two quickly moved onto a platform where others were waiting for a train.

Will glanced in all directions, then whispered to Ridges: "Platform three." He kept his hands in his parka and led the way with his head covered by a cap. The fur hood was pulled up close to his neck. He knew where the cameras were, but skillfully took a path that kept his back facing each one. Ridges followed him like a man following another through a minefield. When they got to platform three, Will stopped at a pole next to a wooden bench. An old woman, with a blue scarf over her head and a brown coat with a cheap fur collar, sat on the far end of the bench. She had a plastic bag on her lap almost overflowing with goods. The scarf had colorful flowers of green and yellow. And she wore black boots that seemed like something issued at a military post. The woman kept her face and nose pointed to the ground, clearly having no interest in engaging with others.

Perfect.

Will pointed to the bench.

Ridges took a seat, near the end and next to the pole. He kept his head down, acting as if he'd finished his last bottle of vodka only a few minutes before.

Will pointed a finger in the air as if to say, "I'll be right back," and crossed back into the station.

The loud announcement echoed off the walls of the cavernous Leningradsky. A train was getting ready to depart. The military was out in force throughout the station. Will moved up to a ticket window with no line.

He pulled up his hat just before stepping to the window.

"Two to Helsinki." He said the words in perfect Russian with a Moscow accent.

"Which one?"

"Tolstoy thirty-two A."

"You need to hurry up." The agent made a point of looking at the clock.

Will took the tickets, pulled down his cap, and gathered his hood close to his neck, then returned to Ridges and the old woman. He helped Ridges up, as if the man were beyond establishing his own equilibrium.

"Come on, friend," Will said loudly in Russian.

They climbed onto the train just as the door was closing. Ridges followed him as Will went down the corridor until he reached the third car. They passed several guards; Will looked briefly but directly in the guards' eyes, greeting them in Russian. The guards didn't respond or stare back.

Tradecraft again, Will thought. The face least likely to be remembered was the one that looked directly at you. It sent a subliminal message that you had nothing to hide.

At the end of an empty corridor in the train, Will pulled Ridges into a bathroom. The toilet compartment had a large window of fixed glass with a small partition of glass at the top, through which one could let in some air. The window was frosted by both the tint of the glass and the buildup of ice and snow. A steel toilet and steel sink took up much of the room.

"We wait," Will whispered in English as he locked the door.

Michael Ridges's face expressed relief at the sound of Will's voice. It seemed as if the young man missed the language as much as he surely missed his country and the girlfriend who had returned home nearly a month ago. The train gained speed as it cleared Moscow. A cold wind came through the cracked window, helping clear the stench of the toilet compartment.

The door rattled once.

"Shortly," Will grumbled in Russia to the person trying the doorknob. It seemed the answer was accepted as the person seemingly moved on to another car.

In less than an hour, the screech of brakes passed through the train as it began to slow. The two were jolted against the wall.

"Tver," Will whispered.

"Tver?" Ridges seemed to know of it. "You do realize what it's known for?"

"Yes." Will was keenly aware of the small town on the outskirts of the Moscow district. "Let's go."

Chapter 54

The FSB Hideout

"Will he live?" Lt. Col. Mikhailov stood over the couch in the dacha where the injured guard was lying, hands pressed to his head.

"Yes, sir." The head of the guard detail was holding the FSB soldier's white fur cap, which had been retrieved from the backyard. "It looks like a concussion. His nose is broken."

"So, our stranger didn't kill him." Mikhailov studied the man and turned to the porch, thinking about the American operator. It would have been easy for a man of this skill level to have slain the guard. In fact, it was a risk not to. A scream or cry for help would have brought all of the guards with their AK-47s. And even after a successful escape, the injured guard might still remember some detail or important fact.

I certainly would have killed him, thought Mikhailov. Until now, he had judged every move made by the American as one he would have chosen himself.

"What did you see, Corporal?" Mikhailov actually knew the young enlisted man. He had served under him during a short combat tour in the Ukraine. The guard had handled combat with distinction and became an instructor in his unit for hand-to-hand combat.

"A shape came out of the woods." The guard tried to sit up. Clearly still dizzy, he lay back down. "He was taller than me."

"How was he dressed?"

"I...don't know."

"What of Ridges?"

"He turned off his computer and said he was going to bed." The guard looked up to his superior. His eyes were bloodshot and face red. It wasn't from any drink. The blow to his throat had caused a welt.

"Did you check on him?"

"It was only a minute or two after he said that. I went outside for a second."

Mikhailov looked out through the open porch door. He saw the stain of yellow on the snow and realized why the guard had gone outside. He also noticed something else: a small drop of red had stained the spot where the snow had been churned up by the fight.

"Your knife?" He turned back to the corporal.

"Yes, sir, I think I got him."

He handed the blade over to Mikhailov, who examined it in the light of the fire. It showed a streak of blood.

"Where do the tracks go?" he called to the men in the back of the cabin.

"They go out onto the lake." The detail's sergeant carried a radio, and the squawk of communications kept coming in over the air.

"He's gone, but let's start here." Mikhailov headed toward his car and radio.

"This is Alfa Group commander." He spoke to the operations center of the FSB, deep within the old KGB headquarters. "Is the Dozor up?"

The sky had cleared and the drone should have been able to reach the cabin by now.

"Sir, we have real-time coverage."

What are we looking for? he asked himself. The trail from here would be the start. His quarry had almost surely stolen a car. Since it was just after midnight, the theft would probably not be reported until daybreak.

The guard sergeant came running to the car.

"Sir, we followed the trail back to the east and to a closed cabin, where we found the tracks of a Lada."

"Good. It's a start."

"We think it's a four-wheel drive."

Mikhailov nodded. "He wouldn't steal anything in this snowstorm that isn't winter-ready."

The radio in the car buzzed with a transmission.

"The drone is not responding to the location," the duty officer at the operations center reported.

Mikhailov stared out into the darkness; the temperature had already plummeted following the passing of the snowstorm.

He can't be that *good.*

"Alert all the airports." He paused for a moment. "And train stations."

Chapter 55

Anchorage

Darkness started to fall on Ted Stevens International Airport in Anchorage as the storm rolled in from the west. The Gulfstream was parked directly in front of the Ross Aviation operations center. Next to the jet, a Bell helicopter was tied down for what looked like the night. Its windows were already banked with snow.

"We can't make it tonight," the chopper pilot said simply. "Besides, you don't want to take on that mountain range and wilderness in the dark. Trust me."

"I got you." Frank Caldwell fully understood and agreed with what he was saying. He just didn't want to relay it to the other man sitting in the FBO.

"The weather shows a clearing about dawn."

"Good."

"But first light isn't until about ten."

Caldwell gave him a look, as if to ask, "What else?" He knew the troops wouldn't mind. They'd be heading for the first open bar and hunkering down.

"Thanks, then we'll need to launch then."

"Should be okay. Weather's moving fast."

* * * *

Caldwell gave the thumbs-down to the three black-ops types sitting on a couch outside the visiting-crew rest area. Paul sat inside the small room, working both his phone and laptop.

The door was closed. Caldwell knocked lightly.

"Yeah?" Paul looked up.

Caldwell entered the room. "No helicopter tonight, but we should be able to roll at first light." As Caldwell spoke, he noticed another person in the room, directly to his left. A stranger, filling up the small chair with his large frame. He was dark, Hispanic-looking, and had an unfriendly expression on his face. He had on what appeared to be a new winter coat, tan jeans, and combat boots. He wore no jewelry. The stranger seemed uncomfortable, his hands gripping the arms of the chair. Caldwell looked away.

"Goddamn it." Paul was showing signs of stress. Clearly, time was not his friend.

Caldwell didn't attempt to tender an argument.

"Got all the cold gear?"

"Yes, sir."

"Weapons?"

"The men have their HK416s, and HK p30s with suppressors."

"Get him one of the P thirties." Paul pointed to the stranger. "One with a can."

The semiautomatic HK pistol with a .40 caliber Smith & Wesson round had punch and accuracy. The suppressor, or silencer, or "can" as they were sometimes called, didn't fully silence the weapon, but did reduce the noise significantly, often preventing the enemy from getting a sense of the direction the shots were coming from.

He isn't going to introduce me, Caldwell thought. The lack of introduction signaled much. The man would come and go without any record of who he was or where he had come from. Things were getting progressively bizarre by the minute. If this was occurring in the back end of a C-130 heading into deepest Africa, it would have made more sense than Anchorage, Alaska.

"We got a bunk room here we can use," said Caldwell, trying to cover the remaining logistics.

"Good. Less of a trail." Paul checked his phone and laptop again. It seemed to be almost a tic at this point. "What about Parker?"

"Do you want me to try to call him?" Caldwell had a cell number. He wasn't sure it would work and, thus far, had held off trying to reach him directly.

"Nah. Wait till we get to Snag." Paul looked back at his laptop. "The FSB's closing in on him anyway."

The last comment was troubling and it didn't make immediate sense. Paul was hoping that Russian intelligence would stop an American? How would he know the status of the hunt?

More to the point, Caldwell asked himself, *why is he so scared of Ridges?*

He went back out to the main room to tell the others of the plan. They were being paid triple what they ever made when serving with Delta or Rangers. No one had any complaints.

"Hey, Captain?" One of the black-ops types with a curly red beard stood from the couch and approached Caldwell. The man was taller than he, had the muscular frame of a linebacker, and smelled of Aqua Velva and cigars. Caldwell noticed his strikingly blue eyes. He seemed a modern-day warrior from the family tree of William Wallace. His face was rugged and red-freckled, making him look as if he had been raised in the backcountry of the Lake District and drunk warm scotch since childhood. The man moved closer to Caldwell so that the conversation would be limited to only the two. "What's the story?"

Caldwell knew what he was asking. It wasn't about the weather, or the mission, or even the times of launch. It was about the stranger.

"Just keep an eye on him."

The redheaded soldier tilted his head. "Really? Okay, well, the dude didn't give his name. That's cool and all, but we're gonna keep him in front of our sights."

Chapter 56

Snag

"I'm going to hike around a little tomorrow." Kevin Moncrief sat on a stack of MRE cases near the potbelly stove in the cabin at Snag. He had just finished a meal of chili with beans. "Your MREs are just about expired."

"Probably." Karen had her boots off, in her stocking feet, sitting on the corner of her cot.

The CDC did get the leftover of government gear, such as MREs. The organization's hazmat suits, masks, and gloves were the best in any industry, but the food didn't hit so high on the list.

"You enjoy this?" Moncrief looked around the tiny cabin, his eyes settling on his sleeping pad and bag in the corner. The night was quiet, except for the crackle of wood in the stove. The room was warm, too much so for his taste.

As if reading his mind, Karen stood to open the window on top of the door. "Yeah, I do."

"What's it all about?"

"The north is getting warmer so animals are traveling farther north. Diseases are spreading like wildfire."

"Oh."

"Why have you stuck with Will all these years?" she asked in a counterpunch question.

"Good question." Moncrief leaned back against the wall with his rifle across his lap. He had a cloth with which he was cleaning the Marlin. "I just know he's got my back. Can't say much more than that."

"So, what's this all about?"

"A man's son got in the middle of something much bigger than himself."
Moncrief put the action back in the rifle, cocked it, and dry-fired the
weapon to ensure it was ready.

"And that could affect me—er, us, here?"

Moncrief nodded.

"Should we head back to Anchorage?"

"No, we decided that you were safer here." Kevin loaded the rifle with
a handful of shiny brass casings that were thick as Magic Markers and
had lead bullets the size of marbles.

"I have to check a trap in the morning." Karen changed the subject.

A howl started up in the distance, in the direction of the mountain range
to the west. The wolf's voice was followed by another closer to the cabin.

"Just like clockwork," Karen said and turned off the lamp.

Chapter 57

Tver, Russia to the East of Moscow

"I need a room with two beds."

The hostel in Tver had rooms for rent at less than four hundred rubles a night. That translated to approximately $6. The inn stood a block away from the tracks, behind the town's small train station. A green and yellow fluorescent sign marked its name. The doors and windows were painted a moss green and the cement-block structure had been covered with whitewash, which did a poor job of hiding the dirt and grime.

Tver stretched to both sides of the Volga River and was split again by the Tvertsa and Tmaka Rivers. At one time, it had been in the running for capital of Russia. Like much of Russia, Tver hosted people from a variety of religions: Russian Orthodox, Muslims, and Jews competed for the souls of the local youth.

The train station was south of the Volga River, near the heart of the old city, where the streets were tight, some no more than narrow alleys.

The old man behind the desk grunted. He had a cigarette hanging out of his mouth with the ash collecting on the desk. He took his hand with long, yellow fingernails and slid the ash to the floor. The walls behind his desk and in the hallway seemed to have been decorated by a color-blind painter. Patterns of yellow, brown, and black flowers sprawled across the walls, hemming in bright velvet red chairs with orange pillows.

"Also, we need some fun." Will smiled a crooked smile and spoke the words in near-perfect Moscow Russian. "My friend and I."

Again, the clerk grunted, turned, and picked up an old telephone that looked like a prop in a Hollywood movie from the fifties.

"And a bottle." Will tossed another two hundred rubles on the desk. The three bucks would buy a gallon of Russky Standart vodka if the clerk didn't keep the change. More likely, he'd bring them a 750-ml. bottle. "With some zakuska. Maybe some black bread?"

The man gave him a strange look.

"How about herring?" Will suggested.

The hostel was not known for food, of course: Only vodka and a warm place to sleep. Most of the short-term tenants were railroad workers from the nearby rail yard. Will's requests and money would seem suspiciously generous here. The clerk appeared torn between temptation for cash and worrying about what he'd need to report to the local police.

Tver was the Wild West. It also had become known as the home of hack central. Investigators chasing hackers from around the world often followed the trails back to Tver. The digital exploit might run through France and Italy and India before it hit a company like ITD, but it always started in Tver. The FSB had been known to use Tver as a base for its cyber-attacks on the "payment space," as ITD's financial subsector was called. The creator of the famous program SpyEye had been from Tver. He'd lived with his grandmother in a small apartment while he was stealing data from more than a million computers worldwide.

Ridges looked ill as they closed the door to their room. A single bulb hung from the ceiling over two metal-framed beds. Pale green paint peeled off of the walls.

"They said I'd be dead if I ever tried to leave Russia without Putin clearing it."

They sat across from each other on the small beds as they spoke.

"You would be dead if you stayed," said Will. "Why does Alexander Paul want you so bad?" he asked, figuring the tiny motel room was as safe as anywhere in Russia for a frank conversation. "Why aren't you already dead?" Both questions had been lingering in Will's mind for some time.

"That one's easy." Ridges ran his hands through his hair. "Putin isn't ready for me to be dead."

It made sense. Putin hadn't figured out the endgame as of yet. Ridges was a bargaining chip that could be played in a million different ways.

"So, Paul?"

"He's not sure exactly what I know."

"How about the two Marines?"

Ridges rubbed his face, stared at his feet, and shrugged. "They just got caught up in it."

"How?"

"Paul must think they know what I know and what I can do."

"How did you get into this fix?" Will kept firing questions. "A son of a housebuilder from Richmond. Smart, but not smart enough to get out of college."

"I was smart enough, just didn't care," Ridges said, defensively. "Hell, I was an Eagle Scout."

"And?"

"Just saw too much at DIA. I knew that these guys play for keeps. I didn't want a bullet in the back of the head in some fake robbery in DC. Russia became the only option." He didn't realize how close his example was to the truth.

Will leaned back against the wall.

"What about you?"

"A father needed help in finding his son. He thought you were the only way."

"You're talking about Todd's father? I thought they didn't like each other." Ridges seemed to know more about his past friend than was expected.

"The father is betting a lot on getting you out of here."

"Really?"

Much more was not being said.

"Both of you must be crazy!"

"You may be right."

In less than an hour, two Russian women, both blond and torn up, knocked on the door. One looked like she had visited hotels near the train station for too many years. The other, dressed in a lipstick-red dress, seemed barely out of high school. The older one seemed the boss, with the younger one following her lead. They already smelled of cigarettes and liquor.

"Vodka?" Will spoke in perfect Russian with an accent from Moscow. Ridges kept quiet.

He took the bottle, gave them each a thousand rubles, and started to pour drinks. One woman pulled up next to Parker and the other sat on the bed across. They drank from one glass.

"What else do you have for fun?" Will asked.

The girl pulled out a small packet of heroin. She raised an eyebrow inquisitively. Will shrugged, palms up, giving her the universal sign for *Be my guest.*

Will and Ridges declined to participate as the two women drank, shot up, and shortly fell into a doped-up sleep. One started to snore almost immediately.

* * * *

"I'll be back," Will whispered to Ridges. He grabbed his backpack, went into the bathroom, and quietly pulled the door closed.

Ridges listened for something, but heard only silence. He huddled up in a chair, hands in his pockets, waiting and listening. From underneath the bathroom door, a bright light shined, as if inside a bare light bulb swung back and forth from a wire.

What the hell have I done?

There was only one reason he trusted this stranger. It was only going to be a matter of time before the Russians got out of him what he had discovered...either that, or else Putin would soon tire of the distraction.

Ridges had found out something that could tilt the world on its edge. The flash drive he had given to Will held a secret that went well beyond his troubles with Alexander Paul.

Ridges had originally gone to Russia because it was his only option. In Russia, as long as they thought the DIA computer geek had something of value, he would be safe. Using that safety, while theoretically out of the reach of Alexander Paul, Ridges had made his move, sending a message to Paul in the form of the ITD breach.

"It was pretty ingenious, if I say so myself," he whispered for the benefit of the sleeping Russian women.

Alexander Paul had signed a contract with ITD to protect the company from hacking attacks. As soon as Ridges had learned about the contract, he'd known exactly how to get Paul's attention.

So far, Paul had been held at bay. Or, if he'd had the ability to see Ridges murdered in Russia, he'd chosen not to do so, perhaps because he'd rightly assumed that Michael Ridges had a backup plan in place in case he suddenly died.

The death of the two Marines had changed everything, though. It meant that Paul was willing to take chances. And that had scared Ridges into reaching his ultimate conclusion: He was no longer safe in Russia.

A draft of cold air from under the bathroom door caused the two women to stir. The older one leaned up, looked around, and then fell back to the bed, her snoring only growing louder. The younger one clutched a brown pillow and had her body curled up around it. The spent needle used by the two and a scorched spoon from the heroin sat on the nightstand. Next to the drugs, the half-empty bottle of vodka was missing its cap. He stood up and walked over to the nightstand and took a swig from the bottle. The vodka tasted like a bitter swallow of gasoline. It burned as it went down. Ridges wiped his lips with his sleeve and put the bottle back down.

It seemed an eternity before the door to the bathroom cracked open. The interior light had gone out, leaving the room lit only by a small lamp in the corner. Along with Will Parker, a stronger rush of cold air came into the room, causing the women to stir again but not to wake.

"Do you have gloves?" Will asked as he closed the door behind him.

"No." Ridges had left his gloves in the Lada somewhere in the rush of the last few hours. A major mistake in the bitter cold.

Will rifled through the coat of one of the women and pulled out a pair of leather gloves with white and black fur on the trim. He replaced them in her coat pocket with a wad of rubles. He did the same with the other woman. For days they would be held in a cell. The FSB rarely believed the truth, even when it was true. The wad of rubles might be of some help.

"These might fit." Will tossed a pair of gloves to Ridges.

"Okay." He pulled the gloves on and held them up to show that they were a tight fit, but would work.

"Now we wait." Will reached over and turned Ridges's wrist to look at his watch.

The placing of each piece of this puzzle was timed to the minute. They sat in the room, the vapor of their breath visible. Off in the distance they could hear the whistle of a train and the click-clack of rail cars as they passed over the tracks. The train to Helsinki was long gone.

Chapter 58

The Casa

"I think he's dead." The smaller of the two Mexican men stood over the bunk in which Todd lay unconscious. He pushed the body with his hand like someone who thought the creature's corpse would suddenly bite back. Newton's vomit covered much of his blanket.

"*Mierda*," growled the man with the silver-plated .45 revolver. He knew that if Todd died, they would be next. "Get him up."

The smaller man had felt dead bodies before. He was the one assigned to the job of burying what was left. A dead body would be stiff and cold. As he lifted the Marine up, he felt the same cold flesh, though the body remained pliable.

"Does he have a pulse?"

"I don't know!" the small man shot back.

The two struggled with the limp body, shaking him as if that would help. The body stank from days of being locked to the rack with no shower or bath, only able to use a bucket in the corner of the room. The task was nearing unbearable for the two of them.

"This won't be good," said the smaller man. His face was pale white with fear. To kill a man was something that they had often done, but to lose something entrusted to them was far different.

"Get some water."

The little man scurried up the stairs and came back with a small plastic bucketful. He cupped the water in his hands and then let it drip onto Newton's face.

"Oh." Todd's eyes suddenly flew open and he gasped for air like a drowning man.

The smaller man jumped back, startled by his suddenly coming to life.

"Help him up," the killer ordered the other guard.

"I need a doctor." Todd mumbled the words. He was shaking with a chill. Sweat from the fever and the water used to awaken him soaked his hair and clothes.

"No doctor." The big man paced around the room as the little one helped Todd drink from the bucket. "I'll get you some aspirin."

The prisoner nodded, still semiconscious.

"And some food. I will bring you some." The killer's tone remained flat, as if he were taking care of livestock on a farm.

* * * *

"He ain't good." The little one stood outside when the van pulled back up to the hacienda some hours later. A cloud of dust engulfed the van and swirled around it.

The Mexican wasn't as fearful for Todd as he was for himself. He had seen Angel use a chainsaw on a man strapped to a chair, blood and tissue flying as the man screamed and gagged. His eyes had still been open and looking at them when it fell to the ground. Angel had stuck the skull on a spiked fence post.

The dead man was one of six that Angel had murdered that day, using his preferred method of execution. His video of killings often appeared on the internet. It was one thing to put a bullet in the brain of another, but Angel chose a manner of murder that caused the most fear.

"I have some aspirin for you." The smaller man acted as if he were Todd's savior.

He had a plastic bag in one hand and a small bottle of tequila in the other; leaning back against the dust-covered van, he took a long swallow.

"I spoke to Angel."

"What do we do?"

"He said we'd have an answer in the morning."

"*Bueno.*"

"He said make plans to get rid of the body. He doesn't think we'll need him after tomorrow."

"What do you want to do?"

"Same as her." The killer was referring to the other Marine. They had decided early on that only one was needed. Angel had used the chainsaw on her, blood spattering onto the desert sand as her screams reached out to no one.

"Make sure nothing with fingerprints or teeth?"

"Yeah. But this one we can bury in the desert." He tossed the plastic bag to his partner.

"His last meal."

The smaller man smiled. The coming permission to kill their prisoner was good news. And to think that only minutes before, they'd worried that the Marine had died too soon.

Chapter 59

In the Center of Moscow

"What about the woman?" FSB Lt. Col. Mikhailov sat in a steel chair behind the computer operators at the operation center in the basement of the FSB headquarters.

"Yes, sir. We followed up on that." The junior officer turned around from his chair. "She knew what she was doing."

"What makes you say that?"

He pulled up the surveillance footage from around the hotel. It was uncanny: The woman seemed to know the location of each camera. Her head was down and her fur hood covered most of her face. The FSB pulled up each camera on the trip until the two disappeared into the metro. In each, she would throw up her hand or arm at precisely the moment she came into focus. "The hotel said she was his Russian bride." Mikhailov lit up a Karelia cigarette while sitting in the chair. The white and blue box had a small seal that looked like something from the age of the czars. As dated and quaint as their chances of catching the blond woman had become. No doubt she had traveled far away from the city by this point.

"We can keep looking."

"No, even if we find her, she'll say the American promised to take her to New York. Even if we got the truth out of her quickly, it'd be too late." Mikhailov knew this coyote was smart; he wouldn't have let his "bride" know anything of consequence, in any case.

"Sir, we've got something." The computer operator at one of the terminals on the other end of the room turned to him.

"What?"

"An old woman at Leningradsky reported two men."

"At what time?"

"About an hour ago."

"Do we have surveillance where she saw them?"

"No sir, but we do have something." The corporal pulled up grainy video of the end of a platform at one end of the station. The shape of two men climbing up on the platform from the dark appeared in the center of the camera's view. Both moved quickly into the crowd with their heads down.

"Can we pull up the ticket windows?"

"Yes, sir."

At times like this, Mikhailov felt like the child he had once been, hunting with his grandfather, sitting in the cold and silence of the woods until they first saw the movement of the musk deer. The buck's gray coat blended in well with the gray, leafless forest. It was invisible until it moved. The adrenaline surged through young Mikhailov's body. Suddenly, his hands became warm despite the cold. His grandfather even let him take the shot. All because the deer had moved.

The American had just moved.

"Here." The camera had a clear picture of the man buying tickets at the window.

"Find out where to."

The operator called the senior FSB officer on duty at Leningradsky. It didn't take but a minute for the radio to crack with a reply.

"Helsinki."

"What train?"

"Tolstoy thirty-two."

"What's its first stop?"

"Tver."

"Alert Tver."

* * * *

The FSB's Kamov 226T helicopter was on the roof of the old KGB headquarters building before Mikhailov and his lieutenant had finished checking out their pistols from the armory and taking the elevator to the top. The twin-rotor aircraft lacked tail blades, but with the stacked rotors, it didn't need one. It also gave a smoother ride than the other helicopters produced by the Russian Helicopters group.

The night sky was clear and the city's lights below were bright with the distant blue, green, and gold domes of Saint Basil Cathedral lit by the floodlights as if it were a ride in a Disney park.

"Tver reports thirty-two has left to Saint Petersburg." The lieutenant was monitoring the digital radio in contact with the FSB officer in Tver.

"Call our unit in Saint Petersburg." Mikhailov would not let that train get to the Finnish border without pulling every passenger off first.

"Sir, Tver reports two men were seen getting off."

"So now where is my friend going?" he murmured to himself. The journey had been an effort to mislead. This was turning into a more complicated plan than even he had anticipated.

"We're more than five hundred miles from any border that would be of help." Mikhailov weighed all of the options aloud. "Find out when the next train is going back to Moscow," he barked.

"Yes, sir."

"Didn't the phone tap from the hotel say he was buying two airplane tickets on Air France?"

"Yes, sir."

"Find out when that flight leaves."

The helicopter's jet engine started to spin up, the rotors' blast pushing the two FSB officers back on their heels. The frigid air burned Mikhailov's face until he was able to get into the cabin and close the hatch. Inside, he inhaled the sweet smell of jet fuel.

He sat back in his seat and donned a set of headphones with a boom mike.

He'd play the man's game for now.

"Take me to Tver."

Chapter 60

Snag

"The sky is clearing." Kevin Moncrief took the rifle off of his shoulder as he came to the front of the cabin. He unbuckled the red snowshoes and checked the safety on the weapon.

"Good." Karen was holding a covered cage full of straw. It seemed to be moving.

"Not good." Moncrief turned to the west and the mountain range. He knew how they would come. The airplane would come in low or the helicopter would make one sweeping turn around the airfield to pick a landing spot and check the winds. They'd assume that their arrival would be unopposed. The aircraft would land and then the men on board would fan out in a three hundred and sixty degree pattern. They would be carrying automatic rifles, their mission clear.

He hadn't heard from Will in some time. They had discussed the options, but at this stage, silence was not good. He needed to be prepared for anything.

"What you got there?" Moncrief asked.

"A new one. In the trap on the other side of the airfield." Karen had the cage covered with a dark-colored towel, which she pulled back for him to see inside. A small arctic fox peered out from the straw. For a moment, the animal stared at him, then it suddenly lunged at him as if there were no cage to stop it. The fox growled and seemed to choke on a foam that surrounded its mouth. It bared its teeth in a desperate, vicious snarl.

"What's the prognosis?"

"Active case. Maybe ten days."

"No hope?"

"None." Karen laid the cage down. "Microbiologists say it's the most dangerous disease on the planet."

Moncrief nodded. Rabies had always been a death sentence, as far as he'd known.

"It's the only disease that's one-hundred-percent fatal if you don't stop it before the first symptom shows," she explained.

"A killing machine." He looked at the poor animal in the cage, locked in the throes of the disease. In all his years of combat missions, Moncrief had encountered few enemies who were so effective. A 100-percent kill rate exceeded that of any other weapon in the world. A lucky man could even survive a nuclear blast.

Karen covered the cage back up with the towel.

"There's an outcropping of rock." He pointed to the south toward a bend in the river. "Maybe two hundred yards."

"Yeah, I know where it is."

"It would be a good place to meet up if we get separated." Moncrief was giving her a plan for a rallying point, the Marine inside him anticipating an attack sooner than later. When the shit hit the fan, if they became separated, they'd know where to go to find the other.

"If I don't show up, you run as far and fast as you can away from here."

He knew he was scaring her, but Will had told him she could handle it.

"Why not call for help?"

"They'll be on top of us before any help can get here."

He didn't need to remind her that any outside help would have to come from the other side of the mountain range.

"So, why don't we leave?'

"Will and I agree that we're best off on familiar ground."

"Home-field advantage, huh?" she asked.

Moncrief nodded. He'd always liked his chances in the wilderness, and he'd studied this particular terrain in detail. He now knew it intimately. It would be a distinct advantage in any fight to come.

In the city, one might never see the bullet or van coming.

"See over there?" Karen pointed to the other side of the ridgeline to the south.

"Yeah."

"Just beyond there is where Will and I crashed his airplane."

"Oh?" Moncrief smiled. "I didn't know about that." In the flurry of events and discussions, Will hadn't mentioned the downed airplane. "Well, no harm."

"No, none at all."

"He's supposed to check in with us. Have you heard anything?" Kevin pointed to her satellite phone.

"I'm not sure he has this number."

"Do you want to call him?"

Karen dialed the number. There was no answer.

Kevin knew that Will needed to be out of Russia by now if the plan was going to hold.

"Isn't he in Paris?"

Karen's question reminded him that she had no idea what was going on.

"When we last talked, he was." It wasn't a lie.

"Oops, I'm supposed to be checking in." Karen dialed another number.

"No one there?"

She shrugged. "He insisted I call every day."

"Well, if the authorities are anything like your boss," Moncrief said, "then we really are on our own."

Chapter 61

Tver, Russia

"It's time." Will put his hand over Michael Ridges's mouth so as to ensure no noise if he reacted.

The shot of vodka and the fear of the last several hours had caused Ridges to fall into a deep sleep. He sat up suddenly in the chair, trying to focus his eyes in the dimly lit room. The two women still lay on their separate beds; if untouched, they'd remain so for hours to come.

"Let's go." Will led him into the bathroom. He locked the door behind him and turned on the shower. The window opened to an alley just below. Will led the way as he climbed through the open window and slid onto the snow below. He signaled Ridges to pass down their backpacks.

Ridges complied, then followed him down to the ground.

They traced the alley to the south until a wooden fence blocked the escape route. There, as with the window, Will led the way over first. Ridges tossed the backpacks, then followed.

At the end of the alley, they stopped for a moment. Will looked in both directions. All the windows looked dark up and down the street.

At that moment, a helicopter flew low, just above the buildings. Will saw the markings of the FSB on its tail. He dropped to his knees and opened his backpack. At the same time, he heard a train in the distance, its whistle approaching the station. He waited several minutes, hugging the wall of the building with Ridges.

"What are we waiting for?" asked Ridges.

Will grabbed his arm, pulled up the sleeve, and looked at the watch. Its analog face glowed in the low light.

"Does it keep good time?"

"Now you ask?"

Will smiled. He pulled one of the burner phones out of his pack and dialed a number. After what seemed like less than a second, a low rumble occurred in the distance. The sound of metal crashing into metal rumbled through the town.

"Let's go." Will crossed the snow-covered street to an alley on the other side. There, he pulled a tarp off of what appeared to be a motorcycle. It had been his most expensive request from the Russian bride. The streetlights reflected off of the snow, illuminating the bike; its BMW emblem shone on the side of the gas tank. The motorcycle had been equipped with knobby tires for traction on the snow. Will climbed on, kick-started the engine, and pulled it out onto the road. Ridges jumped on, fuzzy women's gloves wrapped tight around Will's middle. At Will's advice, he pulled his hood down as far as it would go and cinched the cord tightly, so only his nose was exposed.

The bike moved slowly over the snow-covered road. Lights were starting to come on in the apartments of Tver. Will made a turn at the end of the street, another turn, and entered an entrance ramp on to a highway marked M10. The road had been plowed since the end of the storm, giving the motorcycle even better traction. As the wheels gripped the snow, Will accelerated. For nearly half an hour, they traveled on the highway, which was almost empty of traffic. Given the hour and the recent snowstorm, it seemed that Moscow had not yet awakened.

"I need to stop," Ridges yelled over the sound of the motorcycle.

Will nodded and stopped the bike on the side of the highway near the exit from M10 to M11. The roadway remained empty and western Moscow appeared quiet. On the exit ramp, Ridges dismounted, stamped his feet, and rubbed his arms.

"You need to hold on a little longer." Will knew this was the dangerous time. The minutes were flying and any misstep would spell their doom.

"Okay." Gingerly, he climbed back on the bike and put his arms around Will's torso. "Go."

They got back on the road and took the cutoff from M10 to M11.

Ridges looked up to the sky, hoping that the drone was still acting up with the hack he had made into its operating system. FSB would be everywhere; there was little doubt they'd be back on their trail soon.

They passed a sign that said *Sheremetyevo*. He knew the airport.

The motorcycle took the turn onto the main access road. Near the entrance to terminal C, Will pulled through a gate to a large parking lot. He slowed down, passing cars as if hunting for one in particular. In the corner of the parking lot, he found a black Kia alone in a dark space far from the cameras. He pulled up behind the car, stepped to the rear window.

Will looked around the lot, waiting for a second, took off his parka and, with his elbow covered by the coat, cracked the glass. He opened the back door, put his backpack on the seat, and unzipped it. He pulled out the tape he used to bandage his injury from before and put it on the front console.

"Get in." He started the engine with two wires under the dashboard. Stuck in the driver's visor was the parking pass.

"How did you know it would be there?" Ridges, still wearing his parka and with his backpack on his lap, had buckled his seat belt.

"Even odds." Will shifted the car in gear. "Hand me my backpack."

It was on the backseat.

"Look in the inside pocket."

Ridges felt around and found a pocket with what felt like several cards. He opened the zipper, finding two Visa credit cards. There were also two passports.

Will held out his hand as they pulled up to the gate. He used the Visa under the false Russian name.

This guy knows what he is doing. Ridges held the backpack to his chest like it would somehow protect him from a blow. *I hope he does. It's my life.*

Chapter 62

The freight train's engine derailed only meters past a yard switch on the north end of the railyard in Tver. Two tank cars carrying 14,000 gallons of oil had been riding immediately behind the engine. They derailed with the engine, but the train's remaining fifty-six tank cars remained on the track.

The two crew members jumped from the engine as soon as they heard the wheels strike the ground. The first tank car behind the engine piled up on the wreckage and caught fire. It was followed by the second, which was punctured by a steel rib and poured more fuel onto the flames. The train had been traveling at a yard speed of less than fifteen kilometers per hour. The slow pace helped stop the movement of the trailing cars, which separated quickly from the fiery derailment.

"What happened?" Mikhailov ducked behind the helicopter when the burst of heat passed through the frigid night. The bright yellow plume followed lighting up the rail yard. He was standing near the nose of the aircraft with the local FSB commander.

"Not another one!" the commander yelled out. The yard was one of the oldest in the system. It was the main connector between Moscow and St. Petersburg and well more than a hundred years old. The many switches were continually needing repair.

"Another one?"

"Yes, sir. Happens often."

The rail yard was known for derailments. The main line to St. Petersburg was kept in good repair, but the freight trains used the older tracks, which were known to split and derail trains often.

Mikhailov watched the billowing flames and black smoke. He didn't believe it for a second.

If a clever coyote wanted to pull the FSB off his trail, a derailment would work nicely. All it would take was a small explosive charge planted in the switch coupling. That would cause the rail to move only a few centimeters, but the weight of a loaded train on it would further split the rails, causing the train to derail.

Easy as pie.

"What hotels are nearby?"

"Several, sir. I can check—"

"Have your men canvass each within a mile, looking for two strangers."

The commander nodded and turned to make a call.

Mikhailov opened the helicopter hatch and took the radio. He called the operations center back in Moscow.

"Is the drone working?"

"Yes, sir."

"Get it over Tver. Run a circle around the city."

"What are we looking for?"

"Anything."

"It'll take some time to reposition—"

"Do it!"

As the noise of the conflagration lessened, he heard another train coming north from Moscow on the main line. The tracks followed the river for most of the journey from the capital to Tver. Along with the lone whistle, he heard the sound of a motorcycle off in the distance.

He's somewhere close, Mikhailov thought, *but not close enough.*

* * * *

The radio call the FSB commander was expecting took less than twenty minutes to come in.

"We have him!"

"Let's go!" Mikhailov led the way to the commander's jeep near the helicopter.

"We can almost walk."

Mikhailov would have guessed it was that close. "Do you have it surrounded?"

"Yes, sir."

They arrived at the hostel just as the FSB troops were surrounding the gray and green building.

"Look at the alleyway," ordered Mikhailov. As he rode to the scene in the front seat of the jeep, it occurred to him that this all seemed too simple.

Mikhailov and the commander jumped out of the jeep. An enlisted man, with his AK-47 locked and loaded, stood at the front.

"The clerk said two men checked in. One asked for some women."

"Let's see what we have." Mikhailov took command of the troops. He led the way into the small lobby, where the clerk, scared and shaking, sat in a chair behind the desk.

"I told them I didn't know." He stumbled over his words.

"What room?" Mikhailov followed the sergeant down the hallway to the room. Another FSB soldier led the way. The clerk followed.

"Key?" He whispered the words with his hand extended.

The clerk handed him the master key. The sergeant clicked the safety off of his rifle.

"You can put the safety back on." Mikhailov could see that he'd surprised the commander and the sergeant with the order. He already had a fair idea of what he would find in the room.

The two women were fast asleep, their heroin supply and paraphernalia telling the rest of the story. Mikhailov sighed. It would take most of the next day for them to come out of the stupor of the drugs. The pair would get fifteen days in prison, and Mikhailov would have no problem believing them when they inevitably claimed that they knew nothing about the fugitives.

The door to the bathroom was shut. Mikhailov kicked it open to find fresh snow on the windowsill. They quickly found and followed the tracks through the alleyway to a tarp left on the ground. From it, the knobby tire prints of a motorcycle led the way out of Tver.

The FSB helicopter was in the air moments after Mikhailov's jeep returned. It banked over the rail yard, which was lit in the glow from the derailment fire. Mikhailov was finding it increasingly difficult to anticipate his prey's moves. Everything the man did was so obvious, yet no path led in any direction for long.

From the front seat of the chopper as it flew back to Moscow, he called headquarters.

"What about the Air France tickets?" The microphones in the hotel room picked up the trace of a conversation earlier. "Where's Air France flying out of tonight?"

"Sheremetyevo."

The airport was on the west side of Moscow. It made sense if the diversion in Tver was designed to pull the authorities away from the airport.

"When?"

"Hold on." The operation center called the FSB officer at the Moscow airport. It seemed to take forever.

Mikhailov looked down in the darkness to the highways below. The traffic on M10 was sporadic, with the occasional truck alone on the roadway. As they got closer to Moscow it began to pick up. He scanned each vehicle, thinking that somewhere below Ridges and the American were heading back into the city.

"The plane is boarding now, sir."

"Hold that flight!"

"Yes, sir."

* * * *

When Mikhailov arrived at the gate, the FSB soldiers in their green and black camouflaged utility uniforms and drawn AK-12 automatic rifles, also covered in jungle color and with suppressors and thirty-round clips, stood guard. Each man wore a face mask and special-operations helmet with earphones and microphone built in. Several Air France clerks stood at the desk, looking frightened and tiny compared to the Russian troops guarding the entrance to the jetway.

"Is it surrounded?"

"Yes, sir."

"Have you run the manifest?" he asked the smaller of the two clerks.

"Yes, sir." Although the woman was French, she spoke Russian well.

"Two men with tickets purchased less than forty-eight hours ago?"

"Oh, that's easy." She pulled out the sheet and scanned the manifest. "This flight has only a few who booked at the last minute."

"Right." He looked up as the FSB commander of the airport approached and saluted. Mikhailov returned the salute and then held up a finger so as to hold off any immediate conversation. He looked back at the agent, eyebrows raised.

"Twelve A and B."

Mikhailov pulled his pistol out and put it in his jacket pocket. "Follow me," he told the others.

Onboard the aircraft, Mikhailov saw two men occupying the seats. He could smell the alcohol from several rows away.

It turned out that the men in 12 A and B had been handed the air tickets in the metro by a stranger the day before. Both men seemed to be pleasant drunks and were more than happy to follow the lieutenant colonel off of the airplane.

Chapter 63

On the Outskirts of Moscow

Will knew that his luck was running out. His arm was starting to swell from the knife wound and a low-grade fever was causing a sweat around his collar. He had to concentrate on the turns he was making with the Kia.

"You okay?" Ridges looked both exhausted and worried.

"I've got it." They were close.

The trip took them south on A106. The beltway around Moscow was starting to build traffic as the city awakened. He was noticing more military-type vehicles with their lights flashing. The one benefit of being this close to the city was that it would be nearly impossible for them to shut down the traffic looking for one or two men. They would be using their cameras to scan every vehicle.

He pulled off the highway and stopped at a BP gas station.

"I got to go to the bathroom." Ridges sat up in his seat.

"Just give me a few more minutes." Will didn't want him to go inside where a camera would get a good view. "Hand me the backpack."

Ridges leaned over the seat and pulled Will's backpack to the front. Will reached in and pulled out something and then went to the back of the car. Using the same roll of colored tape he'd used to seal the knife wound, he changed the Kia's license plate's 6 to an 8, and the 1 to a 7. He returned to the driver's seat, threw the roll of tape in the back, and pulled back into traffic.

"Did you just change the plate?" Ridges put the backpack in the rear seat and settled in for the rest of the ride. "You're good, man."

The citizens of Moscow had been in a revolt for some time about the government's implementation of parking meters. For decades, Moscow had been known for its free parking. A rebellion had arisen against the imposed cameras used to fine people for failing to pay their parking fees. The motorists' reply was to change their plates. Will's changing of the plate would not stand out in a city where thousands changed their plates to rebel against the traffic authority. It would hardly stand out, even if seen on the gas station's surveillance cameras, whereas in most other countries it might've caused a call to the police.

They were still ahead of the chase, but Will knew their pursuers must be closing in by now. This could not go on forever. Will took an exit to Highway E115, and then another exit that passed over some railroad tracks. He turned into a parking lot. He grabbed Ridges's forearm and, like before, pulled up his sleeve to look at the watch.

"We're here." Will opened the door, grabbed his backpack, and headed for an enormous building, broader than it was tall. It was still dark and the air smelled of snow. Another storm was coming in on the heels of the first. Floodlights on the top of the building shone down on the lot. "Let's go."

Ridges followed Parker, grabbing his backpack and parka. They walked up to a chain-link fence that was more than ten feet tall. It had razor wire on the top and several signs in bright red and white that said *No Trespassing* in Russian. Near the end of the building, where the fence met the corner of the metal structure, there was a full-height turnstile security gate. It had another red sign posted near it and required a magnetic card. Otherwise it was impregnable.

A man was standing just outside the gate. He had on some type of uniform and was smoking a cigarette as if it was his last before the firing squad opened up. He perked up at Will's approach and said, "Jesus, you ran it down to the last minute." The man handed passes through the gate to both Will and Ridges. Will looked at the pass. It had a different name, but his own picture was on it.

"How?" Ridges looked at his. The picture was dated, but was clearly Michael Ridges, or in this case, Frederick Smith.

"Let's go." The man let them through the turnstile and walked them through a door on the side of the building that led into an open bay with several aircraft under fluorescent lights. He took them to a locker room in the back, where two uniforms were laid out.

"We have five minutes at best."

"No problem. Thanks."

"Oh, Mr. Ridges, you don't remember me. We met once." The man had a flight jacket on, but no name tag.

"We did?"

"I'm Wade Newton. My son's Todd."

* * * *

The fully loaded FedEx 777 cargo jet taxied to the main runway at Domodedovo and was cleared for takeoff minutes later. The final security check noted a four-man crew with Will Parker in the pilot command seat and Michael Ridges in the copilot seat. Their IDs had different names, but both acted their parts. The guards barely noticed the extra crew and didn't doubt the two who were in control of the aircraft.

"Don't touch anything," Will told Ridges in English.

Once the guards left, Ridges was replaced in the copilot seat by Newton.

"You got this?" Wade knew that Will Parker had the flight hours in other aircraft.

"Sure." Will guided the jumbo aircraft onto the center line.

The lumbering jet taxied onto the active runway, called out for clearance, accelerated, and then rose off of the runway as Will pulled back on the yoke. The giant airplane floated as its wheels left contact with the ground. It followed the runway's direction to the west, climbed to altitude, and turned southwest toward Charles de Gaulle Airport.

At 10,000 feet, the backup crew took over.

The flight turned out to be much shorter than Ridges expected. When he had come to Russia, he'd flown from Hong Kong. A crew member told him that the run from Moscow to Paris took only a little more than three hours. The winds above the incoming snowstorm favored their route.

"I'm sorry about your son." Ridges was in the back, drinking a cup of coffee in the cargo hold with Wade Newton.

"I just want to know what happened." Newton sat like a defeated man on the crew seat.

"I think I can find out." Ridges reached for his backpack and notebook. He guessed that one man in particular knew where Todd Newton was. "Does the aircraft have Wi-Fi?"

"Yeah."

Will Parker came back from the cockpit. The fourth man was at the control.

Ridges opened his computer and used the password given by Newton.

"Do you have that flash drive?" Ridges asked Will.

He handed Ridges the small black device.

"What's that do?" Will pointed to Ridge's flash drive.

"I can get into the deep web."

"That's not all that special, is it?"

"Not getting into the deep web." Ridges held the computer up. "Getting into someone's emails on the deep web is."

"What's he doing?" asked Newton.

Will knew the significance.

"Here, look." Ridges opened an email from Alexander Paul to someone with a Hispanic name. "This is only a few hours old!"

Will Parker read the message.

"Todd may still be alive!" The message was giving instructions on what to ask about a back door. The reply also mentioned the name of a place.

"You hacked the deep web?" said Will, sitting in the extra seat in the cargo bay of a FedEx aircraft as he stared at the screen.

Will realized that Ridges's software might be the most valuable shipment the company ever made.

"Wade," Will said. "How do I make a call from here?"

Chapter 64

In the Sky Above the Baja

The Ospreys out of Camp Pendleton held an altitude of 25,000 feet as they passed over the border of Mexico and the United States. The hybrid airships were in flight mode, moving at well more than three hundred miles an hour. The radios crackled with transmissions. A joint-training exercise was kicking off. Except this was not an exercise. The canisters of ammunition were broken open and each Marine in the dark cargo bay loaded their magazines.

Just south of the border, the MV-22s descended to 10,000 feet and reduced their speed to be joined by two dark green UH-60A Blackhawks marked with the insignia of Infantería de Marina. From there, they crossed the Baja and then descended to slightly above the harsh, tan terrain as they closed in on the location. The blades threw up dust as they crossed the rocky hills and sands. It was minutes before dawn when the Marine MV-22s converted to helicopter mode and landed vertically on the other side of the hill from their target.

The Osprey offloaded a fourteen-man MSOT special operations team with its Belgium Malinois dog. The Marines, carrying their automatic HK-416s with the barrels extended by the suppression cans, or silencers, launched a small drone. It flew to a hundred feet above the hill and crossed over the hacienda. The Mexican Marines' Blackhawks hovered behind an outcrop of rocks, ready to spring forward the moment the attack began. Their Blackhawks stood guard in the air with their team prepared to rope down when the shooting occurred.

Since the potential captive was a US Marine, it was agreed between the two commanders that the American MSOT would move first.

The MSOT team commander pulled up behind a large boulder that had likely been moved there a thousand years ago, when the great earthquake caused the Baja Peninsula to slide away from the mainland. He studied the video feed. The drone had a heat sensor as well.

"Is he still alive?" the gunny whispered to the lieutenant.

"Can't tell. Two up top. They're moving around, so they ain't him." He signaled the team to move in.

The attack was followed by another video feed to both Camp Pendleton and Mexico City. Later, they looked at the timing of the tape. In two minutes and fourteen seconds, the attack was over.

The bigger man tried to make it to the basement, but the Belgian Malinois caught him by the leg. The killer had a look of fear that only a combat dog could cause. He tried to turn and train his .45 automatic on the animal, but the Malinois's handler, following closely behind, protected his dog. He emptied the full thirty-round magazine, nearly taking off the killer's head.

The smaller captor was in the fetal position in the corner of the large upstairs room, his face covered by his hands.

"Medic!" A team member called from the basement after jumping over the shredded body of the first killer.

Todd Newton looked near death in the corner of a bunk. The stench was almost unbearable.

"Marine, you *will* be okay. Semper fi." The medic gave him an injection while another member of the team cut the chains. They installed an IV line, and the hydration seemed to bring the wounded Marine back to life.

The stretcher transported Lance Corporal Todd Newton to the OV-22. At its three-hundred-knot speed, the aircraft was on the pad at Balboa Naval Hospital in San Diego in less than an hour.

Chapter 65

The FedEx Aircraft Over the Atlantic

"There's only one answer." Will was thinking of what to do next. Michael Ridges sat across from him in a jump seat of the MD-11F as they flew across the Atlantic. They had transferred to the next leg of the trip after Paris. It had taken less than an hour before N601FE was heading west. Like the thousands of packages the company shipped every day, the two had moved through FedEx's transportation system with lightning speed.

The two were eating a box lunch provided on the flight. It was the first food that either had enjoyed since this all began. Ridges consumed the American ham and cheese sandwich and finished off three Cokes.

"If I go to customs, they'll say I'm a national security risk and bury me so deep that you'll never hear from me again." Ridges opened a fourth can of Coke and took another swig.

Will knew that it wouldn't be long before Paul suspected the silence from Mexico was a sign of trouble. Every move had to be made as fast as possible.

"We need to buy one more day." Will looked at his new watch—a gift from his grateful escapee.

Wade Newton was sitting on the edge of the bunk that the crew used for their rest on long flights.

"Hey, you saved my son's life. What do you need?" Wade had spoken to Todd from San Diego, an emotional reunion that had left the ex-fighter pilot in tears. "As far as the other Fed Ex guys go"—Wade waved to indicate everyone in the company jet—"we have your back."

Will looked to the crew flying the aircraft. The FedEx pilots did seem to be a team, much like those in military service. Each of them could easily be fired for this. Their guests were ghosts who didn't exist. The manifest would be left blank as to the two extra passengers.

"Can you get us to New York?"

"A package from Moscow to New York is guaranteed to be delivered by ten thirty in the morning. Is that good enough?"

"Sure." Will was getting close to making the call. He wanted to be in Coyote Six before doing so.

The connection in Memphis was like the one in Paris. They were airborne within an hour of landing at MEM. On the flight line where the aircraft were lined up, Will and Ridges took a golf cart with Wade Newton to the FDX flight to Kennedy Airport. At the jet, Wade said good-bye.

"I am taking a couple of days off. Going to San Diego." Wade Newton wore the stress on his face. "Do I understand correctly that you know who did this?"

"Yeah."

"Are you going to do something about it?"

Will Parker didn't say anything. He shook the man's hand. They both knew what that meant.

Now in the United States, they were beyond the inspection of customs. Ridges had to stay out of sight for one more part of his journey. Will's only hope was to get to New York before Alexander Paul had any warning. He needed the time to get airborne in his jet, the Coyote Six, before Paul got to Karen. The FedEx flight required no overhead baggage or people struggling for their seats. It would be fast and efficient. The New York bird would be wheels-up in half the time that a passenger carrier took. They were above 10,000 feet when Ridges checked his laptop.

"Look at this." Ridges passed the computer to Will. It contained an email from the commanding general of the Russian FSB to Alexander Paul through the deep web. It noted that a Lt. Col. Boris Mikhailov of the Moscow District advised that Ridges was missing and believed to have left Russia.

"When we land, you need to take a taxi and go straight to this address." Will would not have much time. He knew what the next play would be. Paul had to stop Ridges at all costs. He now knew that Ridges was in the wind and probably with Will. Paul needed leverage over Will, and Snag was the only place he had the chance to do so. Snag would be Paul's only answer.

Will wrote down 620 Eighth Avenue in midtown Manhattan and a name.

"Talk only to him."

* * * *

Will stood by as Ridges got into a taxicab in front of the FBO near the FedEx hub. He handed the driver a paper with an address.

"Here, you'll need this." Will handed Ridges a handful of fifty-dollar bills. "Don't stop for anything."

Ridges understood what he meant. Alexander Paul was still playing a guessing game as to where the two of them had fled, but it wouldn't last forever.

"Thanks." It wasn't for the money.

The taxi took him straight to the address; Ridges paid the fare and walked directly into the building.

When he came out of it later, he was taken to a place that only two men knew of.

Chapter 66

Anchorage

Frank Caldwell's cell was set to vibrate. It started rattling just as they were loading the Bell helicopter in Anchorage. He glanced at the call. There were two numbers: One that he recognized and another that he didn't. Paul and Angel had not come out to the tarmac yet. The helicopter pilot was still standing next to his bird with a bright orange parka on over a flight suit and a white helmet with Bell Helicopters and Grumman stickers on the side. Based on his stance, he didn't seem to be in any hurry.

The brutally freezing temperature had not yet risen above zero degrees. A heater had been set up with an auxiliary power unit and was blowing warm air into the chopper's jet-engine intake—otherwise, at these temperatures, the lubricants would be the consistency of peanut butter. The noise from the auxiliary power unit made it nearly impossible to hear.

"What's up?" Caldwell stood so close to his shoulder that he could see the ice crystals that had formed in the helicopter pilot's beard. His breath, a visible vapor, projected out—with his words—to the man's face.

"There's some cloud cover over the mountain range that hasn't cleared yet." The man was clearly determined to fly safely. A crash into the face of a mountain in the Saint Elias Range was not going to happen. "Keep in mind, those mountains go up to over nineteen thousand feet."

"How about a valley?"

"Yeah, with this bird we can't go over the top."

"So, is a valley an option?"

"Cloud cover. If there's an opening, it closes up fast in this kinda shit. Remember, if we have to put down in an emergency, we ain't gonna be choosing between mall parking lots and cornfields. This is the real wilderness, man."

Caldwell had experienced the same during missions in the Hindu Kush with his Ranger teams. Weather at high altitude in remote terrain was serious trouble.

"So what?"

"Give it an hour and we can get rolling." The sun was climbing as they stood there in the cold. It didn't provide much heat or comfort. The exhaust from the APU stack billowed up into the air and the sun's light was reflecting off of the crystals. "But there may be a fast-mover just behind this last one." Another front was crossing the Bering Sea, heading to the east.

"Okay," said Caldwell, "but the boss wants to roll as soon as we can."

"Got it."

Caldwell thought this was the chance to return the first call. He went into the lobby of Ross Aviation and glanced around. Neither Paul nor the big stranger was in sight. Paul had said something that he caught in a passing word to the stranger. He'd heard the word *Mexico*. The big killer looked like someone who called Mexico home. The other word, which was unsaid but also struck Caldwell as one that fit, was *cartel*.

He hit *return* on the call he'd recognized—the operations supervisor at Baker's client company, Integral Transaction Data.

"Hey, this is Frank Caldwell."

"I don't know what happened, but you are something special." The man's excited voice came through the call as if he had just learned that he had won the lottery.

"I'm sorry?"

"The hack."

Caldwell was still trying to absorb what was being said. He unconsciously pressed the phone closer and felt its warmth on his ear.

"Yeah?" he replied, hoping to show he wasn't totally out of the loop. "We've been off the net for a bit. Just landed."

"Have you seen CNN?"

"No."

"Take a look."

Caldwell scanned the room, looking for a television. One was in the room reserved for pilots between flights. It was empty and the set was on some local channel. A popcorn machine stood nearby, giving the room the ambience of some low-cost cinema. He found the remote and scanned through until he got to the CNN logo.

The lead story was how ITD had found an attempted overseas hack that would have jeopardized millions of transaction dollars and stopped it before a single penny was lost. The company was looking strong at the same moment that it was bidding on several other credit-card, debit, and ATM carriers. The byline below also noted a breaking-news story from the *New York Times*, but it didn't provide any details.

"I see. That's great."

"We got an email that showed us the breach and how to seal it."

Caldwell thought he understood. The man was telling him that ITD hadn't found the hack themselves. Instead, they'd been presented with the key to the breach, which they assumed had come from Alexander Paul's company. As the only ones who knew about the disaster outside of the operations center, it seemed clear that the email had been from Alexander Paul's people.

"Okay…" Caldwell was still trying to hold back on any comment that would show how much he was in the dark.

"Our stock went up by over thirty percent just in today's trading."

"I'll tell Mr. Paul."

The second number was the one that he didn't recognize.

At that moment, Paul came to the door of the lounge dressed in his parka and arctic gear.

Caldwell held off returning the second call.

"Just got a call from ITD."

"Oh?"

"The hack was stopped. They think we did it."

Caldwell's many visits to ITD had paid off. Or at least ITD thought so.

Alexander Paul's face turned a bright red. The muscles in his face started to bulge and then recede as he clenched his jaw. A vein in his neck began to protrude.

Caldwell wasn't getting the reaction he expected.

"You have a very happy customer, sir. Their stock just took off and—"

He looks like he just lost a shitload of money, Caldwell thought. Surely, their success would make Paul several more million.

"Let's get the hell out of here," Paul growled and pushed past him.

Chapter 67

JFK International Airport

The HondaJet HA-420 was out of its hangar, refueled, and waiting for Will Parker as he ended his cell-phone call. There'd been no answer, but it suited him well that no one had picked up.

Just give me some time.

He looked at the weather that was crossing much of Canada. The computer in the flight office at JFK Airport's FBO showed clearing over much of the continent, but more importantly, the winds were coming west to east with one exception.

At lower altitudes, a headwind would slow his aircraft down, but the HA-420 had a feature that beat out its rivals. She could fly at 43,000 feet or flight level 430. And at 40,000 feet, a wind pattern was currently running east to west. He filed his flight plan, asking for air traffic control to clear the altitude that favored the winds. It would take a refueling stop, but Snag was on the eastern side of the mountains and several hundred miles closer. And he wasn't going to Snag.

Instead, his target was an airfield he knew well. It was only a short time ago that he had been to Whitehorse. There, he could get an Otter for the final leg of the journey.

The speedy HA-460 jet climbed up into the rare air of the higher flight plan in a matter of a few minutes. Will set the automatic pilot for the refueling stop and then checked the radar. The aircraft cut through the thin air like a scalpel. In what seemed an absurdly short time, Will crossed over Winnipeg and made a rapid descent to an airfield to the west. The jet landed, refueled, and was back up again in the dark sky. Again, the winds were kind. The sun was starting to shine its bright light from behind the aircraft. Well off in the distance, clouds were forming from one end of the windshield to the other.

Will called Whitehorse airfield and pulled up the air map sectional for YXY, the airfield designator on the sectional displayed on his airplane's cockpit panel. He told them that he was inbound, needing fuel and an Otter with sleds.

The airfield radioed him that the Otter would be ready.

"We have some more weather coming in," the Whitehorse operator added before signing off.

Will called the next most important number.

"Hello?"

Kevin Moncrief's voice was good to hear.

"Are you outta there?"

"Roger that." Their agreement had been no calls until Will was heading for Snag.

The gunny couldn't mask the emotion in his voice. "Well, that's great. Are you gonna be here soon?"

"The winds look good. Chances are I'll be there before you finish your breakfast." It was a joke. Moncrief was known to be a late riser, when possible.

* * * *

"Good." Moncrief was holding the phone near the cabin and Karen Stewart was standing nearby. She stopped cutting firewood, put the ax over her shoulder, and looked at Moncrief with a glance that said she knew who he was talking to.

A wave of static interrupted the call. The words became broken on both ends.

"We're quiet here." Moncrief tried to get the message out.

It was then that he first heard a *whomp-whomp* sound off in the distance. The helicopter flew low over the trees, circled with the door closed, and then made another pass with the door open. A man, dressed in a white and brown camouflage parka and pants, had his white boots on the landing rail of the aircraft as it made another pass.

The combat Marine in Moncrief took over.

"Red flag!" he cried into the sat phone. "If you get this, *red flag*!" No response but static. He repeated the warning again, signaled to Karen, and grabbed his rifle and backpack.

She threw down the ax and picked up her rifle as well. They started to head out into the forest behind the cabin. She stopped, turned around, and headed back.

"What?" He chambered a round in his rifle. The helicopter landed just beyond the tree line and just out of sight. He saw her head around the corner of the cabin and heard the door open.

What the hell is she doing? It seemed to take minutes, but in less than one, he heard the cabin door close and saw her come around the woodpile. The *zing* of a bullet rang out as she turned the corner. It was a blind shot from someone who had glimpsed movement.

Bastards.

The shot meant much more than a passing bullet. It meant that their attackers weren't committed to keeping their targets alive, making their intentions crystal clear.

The rally-point plan meant that he didn't have to explain anything to Karen. The spruces were thick behind the cabin. They could disappear quickly on their way to the rock outcropping.

Together, they raced into the woods, no time for snowshoes. Once in the forest, the snow became deep and exhausting. They both struggled to plunge through the drifts.

Moncrief stopped behind a wide spruce and looked back toward the cabin. His heart was running like a racehorse's. The men he'd glimpsed so far were well-armed and were using military urban tactics in approaching the cabin as if an armed attacker were waiting inside. They wore camouflage white suits and white rubber Mickey Mouse boots. Each carried an assault rifle.

"At least they don't have snowshoes either," he murmured.

She knelt immediately behind him.

"Head to the rocks. I'll be right behind you," he whispered.

She nodded and disappeared quickly into the white-green jungle surrounding them.

Shots rang out, and then screams, and then more shots.

"What the—" Moncrief saw shapes at the edge of the cabin. Two looked like they were down on their knees. They had dropped their weapons and one was holding his arm, bent over in pain.

The rabid fox she'd let into the cabin had done its job.

Chapter 68

The HondaJet Above Canada

The static cut off Will's call to Moncrief. He barely heard the words, but one hit the pit of his stomach. *Red* meant trouble. Will accelerated the jet to nearly five hundred knots and quickly computed the ground speed in his mind. Whatever the jet was doing in the air was not what it was doing on the ground. The winds were giving him a small push that had the aircraft moving at nearly six hundred miles an hour, relative to the ground.

When he began the descent, the speed increased even more as the aircraft followed gravity's pull, but the well-made HondaJet proved equal to the strain.

A short time later, the wheels of the jet screeched as it settled on the runway at Whitehorse. The Air North FBO was a quick taxi; waiting in front of it was an Otter with sleds for landing on snow or ice. A man with red and orange sticks guided his aircraft up to the terminal entrance. Will grabbed a large flight bag; some supplies, and two other weapons bags they had stored in the jet when he left Georgia. He headed inside to suit up with his arctic gear, waved at the two inside, and went into the pilots' lounge. The television inside was turned to another breaking news story. This time, he knew the story firsthand.

Ridges had made it safely to the address in midtown Manhattan.

Will went back into the cold and crossed over to the waiting aircraft.

The Otter was loaded with his other bags and waiting for its pilot. He stopped by its tail and called the other number on his cell phone.

"Hello." The voice sounded excited.

"This is Parker."

"He wants to talk to you."

Will knew who the next voice was.

"Parker. You know what I need." Alexander Paul spat out the words, the strain and fury like broken glass in his voice.

"He's gone."

"Where?"

"The only place he could be safe from someone like you."

"I have your friend." Paul's mistake was that he used the singular, clearly unaware that Karen Stewart had a protector in Snag. "Where's he hiding?"

"You've been there before, a long time ago."

"Don't play games."

Will smiled. "All the news that's fit to print."

He felt Paul's reaction through the satellite phone.

The *New York Times* had broken Ridges's story that the CIA and DIA had a bank in the Cayman Islands and that the former director of the DIA had used it as his personal slush fund. Under the assumption that the CIA could use the bank to follow the funds of terrorism, the agencies had been tricked by one of their very own. Paul had been embezzling millions.

"She's *dead*," Paul growled. The phone went silent.

The morning sun suddenly became dark as snow started to come in. The clouds masked the sunlight and winds began coming across the airfield. Will started the Otter's engine and began taxiing out to the main runway.

Does he really have her? Was Moncrief down? The scenarios ran through his brain like wildfire. The Otter was much slower than Coyote Six, but it lifted off the runway in less than a hundred yards as he turned it into the wind.

Will knew the Yukon well and headed north to a place he had been before. The windshield was pelted by snow as the aircraft fought the moving air, jumping up and down in the sudden shifts of turbulence. He took a compass bearing that sent him in the right direction and then dropped to an altitude just above the tops of the spruce trees. The engine struggled against the pull of the wind as it headed deeper into the storm.

The cabin's temperature dropped. The weather front seemed to be bringing Siberian air in from both the west and north. He felt the Otter struggle in his hands and tried not to fight it. The airplane climbed up the side of a hill and then dropped into the valley beyond. It did it again as he crossed the rise and fall of the terrain. The tops of the trees became more difficult to make out, but the airplane continued to move forward.

I'm going to have to set down. The sooner he put the aircraft down, though, the farther he would be from Snag. The storm was stealing his sense of distance and direction. And it would be suicide for him to land at Snag. The bullets would rip through the Otter before the engine even stopped.

Another hill lay directly before him with what seemed to be trees that filled his entire windshield. His airplane and he disappeared into the white.

Chapter 69

Snag

"What happened?" Frank Caldwell ran up to the front of the cabin, finding two of the men on the ground. One was holding his leg and the other his arm. Blood streaked the snow and their white parkas.

Paul and Angel remained near the helicopter, watching from a safe distance.

"The damn thing came at us." The man with the long beard and tattoos was clearly rattled.

"What?"

"There." He pointed to the snow near the cabin's front door. White fur covered in blood lay at the base of the steps to the cabin. The furry object looked like a tiny rug that had been run through the blades of a lawn mower. Their automatic weapons had shredded the animal.

Caldwell looked at the head and saw its skull cracked open by the bullets.

"Oh, shit." He saw that the fox's lips and jaws were covered in a white, dripping foam. He knew why the doctor had come to Snag, and then ran to Paul. "We need to get these men out of here." Caldwell's sixth code of West Point had kicked in, but it instantly became apparent that he was the only one who cared about the troops.

"What's wrong with you?" Paul phrased the words like he was asking Caldwell if he had never seen men wounded in combat before.

"These men." Caldwell had seen wounded men before, but not wounded by the most dangerous weapon on the planet. "The foxes are infected with rabies. The doc let one loose in the cabin." He jabbed a gloved thumb in the direction of the wounded men. "We need to get them out of here. Now."

Caldwell turned back to the helicopter to signal the pilot to spin up the turbine. He'd made it two steps when the shot rang out. A .45 slug caught him in the center of his back, picked him up, and threw him into a snowdrift at the base of a pine tree. The smell of cordite lingered in the air.

* * * *

Paul put the pistol back in his holster and turned away from Caldwell's body. The former soldier would only be described as missing on a job in the Yukon. His beloved kid would no doubt learn about Daddy's disappearance at a soccer game when the mom got the call.

He never knew the score, from the start.

Paul turned to Angel, who also carried a .45 sidearm. "Those two." His nod of the head was directed toward the two wounded soldiers on the ground.

The man with the beard tried to cover his face. The bullet passed through his forearm and blew out the back of his head. The second man tried to crawl away. He had lost his pistol and rifle during the attack by the rabid animal. Finally, he stopped and tried a desperate lunge at Angel. The bullet caught him in the face. Again, the smell of cordite filled the air.

Paul crossed over to the helicopter pilot, gun trained on the man's chest. "Move away from the chopper."

The pilot, clearly in shock, complied.

"Cover him," Paul told Angel, then reached into his own pocket for the plasticuffs he'd brought on the mission. A minute later, he had the pilot stowed in the back of the chopper, his hands fastened tightly with the zip ties to one of the supports.

Paul pulled out the satellite phone and called a number.

"What is the nearest airport that can handle a jet?" he asked the pilot while the call went through.

"Whitehorse."

Paul said "Whitehorse" into the phone. "I need the Gulfstream to pick me up there in an hour."

The G-650 had been on hold in Anchorage, waiting for the next assignment. Paul had already planned where to go next, if necessary— the one place that would welcome the former director of the DIA. The Gulfstream could pass over the Bering Sea and land in the Russian town of Anadyr before the dogs were on his trail.

The United States would express outrage and lodge furious complaints over the "international incident." Putin would claim that even former government officials have the right to ask for political asylum. Paul would prove a treasure trove of information for his sworn enemy. Putin would have lost one plum in the disappearance of Ridges and gained another with Paul. And it wouldn't hurt that the Russians wouldn't be sure how much money Paul had remaining.

Chapter 70

Near Snag

The shots from the execution of Frank Caldwell and Paul's two men rang out in the valley. The sound echoed through the trees. Kevin Moncrief held his head down for a moment in disbelief. He'd known these dudes were dangerous, but murdering your own men was taboo in every modern military in the world. Karen's life would also be forfeit if the surviving killers found her. The massacre at Snag would be covered by the snowstorm coming in. The CDC had not spoken with their research scientist for some time now and didn't expect her any time soon. They would not be alarmed for days to come.

Will would arrive if he could, but Moncrief feared he'd be too late. Then again, that was better than having his old friend die needlessly if he arrived too soon. Either way, when this was all over, Paul would be long gone. The helicopter pilot would ferry him out to a field on the other side of Whitehorse. Then he too would receive a bullet in the back of his helmet as soon as they touched down.

Moncrief moved to another tree to get a different view of the layout. He saw Paul and a large man standing over the two who had been shot.

There was another, he thought as he scanned the area. Another soldier had climbed off the bird when it first landed. The man was nowhere in sight.

Pow.

The shot missed Moncrief's head by inches. He stuck his face down in the snow, still feeling the heat of the round that had just missed. He pulled back from the tree, crawling in the snow, retreating to another tree and just got behind it when another round struck. This one missed, but he felt the burn of his scalp as it cut through his flesh. Warm blood dripped down his forehead and cheek. Again, Moncrief retreated, this time to a large boulder that was covered in a drift of snow. He pulled behind the rock, grabbed some of the snow, made a tight ball, squeezed it with both hands, and then pressed the ice against the wound. In the below-freezing temperature, it would slow the bleeding quickly.

Moncrief chambered a round, waited at the base of the rock and then, when he saw a shape move a hundred yards away, he fired. The blast of the heavy-caliber rifle missed, but caused the man to duck. As soon as he discharged the weapon, Moncrief ran back to another rock outcropping. Again, he waited for the shape of the man to appear, and again, he fired a round. It served its purpose in that it slowed the man's movements.

I hope she made it, he thought as he moved from tree to tree in a zigzag pattern, gradually making his way to their rally point. They were on their own and it was clear that there was no choice but to fight for their survival. There would be no tie in this game.

Moncrief stopped again at the base of the tree and waited for a shape to appear. Blood dripped into his eye. *Damn it*. The bleeding had slowed but he could see that he'd left a red trail behind him.

This time he saw two figures. The second man was larger than the sniper he'd been hunting. Both were coming in his direction. Moncrief only had three rounds left in the rifle. Their quick escape hadn't enabled him to grab any extra ammo. And the chances of his hitting either target was slim. They were both moving quickly, well aware that he was aiming for them.

The next time he looked, they'd disappeared from sight. No movement in the forest, only a deadly silence. Heavier snow was limiting visibility. He slowly crawled backward, moving away from the two men and also away from the rally point. At the very least, he could draw the pursuers away from Karen.

Moncrief had become the hunted. The ground rose from the spot where he last stopped and gave him a better view. He saw a shape closer than he had expected. He held his breath and stayed as still as he could. Now, there were three shapes in the forest. Two men, one the larger one and a smaller one, were moving together. The third one had disappeared. Moncrief was near a clearing and the next move meant that he would have to cross the opening or stay in place.

As he prepared to squeeze the trigger, aiming at the larger of the two men, blood trickled into his eye, causing him to miss.

He darted across the opening, only to hear several shots fired from his far right. One caught him in the right calf. It stunned him, but he quickly realized it had missed bone. In the woods to the other side, Moncrief realized that he had unconsciously circled around and was close to the rendezvous point. There was no way to lead them away from her without crossing the opening again. He prayed she understood that she had to flee the area as quickly as she could. The killers were not taking prisoners.

He made the dash toward the meeting point as well as he could with his lame leg, plunging through snow and underbrush until he saw Karen, rifle next to her.

"We need to get out of here."

She nodded as Moncrief turned back to the opening, waiting for movement. One of the men tried to cross the clearing. He fired quickly in his direction. One of the men fired back and also missed. They exchanged shots again, leaving Moncrief with one round remaining and three killers.

A movement in the white-green undergrowth. Quickly, Moncrief aimed and squeezed. His bullet caught the third man in the chest and flipped him over as if he had been tackled by a pro linebacker.

Now the Marlin was empty.

"Here." He reached for Karen's rifle, which also had a limited number of rounds.

The two shapes had divided. Moncrief saw one on the far right. He fired a shot, but it ricocheted off of a large branch, spraying snow and pine needles but not finding its mark.

"Watch out!" cried Karen, signaling to the left.

The big man fired and struck the rifle in Kevin's hands. The wooden stock exploded into splinters and the rest of the rifle flew out of his hands, leaving them defenseless.

Chapter 71

The Wilderness Near Snag

"Who are you?" Paul asked Moncrief as he leaned against the rock that they'd used for cover.

The bigger man had his boot on Moncrief's wounded leg. He pushed his heel down into the wound as Moncrief screamed in pain.

Karen Stewart was pulled up at the base of a tree with her knees up to her chest. She was too scared to cry. Her eyes looked out into space as if shock had set in.

"Moncrief." He spat the words out: "Gunnery sergeant, United States Marine Corps, you worthless piece of shit."

Paul shook his head. Checked his watch. "What were you two thinking?" He was verbally torturing them, delaying the inevitable. "Running like that."

The prisoners made no reply.

"You know I didn't come here to kill both of you." Paul held a .45 automatic pistol. It was a Remington model RIA 1911 M15 made exclusively and issued only to general officers. He carried it in a shiny black holster with a belt that had a bright gold buckle. The large 11.5 mm slug was designed to destroy human tissue, causing a ragged, deep wound that caused the victim to bleed out quickly.

"Your friend did this to you." Paul played with the pistol like a gunslinger from a John Wayne movie. "If he had just left things alone, left Mexico alone, and stayed here in this deep-freeze shithole, flying his little airplanes, we never would have met."

Moncrief tried to make a lunge at Paul with a last-gasp effort.

Angel kicked him down and stomped on the injured leg.

Moncrief's scream echoed in the forest.

"Kill them both," Paul said like a dispassionate executioner at the gallows.

Angel took his .45 semiautomatic and aimed it at Karen first. Another perverted form of torture, in which he'd put the 11.5 mm slug through the face of the doctor before killing Moncrief, leaving him to see Karen's brain scattered against the tree trunk before the barrel turned on him.

And then...

Whomp.

The .338 Lapua Magnum is known in the African country of Namibia as the "big-five killer." Its slug can take down a Cape buffalo on a charge.

The big man would not have felt pain. Instead, it would have been like having his chest struck by a runaway freight train. The force of the bullet lifted him off his feet and threw him back against a rock. He was dead before his body slid to the ground.

Paul froze, motionless with fear.

"Put your hands behind your head." Will Parker stepped out of the woods with the Windrunner in his hands. He and the rifle were covered in white camouflage. But for his movement, he melted invisibly into the snowy air. He approached Paul and nudged the fluted barrel of the rifle into Paul's neck as he used his other hand to unbuckle Paul's holster. The pistol fell into the snow. Will backed up and helped Karen to her feet. He turned to Moncrief.

"Gunnery Sergeant United States Marine Corps?" Will repeated Moncrief's cry with a smile.

"Sir, yes, sir."

He looked over Kevin's injured leg, then helped the gunny to his feet.

"You think you can make it back to the helicopter?"

Moncrief tested putting weight on the injured leg. He winced but felt steady on his feet. "Hell, yes."

"Lead the way." Will gave Paul another nudge of the Windrunner, keeping him ahead of them as they made their way through the brush and snow to the cabin. He kept the long barrel trained on Paul's head as they neared the helicopter.

"They won't do what you're thinking they'll do to me." Paul regained his swagger as they moved past the cabin and to the helicopter. "I know too much."

The comment had some risk of truth to it. Paul possessed a decade of the worst of America's secrets. If Ridges could be spared because of his knowledge, Paul too might avoid the gallows.

"We'll take the chance," said Will.

"Like hell you will. You think—"

Pop.

Paul's words were lost in the snap of the bullet as it passed through his neck. His voice started to gurgle as blood poured out of his neck. He grabbed the wound in a desperate attempt to stanch the bleeding. He fell to his knees, still holding his neck with both hands. The sound of him drowning in his own blood filled the air as Karen, Moncrief, and Will stood back, searching for the source of the gunfire.

A man came out of the trees with his pistol still extended. He walked up to Paul and looked him in the eyes.

"I could have shot you in the head and made it less painful," Caldwell said as he stood over his former employer, watching him gasp his last breaths. He turned to Will. "The Agency suspected he was a danger. I was told what to do if he left the United States."

Frank Caldwell worked for Langley.

Will lowered his weapon.

"For some time, the bank in the Caymans had money coming out. They thought it was going to the UAE and frankly they thought it was terrorist money."

"So, no one cared."

"Exactly." Caldwell leaned against the helicopter, clearly in some amount of pain. "Then it became agency money."

"Are you hurt?" asked Moncrief.

The man that Paul and everyone else had known as Caldwell opened his parka, revealing a bulletproof vest badly damaged in the back.

"Nothing worse than a couple of broken ribs, I hope."

"What now?" Will asked.

"Nothing. We're done. A tragic mishap in the Yukon left Alexander Paul missing. Probably a downed aircraft near Snag. Not unusual, I understand."

Caldwell opened the hatch on the chopper and, with some effort, pulled the pilot into view. He reached into his pocket, pulled out a folding knife, and freed the pilot from the zip ties. "Let's get the hell out of here."

* * * *

It turned out that the helicopter pilot also worked for the Agency. Paul was never going to leave Snag, no matter what he did.

"Can we make it?" Will asked the pilot.

"Sure."

"I need you to drop me off at a lake on the other side of that ridgeline." Will pointed in the direction of the lake where he and Karen had survived the nights. His Otter had made it back to the same lake. He'd been crossing the ridgeline when he heard the shots ring out in the valley.

"Get him to the infirmary in Whitehorse." Will pointed to Kevin Moncrief.

"I've already called in." The man they knew as Caldwell held up his radio. "They're waiting for us. You know…." He paused. "It's probably best that we forget about all of this. Doctor, you might want to leave Snag alone for a while."

Dr. Karen Stewart nodded.

There was nothing left of Snag other than the bodies. The wolves and foxes would take care of much of the corpses before anyone returned to the scene. A false story would leak that Alexander Paul was lost somewhere in the Yukon in a small airplane crash. The hope would be that searchers returning in the spring would find the missing airplane.

"What are you going to do?" Caldwell asked Will.

"There's a cabin on a lake way north." He smiled. "I might go up there for a while." He looked at Karen meaningfully.

"Need a little company?" she said.

"Yeah." Will smiled. "I've been meaning to train a copilot for some time now."

The turbine of the helicopter started to whine. The blades began kicking up ice and snow.

"How about you, Gunny?" he asked Moncrief, who was limping to the helicopter.

The gunny turned and sighed. "Me? I'm going to get these little scrapes fixed up and then take a long nap."

Epilogue

Six months later

The long nights became long days again.

Pontoons replaced the sleds on Will's Otter. It lumbered over Snag, heading toward the familiar ridgeline, then swung down to the pothole lake on the other side. The forest was now green and dense with undergrowth. Even from altitude, Will could make out giant ostrich ferns crowding the forest floor.

He made the turn to the lake, slowed the aircraft, and dropped on to the glass-like surface. He taxied the Otter to the same shoreline where they'd crashed and spent their frozen days and nights until the airplane's pontoon nestled up against a rock.

As he climbed onto the pontoon, Will extended his hand.

"Here you go."

Karen Stewart slid out of her copilot seat and placed her foot on the float. Will stepped on to a rock on the shore. "Pass me the rifle."

The bears were out and the days were warm, the sun lighting the Yukon for nearly twenty hours a day, earning its moniker as the land of the midnight sun.

After the lake settled down from the wave motion caused by the landing, Will didn't need to moor it with a rope. It wasn't going anywhere. They climbed up the hillside, following the path of fallen and broken trees that had served as an opening when they were seeking shelter last winter.

"Are you gonna tell me now?" Karen jumped from the pontoon to the shore. "Why'd we come back here?"

"I wanted to check on something."

He took a closer look at what had once looked like a giant rock, the same outcropping that had sheltered them from the killing cold during their fight to survive.

"Is this it?" She held up the piece of tin that he had used to carve out the snow for them to shelter. The dish-shaped metal object still looked oddly out of place in the wilderness.

"This wasn't supposed to be here." He held it up, scrutinizing it. It was the reason he'd returned. He scanned the area above them once more. Moss and ferns covered the big rock. Using the same piece of metal, he began scraping away the moss and weeds from the outcropping.

They both stared at the rock overhang, which clearly wasn't made of rock.

"I thought so."

He pulled the weeds away, using his bare hands, revealing another piece of metal and, soon, a number.

"Forty-two-seven-two-four-six-nine." He read the number out loud. He pulled more of the moss away. Above the figure were four letters.

"USAF," said Karen, looking over his shoulder.

Like seeing the solution to a puzzle for the first time, Will looked across the hillscape. Now it all made sense. The fallen trees had been cut down by the fuselage as it bored into the hillside. He pushed through the undergrowth and saw the glimmer of another third piece of metal buried just below the brush. This one was no larger than a dog tag. He held the newly discovered, small shape in his hand, walked to the shore, and used the cold water from the lake to wash off the dirt.

"Sergeant John A. Jones, USMC."

The C-54 Skymaster had been missing for nearly seventy years, with its thirty-six passengers and a mother and her child.

That night, the news story hit CNN, and a son, now well into his seventies, learned of the airplane's grave.

The news that night also reported on the FBI investigation into the Cayman Islands bank fiasco. It exposed a conspiracy that connected the Defense Intelligence Agency and banks in the United Arab Emirates and Great Britain, resulting in forty-six federal indictments.

Also on the news, a smaller, human-interest story about a young Marine with an 0651 military occupational specialty who had been missing was promoted to corporal. His father, a retired Marine colonel, attended the ceremony and helped his son pin on his new stripes.

Michael Ridges was indicted for his release of intelligence information and ultimately pleaded guilty to a lesser crime, serving one year in the federal prison in Montgomery, Alabama, under special protection. After his release, he was hired as a consultant to the ITD corporation.

Kevin Moncrief returned to painting houses in the Atlanta area and keeping an eye on a certain seldom-visited farm, cabin, and airstrip well to the south.

Acknowledgments

I wish to thank the many who have followed the Will Parker series from its beginning. In addition, my thanks to Kevin Harcourt and Meed Geary for their advice and counsel on much of the aviation. Likewise, I appreciate the help and advice of Ed Stackler, Doug Grad, and my editor, Gary Goldstein, as well as my many fellow authors who have provided so much over the years. Of course, the help of my brothers-in-arms, especially the Marines, will always be appreciated.

—AH

Don't miss *Northern Thunder*, a Will Parker Thriller by Anderson Harp.

INTO THE LION'S DEN

North Korea. 2011.

For Kim Jong-un, the time has come to position his country atop the world's pecking order. To do so, he has invested his nation's resources in one rogue scientist. Peter Nampo is a nanotech specialist who has developed a nuclear missile not only capable of reaching the heart of Los Angeles, but also capable of knocking out America's eyes in the skies—the GPS satellites overseeing the Korean Peninsula. Kim Jong-un has funded Nampo's secret laboratory somewhere in a valley of the Taebaek Mountains.

Marine recon veteran and small-town prosecutor William Parker has a history with Peter Nampo—and is the only one who can identify him. Recruited into a joint CIA and Pentagon Dark Ops task force, Parker must infiltrate the Hermit Kingdom, find Nampo, and end the scientist's threat. But there's more to this mission than Parker knows, and what he discovers is a danger far greater than being trapped behind enemy lines...

Look for *Northern Thunder*, on sale now in eBook and paperback.

Printed in the United States
by Baker & Taylor Publisher Services